**"I don't have any r... that you weren't a ... studied her. "Do yo... believe differently:**

"Of course not. I don't even know anybody in this town. How could anybody be upset with me?"

He seemed to hesitate before smiling. "That's what I thought. Do you need any help getting ready for bed?"

If she'd been revved up before, she was now a driver on the last leg of the course. Full throttle ahead. She might spontaneously combust and he hadn't even touched her. "Uh...no."

He stared at her. "There's something here, isn't there," he said. "Between us. Something different."

Her throat felt tight. "Different how?" she managed to say.

"Something different than what I've experienced before," he said, his voice soft.

"Yeah. That's what I thought you meant. Same," she admitted.

"I thought so," he said. He didn't say it as if he was happy or sad, just accepting.

"What now?" she asked.

He reached out and with two fingers gently tipped her chin up. Then every bit as gently, he kissed her.

Dear Reader,

*Trouble in Blue* is the second book of the three-book Heroes of the Pacific Northwest miniseries set in fictional Knoware, Washington. At the peak of the summer tourist season, Marcus Price, interim police chief, receives word that there is a credible threat of an imminent terrorist attack and to be watchful of strangers. He doesn't need any particular urging to pay attention to Erin McGarry, a stranger who has arrived to temporarily run her sister's gift shop. Unfortunately, however, trouble has followed Erin to town, and neither Erin nor Marcus may survive it.

*Trouble in Blue* is ultimately the story of trust and forgiveness and having the courage to believe that your past does not have to dictate your future. It's a story of friendships—those that have lasted a lifetime and those that are much newer. And, ultimately, a story of the joy of finding a great love when you weren't really looking.

I hope you enjoy meeting Marcus and Erin.

All my best,

*Beverly*

# TROUBLE IN BLUE

## Beverly Long

HARLEQUIN
ROMANTIC
SUSPENSE

# HARLEQUIN®
## ROMANTIC SUSPENSE™

Recycling programs
for this product may
not exist in your area.

ISBN-13: 978-1-335-75964-1

Trouble in Blue

Copyright © 2022 by Beverly R. Long

All rights reserved. No part of this book may be used or reproduced in
any manner whatsoever without written permission except in the case of
brief quotations embodied in critical articles and reviews.

This is a work of fiction. Names, characters, places and incidents
are either the product of the author's imagination or are used fictitiously.
Any resemblance to actual persons, living or dead, businesses,
companies, events or locales is entirely coincidental.

This edition published by arrangement with Harlequin Books S.A.

For questions and comments about the quality of this book,
please contact us at CustomerService@Harlequin.com.

Harlequin Enterprises ULC
22 Adelaide St. West, 41st Floor
Toronto, Ontario M5H 4E3, Canada
www.Harlequin.com

**Printed in U.S.A.**

**Beverly Long** enjoys the opportunity to write her own stories. She has both a bachelor's and master's degree in business and more than twenty years of experience as a human resources director. She considers her books to be a great success if they compel the reader to stay up way past their bedtime. Beverly loves to hear from readers. Visit beverlylong.com, or like her author fan page at Facebook.com/beverlylong.romance.

## Books by Beverly Long

### Harlequin Romantic Suspense

#### *Heroes of the Pacific Northwest*

*A Firefighter's Ultimate Duty*
*Trouble In Blue*

#### *The Coltons of Roaring Springs*

*A Colton Target*

#### *Wingman Security*

*Power Play*
*Bodyguard Reunion*
*Snowbound Security*
*Protecting the Boss*

#### *The Coltons of Grave Gulch*

*Agent Colton's Takedown*

Visit the Author Profile page at Harlequin.com for more titles.

To my sisters, Mary, Linda and Karen.
You taught me all the important things.

# Chapter 1

Erin stood in the dark alley, shifting from foot to foot, fumbling with the unfamiliar keys in her hand. Nerves. Scared for her sister, Morgan, who had been hospitalized two days ago. Twenty-six weeks along, much too early to have a baby. Scared, too, that she wasn't up to the task of running her sister's beautiful store for the foreseecable future.

She knew nothing about retail, nothing about the Pacific Northwest and the little town of Knoware. Other than it really was nowhere.

And that it had taken her more than twelve hours to get here.

What if she screwed it up? Morgan had assured her she wouldn't when Erin peeked into her hospital room. But who really knew? She had a history.

She'd left her sister to sleep and accepted the keys to

Tiddle's Tidbits and Treasures from Brian. Her brother-in-law had told her to park in the alley and enter via the back door.

She tried a key. Then a second. She really should have listened to Brian's explanation more closely. Put the third key in. Oh, good grief. She only had one more. Fortunately, that was all she needed because the lock clicked. She pushed the door open and walked inside. She'd been in the store only once before. And it had been at least a year. But she knew the back hall led to a storage room, a small kitchen and a restroom. The rest of the storefront was devoted to merchandise. She walked that direction.

A light was on above the cash register. The change drawer was open. That didn't surprise her. Brian had told her that they took all the cash out every night. Everything in excess of a hundred dollars would be dropped in the night depository at the bank. The hundred, hopefully mostly in ones and fives with just a bit of change, would be left in a money bag and hidden in the tea cabinet in the kitchen.

She was hours too early but there'd been little to do except drop her suitcase off at Morgan and Brian's house. She hadn't even considered sitting down. Wasn't going to risk falling asleep and opening late on her first day. Fortunately, she'd caught a few hours of rest on the first leg of the trip, but once she'd hit the States and caught a connecting flight that took her from New York to Seattle, she'd been too keyed up to even close her eyes.

Now she absolutely yearned for a cup of tea.

Marcus Price had been on duty for more than ten hours. Another two and he should be off. *Should be.*

Not going to happen. It was the middle of June and the tourist season was in full swing. That always necessitated some extra shifts. Now, because he'd been named interim chief after his boss's recent heart attack, he was pulling extra upon extra.

He had a whole host of new things on his plate. Certainly hadn't needed the call from Homeland Security yesterday advising that law enforcement across the country needed to be on high alert. There was a credible threat about an impending terrorist attack on US soil.

Unfortunately, the actual target was unknown, which greatly complicated things. Meant that everywhere had to be watched at all times.

He wasn't a novice when it came to responding to domestic terrorism. Ten-plus years of work experience in the Los Angeles Police Department had ensured that. And while much smaller and quieter Knoware, Washington, was unlikely to be a target, still, he had listened carefully to their direction. *Be watchful. Extra diligent about following up on odd things. Overcommunicate information up the chain of command. Pay attention to strangers.*

It was that last bit of advice that had him shaking his head. Knoware had about 1,500 year-round residents, but that tripled in the summer as tourists poured in. That meant that most of the people he saw were strangers.

Speaking of strange, he thought as a call came over his radio. The alarm at Tiddle's Tidbits and Treasures had gone off. Calls had gone out to the store owner and there had been no response. Per protocol, the alarm company had notified the local police for follow-up.

He couldn't recall that ever happening before. Just months ago, Marcus might have been less concerned.

But then Gertie's Café and Feisty Pete's bar had been broken into and robbed. Those businesses sat on either side of Tiddle's. The perpetrator had not been captured.

He left his lights and siren off. It was early enough that he didn't need them to prompt traffic to get the hell out of his way. There was hardly anybody moving about in Knoware yet. He pulled into the alley. One car behind the three-story building. Tiddle's was on the ground floor. Apartments on the second and third. He knew the residents parked in the corner lot, same place the help at Gertie's parked. He got out, approached the door. No sign of damage. He put his hand on the knob.

It turned easily. That wasn't good. It should have been locked.

He pulled his gun and stepped inside a dark hallway. He listened. Heard something in the room up the hall and to his left. Dim light spilled out into the hallway. He approached, hugging the wall. Rounded the corner.

And the woman in the middle of the room dropped her teacup. It hit the floor hard, but it did not break. Black tea spilled widely, including some splatters on her bare legs.

"Keep your hands in the air," he said. He was confident that he'd never seen her before. She would not be easy to forget. Her reddish-gold hair hung to the middle of her back in ringlets. Her eyes were green and her skin was fair with a dusting of freckles. "Are you the only person in the building?" he asked.

"I'm not at all confident about the whole building. In this shop, yes, I'm fairly certain."

He assessed her.

"Are you here to arrest me?" she asked, not sounding terribly concerned.

"That depends. Did you break in?"

"Absolutely not."

"The burglar alarm rang. The police were called."

"You responded to the wrong address," she said, sounding satisfied. "No burglar alarm here."

Gun still in hand, he motioned for her to follow him. Then he pointed to a panel on the wall, near the cash register.

"Well," she said, her lips pursed. "I believe this is a salient detail that Brian neglected to impart. Understandable, you know. Has his mind on other things."

He was generally pretty good with faces and the puzzle pieces started sliding into place. He slipped his gun back into his waist holster. "You're Morgan Tiddle's sister?"

"Guilty. Erin McGarry."

"I'm Officer Marcus Price, Knoware Police Department. What are you doing here at barely six o'clock in the morning?"

"Can we have this conversation while I mop up my spilled tea?"

"Of course." They returned to the small kitchen.

She grabbed paper towels from the counter. First she patted at her bare legs. "Well, it's a good thing I'm not wearing pants," she said.

Good, indeed. She had great-looking legs. Nicely shaped, very tan. She was wearing a blue-and-white-striped skirt, a white shirt and flat blue shoes. She wasn't very tall, maybe five-three, not skinny but rather nicely proportioned.

She squatted down. Her thick hair fell in front of her face. She handed him the now-empty teacup. "Thank goodness this was made of sturdy stuff. Would hate to start breaking dishes on my first day."

"Your first day?"

"Yes. My sister has been confined to bed rest for the duration of her pregnancy."

"I'm sorry to hear that," he said. He liked Morgan Tiddle. Could always count on her store for a perfect gift. Her husband was also a nice guy. "I know both your sister and brother-in-law. In fact, my path crosses with Brian at city hall sometimes."

"He told me once that he actually likes crunching numbers. Accountant extraordinaire, Morgan likes to say. Not that she isn't pretty great herself. And if you know Morgan, you'll know this to be true."

"You're filling in for her now?" he asked.

"Well, in Morgan's generally unflappable and efficient way, she had secured someone to watch over the shop for a few months once the baby was born. But said person was anticipating mid- to late September, not early June. And she's not available at this time. There's a part-timer. Jo Marie. Perhaps you've met her. Anyway, she's not interested in more than fifteen or twenty hours a week. Thus, I've been drafted, if you will, to steer the ship."

She had a slight accent, but he couldn't pin down the geography. He thought of the counsel he'd received just the previous night. *Pay attention to strangers.* "Where are you from?"

"That, my friend—can we assume we're friends since you didn't shoot me?—is a long story that I'm sure you do not have time for."

"There would have been a lot of paperwork to do if I'd shot you," he said.

She smiled and her face lit up. "Well, there is that."

"It was good you could come," he said, having some empathy for anybody suddenly asked to take on a new role. "Not easy I suspect for you to suddenly leave your job and your home. That's quite an interruption to your life."

She stared at him. The smile faded and her eyes looked sad. After a long pause, she answered. "Indeed. All kinds of interruptions in my life lately. But then again, those are stories best told over cocktails and a dinner that includes dessert," she said with a wave of a hand.

"Tonight?" he asked.

"What? Oh my, I wasn't angling for a dinner invitation. Erin McGarry can feed herself, thank you very much."

"I did put my gun away," he reminded her.

She cupped her chin in her hand and considered him. "This is a bit of a conundrum."

"Conundrum," he repeated.

"A difficult question, to which there is no easy or right answer," she explained.

"I know what a conundrum is," he said, slightly amused. "I'm just not used to having my dinner invitations labeled as such."

"I'd like the day to think about it," she said finally. "I've had no caffeine, no real food of any substance for more than twelve hours, and I'm a bit thrown off by my new responsibilities. I can't make any more decisions."

It stung a bit. "I'll need an answer by four. It's a Friday night, we're in season and reservations are required at most restaurants." It was a stretch. He could generally get a table most places, but there was no need for full disclosure.

"Four is adequate," she said. "Shall I ring you?"

"Sure. *Ring* me," he said. He pulled a business card from his pocket. Picked up a pen that was on the counter. He added his cell. "What's your number?" he asked. "So I can recognize it when the call comes in," he added.

She rattled if off and he entered it into his cell phone. "When you come in, make sure you lock the door behind yourself. In the last several months, we've had a couple break-ins on this block."

"Morgan never mentioned that," she said, looking concerned. "But it does explain the addition of the security alarm."

"I don't think there's a need to worry. But it's always good to be cautious."

"Of course," she said.

"If you need something to eat," he said, "Gertie's Café next door has the best breakfast in the area."

"That *is* something that Morgan chatted on about. A meal sounds like a fine idea."

"Dinner is a meal," he said.

She said nothing.

He decided that he'd pressed hard enough. "Goodbye, Erin McGarry. Good luck on your first day."

"Goodbye, Officer Marcus Price. Lovely to know you're here to serve and protect."

Two hours later, Marcus sat in Gertie's Café, sipping his hot tea. Thinking about another hot tea that had been spilled next door. The door of Gertie's opened and he found himself looking for a redhead.

Instead it was his friends Blade Savick and Jamie Weathers. They slid into the booth. Within seconds, Cheryl, their favorite server at Gertie's, brought over two coffees. She had a cream pitcher for Jamie.

They placed their order and settled in to catch up. They'd been friends since kindergarten, but had all gone their separate ways after high school only to reconnect back in Knoware a few years ago. There'd been times over the years that they were out of contact for months. Now it seemed odd if they didn't talk every couple of days.

It had been a week since he'd seen either of them. "How was the conference, Jamie?" Marcus asked.

"Good."

"Did you present, Dr. Weathers?" Blade asked. "Brag about the emergency medicine department at Bigelow Memorial?"

"Not this time. The people who did were good and the weather in San Diego was, of course, wonderful. Got some sailing in."

"I miss California," Marcus admitted.

"Too many people," Blade said. He liked small towns.

"How is Daisy feeling?" Marcus asked him.

"Sick every day," Blade said. "But she's a trouper. Wakes up, throws up a couple times, and then showers for work."

"She's just ten weeks along, right?" Jaime said. "Another month and she'll likely be easing out of that phase."

"That's what she tells me," Blade said. "She takes it in stride, but it's driving me crazy. I wish we could have waited on the house, but it was perfect and we didn't want to lose it. Plus, I had a buyer for my duplex."

"With twins coming, you'll need the space," Marcus said. "Plus, you're going to love the neighborhood." Blade's new two-story brick home was just two streets over from the house Marcus had been fixing up for the last two years. It had great character, beautiful woodwork and a chef's kitchen that was as nice as his own and totally wasted on Blade.

"I know. It was good to have a week off for the move. Back to work tomorrow. What's been happening in our fair city?" Blade asked as Cheryl dropped off the food and refilled coffee cups.

"We live in a city?" she said. "I thought it was mass confusion." She looked at the window where outside at least twenty people were waiting for a table. She hurried away.

"Well?" Jamie prompted, reminding Marcus that he hadn't answered Blade's question.

"Busy, you know." He leaned forward and spoke quietly. "Confidentially, I heard just yesterday that there's chatter that is getting picked up about an upcoming attack on US soil. Homeland Security thinks it's credible." He could trust his friends to keep the information to themselves. Plus, they were in jobs where they were either out and about in the community or seeing a steady stream of strangers in the emergency room. It wouldn't hurt to have more watchful eyes.

"At least a third of our sessions at the conference had something to do with responding to terrorism," Jamie said, shaking his head. "It's a crazy world right now."

"Yeah. I doubt Knoware, Washington, is the target but still, aware and watchful beats the alternative. Anyway, closer to home, I answered an alarm call at Tid-dle's this morning."

Blade put down his fork. There'd been reason to think that the break-ins at Gertie's Café and Feisty Pete's had been the work of a group that had nearly killed Daisy just a few short months ago. But they'd never been able to successfully tie them to the break-ins. Blade was interested in anything that might lengthen the already-lengthy prison sentence that the three in-dividuals were serving.

"False alarm. Set off by Erin McGarry, Morgan's sister. She's taking over for Morgan, who's been put on bed rest for the remainder of her pregnancy."

"I don't think I knew she had a sister," Blade said. "Does she look like Morgan?"

"Every bit as Irish. Not blonde like Morgan. A red-head. And…well, she's…um…not really all that tall. She drinks tea."

Blade and Jamie looked up from their plates. Then at each other. "That's it? That's all you have to say about her?" Jamie asked.

"Yeah. She's…fine."

Blade put down his fork. "I think I have a sudden need for chocolate."

"No way, you got the last girl who came to town. And you married her. This one is mine," Jamie said.

"Dibs," Marcus said, using his cop voice.

"What?" Blade and Jamie said together. *Dibs* hadn't been uttered since Marcus and Jamie fought over the senior prom queen.

"I already asked her to dinner," Marcus said.

"Where are you taking her?" Jamie asked.

"I don't know," Marcus admitted. "She...hasn't exactly said yes. She wanted the day to think about it."

"Oh my God," Blade said. "She didn't say yes right away. This is great. It almost makes up for having to paint every room of my new house."

"So you really don't have a date yet," Jamie clarified.

"Dibs," Marcus said again. "Listen, she's a stranger in town. We were told to pay close attention to strangers."

Blade pointed at the people waiting outside. "You plan on taking all those people to dinner, too?"

"I called it," Marcus said. "That's how dibs works."

"That was how it worked twenty years ago," Jamie said.

Marcus said nothing.

"Oh, fine," Jamie said, shaking his head. "But I'm still buying chocolate today."

"I'll go with you," Blade said. He looked at Marcus. "Perhaps you could benefit from a character witness. Want us to put a good word in for you?" he asked innocently.

"No. What I really want is for the two of you to shut up."

Erin drank her tea and thought about the very handsome police officer who had responded to the silent alarm. He'd been polite and professional until they'd cleared the air that she was Morgan's sister. Then he been a bit flirty. Not in a sleazy way, but in an *I'm very good at this* way.

He wasn't used to being put off, that much was clear. But as charming as he'd been, she hadn't come to Knoware to meet a man. She'd come to help her sister. There was no one else. It hardly seemed possible that their parents had been gone for almost ten years.

Morgan had been the rock. Steady. Settled. She'd been the rolling stone, moving from place to place, shaking off any moss that had the tenacity to attempt to cling to her and slow her down.

Nothing had changed. She would only be here as long as Morgan needed her. Next stop, unknown. She'd enjoyed saying that over the years. Now, oddly, not so much.

Perhaps the stone was simply tired. Perhaps it was bruised from the unpleasantness that had precipitated her leaving her last position, or rather, being told in no uncertain terms not to come back.

Her pride was hurt. No doubt about that. While she'd been a rolling stone, she'd been a valued contributor according to every one of her former employers. Until her last position at Preston's Automobile Exchange in Paris had ended badly.

But that was a worry for another day. Today's task was to open the store, delight every customer, and sometime along the way, make a decision about dinner with Officer Price, who had caused her to spill her first cup of tea.

She'd just turned when he came around the corner, not a sound betraying his arrival. And she had very good hearing, which meant that he was pretty quiet on his feet. She'd seen the gun first, thus dropped cup and spilled tea.

She'd seen the police uniform next, which had quieted her racing heart. Not quite still a believer that those in positions of trust can always be trusted—an arrest and a brief stint in a South American jail three years ago had forever destroyed that illusion—she had re-called her sister saying that the police in Knoware were quite nice.

She noticed the man then. He was handsome, with perfectly symmetrical features. Dark hair, dark eyes, tan skin. Tall, but then everybody was tall compared to her. Maybe six feet. Lean and muscular, the uniform had hugged him in all the right places.

He was really one of the sexiest men that she'd en-countered in a long time. And for some reason, even though the gun had still been pointed in her direction, she had not been afraid.

She truly had not been angling for a dinner invita-tion. Just trying to put off any more questions about leaving her job. That was still a little raw. But he'd been so quick to offer that she hadn't had time to dance her way back from the awkward gaffe. She wished she could call up Morgan, bend her ear a bit, and casually inquire about Officer Price. But her sister had more important things to think about now.

Erin would have to go this one alone. But then again, wasn't that what a rolling stone generally did? Even when there were other stones, rolling along, they were generally never going at exactly the same pace or po-sitioned on exactly the same path.

She wandered about the front of the store now, fa-miliarizing herself with the merchandise. Morgan had found herself a cadre of local artists and she used their work strategically through the storefront to create depth and texture. There were paintings and prints and mixed metal sculptures. Interesting jewelry popped up in un-usual places, and a lovely selection of scarves tossed over an antique sofa likely made shoppers think about sinking in.

She rubbed her hand across the stack of Irish sweaters and smiled at the Irish proverbs hand-painted on glass frames. She passed by the chocolate case and made a resolution to limit herself to one per day. Morgan had been sending her chocolate for years. She could recommend it unconditionally.

She retrieved the money that was hidden in the kitchen and got her cash register ready. Then she walked to the front window and flipped the lovely hand-painted sign to Open for Business. She would watch over Morgan's store and would not give her sister any reason to, once again, be disappointed in her. Morgan could rest easy with her decision to reach out for help. Erin would be the steady rock this time.

The two men sat on their beds in the cheap hotel room. The television was on, but neither of them watched it. The younger man finished his food, crumpling up the wrapper into a ball. He tossed it toward the garbage container in the corner. It fell short. He did not get off the bed to fetch it.

The older man sighed. "Pick up your mess. Were you raised by pigs?"

Ivan didn't answer. It didn't matter. They both knew who had raised him. But he did get up and toss the garbage into the can. "This is stupid. We're wasting time. She was a bad choice."

"She was a good choice and a necessary one," Gasdrig said. He'd been confident that the flight attendants were studying him, and he'd fully expected that he and

Ivan would get extra scrutiny when going through customs in New York.

"But you said it would be easy to retrieve once we were in New York," Ivan whined.

"I was wrong. She protected her bag too closely. We couldn't cause a spectacle."

"So we chased her across the whole damn country only to lose her because of a train."

"That was unfortunate," Gasdrig said calmly. The previous night he'd cursed the freight train that had gone on forever, allowing her to get so far ahead that they lost her. "But she's not gone far." He pointed to the map that was spread out on the small table in the corner. They'd purchased it at a gas station after they'd lost the woman. "The road only leads to a few places. We'll find her."

"It delays us."

"A delay is not bad. Bad would have been the information being seized. The whole operation is contingent upon those plans."

"So now what?" Ivan asked.

"We start looking for her and we retrieve what is ours."

"What if she's discovered it? What if she resists?"

"She won't have found it and she is but one woman, easily disposed of. And then we will do what we came for. America will pay," Gasdrig said, closing his eyes. "We will keep our promises."

# *Chapter 2*

By the time Marcus finally went home, it was almost noon. He'd intended to stay for maybe an hour to do some paperwork, but it had taken much longer when he'd had to play referee between Dawson and Serenity, two of his junior officers.

They were both decent cops and he thought Chief Ralley had made good hiring decisions when bringing them on. But they were both high achievers and instead of cooperating and watching each other's backs, they were both demonstrating some competitive behaviors that could be a detriment to their safety, the department's performance and ultimately, the department's reputation.

*Not on my watch.* That was what he'd told them. Got them both to acknowledge their role in the morning's snafu and then spent another forty-five minutes walking them through how the assault-and-battery investigation involving one vacationer against a second vacationer, who both should have been spending their time fishing on a Friday morning versus throwing punches, should have gone.

Finally satisfied that he'd done what he could, he'd left and driven straight home. Well, almost. He'd driven down Main Street, past Tiddle's. He'd looked in the windows as he passed and had seen movement, but hadn't been able to distinguish much more.

He wondered if Blade and Jamie had made good on their promise to stop in the store, on the pretense of desperately needing chocolate. He wasn't worried that they'd say anything inappropriate about him, no matter how much they teased. They'd been friends for thirty of their thirty-five years.

After high school, he'd gone to college and then did his time with the LAPD. Jamie, supersmart Jamie, had done college and then medical school and a residency. Then had surprised everyone and joined the army. Finally, he'd come home to run the emergency medicine program at Bigelow Memorial.

Blade had never left. After his girlfriend had gotten pregnant, they'd married and Blade had done his best to make it work. He'd gotten a job as a firefighter and had earned his paramedic license. The marriage hadn't lasted, but he now had a wonderful sixteen-year-old daughter. And just months ago, he'd rescued pretty Daisy Rambler, who had her own sixteen-year-old daughter, off a ledge in Headstone Canyon; now they were married and expanding their family.

Marcus pulled into the detached three-car garage that sat behind the hundred-year-old house that he was almost done remodeling. He walked inside and straight to the bedroom. He put his gun and badge in the drawer next to the bed. Then he took off all his clothes and headed for the shower.

Ten minutes later, feeling almost human, he pushed open the bedroom window to let in the warm fresh air. Then he crawled into bed and closed his eyes.

He had one final thought before falling asleep. Erin McGarry with the pretty red-gold hair had not yet called.

Erin looked at her watch. Ten minutes after four. She'd missed the deadline. But really, there'd been barely a minute of time in between customers to sneak a second cup of tea. But she'd done exactly that, because the slice of cherry pie that Gertie from the café next door had brought by shortly after noon demanded a good cup of tea.

*Welcome and let me know if you need anything,* Gertie had said.

On her way out of the store, several of her customers had stopped the woman. S*o nice to see you back working. Gertie, we knew nothing could keep you down.*

It had made Erin think that there must be a story there and she'd made a mental note to ask Morgan or Brian when she got the chance.

The customers had been such an interesting mix. Moms and dads with children in tow. Women by themselves, shopping for a variety of things. Two handsome men, not as handsome as Officer Price, but definitely lookers in their own right, had come in and bought copious amounts of chocolate. One said his wife was pregnant and the other said he had recently been absent from work and his coworkers would expect something to compensate for picking up extra shifts. They'd stayed around to chat some, mostly about Morgan and how nice it was that she'd come to help out her sister.

There had been a group of young women looking for bridal shower gifts. Her most recent customer had been a pretty woman with dark hair and striking blue eyes. She'd wandered about the store a bit before buying some scented lotion. She'd seemed pleased to run into a woman with blond and pink hair. Erin had been close enough to hear that the dark-haired woman's name was Daisy and the blond-and-pink-haired woman was Sheila, who was buying an anniversary gift for her parents. Daisy had left first, then Sheila with a dazzling glass bowl. On her way out, Sheila had given Erin a coupon for 50 percent off a dozen pastries at the Knoware Bakery & Café.

For the first time all day, there was nobody in the store but her. She would flip the sign to Closed in another fifty minutes and would have nicely survived her first day. She should be exhausted. Instead, she felt revved up, ready to take on the world.

But oddly enough, not ready to take on handsome Officer Price. She was going to call and politely decline his offer.

She pulled his business card from her skirt pocket. It was already looking rather rumpled. At least ten times during the day, she'd reached in her pocket and folded and unfolded the poor paper. Considering.

Now, at peace with her decision, she dialed. Maybe it would go to voice mail and she'd leave a polite and decisive message. When it was answered on the second ring, she almost bobbled her phone.

"I thought you might not call," he said.

She'd expected a hello. "I…uh…well…"

"But then again, you didn't strike me as the type who considers avoidance much of a strategy."

She was exactly that type. She'd made avoidance into an art form.

"What time should I pick you up?" he asked. "Or would you feel more comfortable meeting there?"

"I…"

"At first I thought steakhouse. But then I reconsidered. We've got a place that makes the best shrimp and grits and corn bread that you'll find west of New Orleans. And they've got a bourbon pecan pie that will make you swoon."

She loved shrimp and grits. "I'm not the swooning type," she said.

"You will be after tonight."

That was what she was a little bit afraid of. Officer Price was charming. But then again, her feet hurt, her only sleep had been sitting up on an airplane, and she was starving. The pie from Gertie had been lovely, but she needed food.

"I can meet you at six," she said. "It won't be a late night because afterward, I need to stop in and see Morgan at the hospital."

"How is your sister?"

It was nice of him to ask. "Doing fine. Her blood pressure is staying where they want it and contractions have stopped. They want to monitor her for a few days, but if it all stays well, they have told her that she'll be released from the hospital and can continue her bed rest at home."

"Good to hear," he said. "Must be hard to focus on

anything else when you're worried about her and the baby."

He'd given her the perfect out. But suddenly she didn't feel quite so strongly about taking it. "I'll need some directions," she said.

"I'll text you. There'll be a reservation under my name."

She hung up, thinking Officer Price had rather easily gotten his way. But she wasn't too bothered. Shrimp and grits awaited.

She heard the bell above her door jingle and she walked back to the front. By the time she locked the door at five, there had been six more customers She counted her cash drawer, readied the bank deposit and put the money to start the next day in the kitchen, behind the tea canisters. She walked to the front of the store to double-check the lock and was just about to leave when her eyes caught the shelf of lovely leather purses that Morgan stocked. They were bright summer colors and a perfect size, much better than her big brown shoulder bag.

She got cash from her wallet and slipped the money under a flower pot that sat near the cash register. She didn't want to recalculate the deposit so she'd ring up the sale tomorrow. But she wasn't waiting to use the new gem. She transferred her wallet, some gum and lip gloss from her shoulder bag to the purse. She left her comfy shoes, her scarf and two new books she'd purchased in the airport in her shoulder bag. Those things were essential for travel, but she didn't need to lug them around every day.

She paused when she came to her passport. In Europe, where she often traveled between countries, she routinely carried it. But there was probably no need of that here. It would just take up space. But old habits were hard to break and she knew she'd want to keep it close. And given that she'd be spending most of her time at the store, that was probably the best place.

In the back room, she found the drawer where Morgan kept a laptop and other office supplies. She pulled out a manilla envelope and put her passport in it. She took one last look in her brown shoulder bag and unzipped the inside compartment. There she found a thumb drive.

She had no idea it had been in her purse and certainly didn't know what was on it. But it rather looked like one she'd used several years ago and she suspected it had been in the shoulder bag for a long time. She'd have to look at it later. Perhaps when the store wasn't busy, she could borrow Morgan's computer. She added the thumb drive to the manilla envelop, sealed the adhesive tab, and tossed the envelope on a shelf in the back room.

Before leaving the store, she set the alarm and double-checked to make sure the door was locked behind her. Her car was warm and she turned on the air conditioning. On her way to Morgan and Brian's house, she swung by the bank and dropped the deposit in the overnight banking slot, as Brian had instructed.

She parked on the street in front of the house, since Morgan and Brian both parked in the two-car garage. She used the key that Brian had given her to let herself in. There was a guest room on the second floor where she'd stashed her suitcase that morning. She tossed her shoulder bag on top of it. Glancing at her watch, she realized that she was going to have to hurry in order to make dinner on time.

She took a five-minute shower and pulled on a soft black dress and some strappy black sandals with just a little heel. Then she walked through a spritz of perfume and brushed her teeth. There wasn't much she could do with her hair. It had a mind of its own. She kept it long to give the corkscrew curls some weight. That helped keep her from looking as if she'd stuck her finger in a light socket.

At fifteen minutes to six, she left the house. Fortunately, it was only a mile away although that mile took a bit since there was heavy car and foot traffic along the way. She walked in with one minute to spare.

"Officer Price," she said, seeing him in the corner of the small lobby. The place had rough wooden floors and wide-plank walls. She peered into the dining room. There were big wooden tables and comfortable-looking chairs. Ceiling fans were whirling and some jazz was playing in the background.

"Marcus," he corrected her. "You look nice."

"Wasn't sure of the dress code."

"You're bringing up the standard," he said easily. "Come on. Our table is ready."

If he'd thought she was pretty this morning, she was downright adorable in her black dress that was fitted at the top and then swung a couple inches above her knees. Her shoes were sexy and her toenails were a shocking blue. And she smelled really good.

"They sell that perfume in the store?" he asked.

She shook her head. "In Paris."

"Ah, the beginning of the story that will take us from drinks to dinner to dessert."

Again, she shook her head. "I wouldn't want to bore you with the details."

He had been a cop for way too long not to wonder if there was something nefarious about Erin's unwillingness to tell her personal story. "I don't think that's possible," he volleyed.

The server came up to the table, saving Erin from having to answer. They ordered cocktails, a white wine for her, a Manhattan for him, with his favorite whiskey. Then it was time to study the menu. They both went for the shrimp and grits with a side of succotash.

"You won't be sorry," he said.

She took a sip of her wine. "Oh, that's good. Tell me about Knoware."

Not "tell me about yourself," which would have ultimately reverted back to an inquiry into her. But rather a safer nonpersonal topic. "First time here?" he asked. He would get to the information he wanted, even if he had to take the long route.

"No. I breezed through for a few hours about a year ago. So I've heard the 'Knoware is really nowhere' jokes. But not much else. I had a layover in Seattle and wanted to see Morgan and Brian and the store. There was no time to see any of the community."

"The *community*," he emphasized, "is busting at the seams right now. Every hotel, B and B, short-term rental and camping ground is likely above an 80 percent occupancy rate, with the more popular places at 100 percent. There's good boating and water sports, excellent fishing and lots of hiking and bike riding trails. The views of the ocean are spectacular and the mountains are an easy drive. We've got highly skilled chefs in the area, so foodies like to visit. Most of the vineyards are east of the Cascades, but we've got a few of those, too. And the weather this time of year just can't be beat."

"It was lovely today. Every time the door opened, I drew in a deep breath of air. It just felt good in my lungs."

"Locals and tourists alike appreciate this. Off-season can be wet and cold and generally unpleasant at times."

"Well, I'm glad it's June then."

"Hard to believe that July is just around the corner," he said. "How did the day go?"

"I had fun meeting all the customers today. And they weren't just lookers. A lot of them bought something."

"These months have to be good to sustain the merchants over the leaner times."

"But I suspect the influx of people strains local services, everything from garbage collection to police protection," she said.

"Indeed. From Memorial Day to Labor Day, firefighters and police work extra shifts, as do the medical providers in the urgent care centers and the emergency room at Bigelow Memorial. Every high school kid who wants a job has one at one of the local eateries or at the boat and water craft rentals down by the harbor."

The server returned, carrying their steaming plates. Erin added a generous pat of butter to her grits and then took a bite. "Delicious. I may try the steakhouse some night, but this was definitely worthy of a first dinner."

"I'm glad I guessed right."

She glanced around the busy restaurant. "Hard to believe this all goes away at the end of season."

"Not all. We get some fall hikers because the foliage in this area is pretty amazing. But by winter, it's pretty quiet. But the locals, who may have stayed away from the stores and the restaurants and the bars at the height of the season, come back."

"And those of you working extra shifts actually get a day off?"

"A true luxury," he said. "But I knew what I was in for when I came back."

"Came back?"

"I grew up here. My mother moved here after she and my father divorced." If he gave her some personal information, maybe she'd reciprocate.

"But then you moved away?" she asked.

"I did. College in California. Then more than ten years with the Los Angeles Police Department."

"Why did you come back?"

"My mother was ill. Ovarian cancer. She died about two years ago."

"I'm sorry," she said. "I know what a terrible loss that is. Morgan and I lost our parents more than ten years ago. Are you close to your father?"

He thought about the three unopened voice mails that were sitting on his cell phone. All had come in within the last two weeks. "My father is not close to anyone. Not to me or to either of his two living ex-wives. Not sure how he feels about his current wife. We haven't met."

"If I'm doing the math right, that's four marriages," she said, looking faintly astonished.

"That's right."

"Oh."

Shock. Maybe disapproval. It was probably why he should never talk about his father. "He's career-driven. Was early into the tech industry in California. Made a ton of money, or so he says. But enough about that."

She studied him. "Did you go to school and work for all those years in California in hopes of having a relationship with your father?"

No one had ever asked him that. If Blade or Jamie had connected those dots before, they hadn't wanted to stick their necks out. "I like the weather in California," he said easily. It was what he told everyone.

"I see. Does he have other children?"

"Nope. Just me. Wasn't lucky enough to have a sibling."

"I don't know what I'd have done without Morgan. She's been the constant in my life for the last ten years, serving as parent long before she should have."

"Now you get a chance to return the favor."

"Yes. And I'm going to work very hard not to disappoint her."

That was an interesting way to put it. "I doubt that will happen," he said.

She just shrugged. "It must be very different being a police officer in Los Angeles and then coming to Knoware."

Again, she was deftly changing the subject. He let it go. "Different, of course. And even though I was coming home to friends, I missed a few of the other officers I served with in Los Angeles. Oddly, though, I'd talked about Knoware enough over the years that a couple of guys who were older than me and able to retire moved here about six months ago. Like a lot of former cops do, they'd transitioned over into security work and started a small company. When I need a fix from the old days, I call up Jim and Tyson and we go get a beer. When I'm buying, they never turn down the invitation."

She smiled. "Smart guys. Well, I for one am grateful that I didn't turn down this invitation."

"Speaking of grateful. You'll be filled with gratitude if you have the pie."

She put her hand on her midsection. "I want to. I do. But I'm stuffed and quite frankly, it would be my second piece of pie today and that might just be excessive."

"Second piece?"

"Yes, Gertie from the café next door brought one over. Several of my customers seemed to know her quite well."

"Gertie Biscuit is an institution in Knoware. Runs a great restaurant, caters amazing events and always has time for somebody who needs a minute."

"Was she recently ill? I overheard several people telling her that it was nice to see her back at work."

"She was shot."

"In Knoware?"

"Yeah." He held up a hand. "I don't want to scare you. This is generally a pretty peaceful community. But she got in the middle of a situation that involved my friend Blade Savick, the woman he recently married, Daisy Rambler, and some bad actors."

"There was a woman in the store today named Daisy. Brown hair, lovely blue eyes."

"That was probably her."

"Well, she seemed nice so I'm glad that she wasn't hurt. And I'm also glad to hear that Gertie recovered. Which reminds me, I should get going if I want to make visiting hours at the hospital."

He signaled the server for the check. Once he had it, he left cash for the bill and a nice tip. "I'll walk you to your car," he said.

"I guess that's a good idea."

He'd probably scared her with Gertie's story. That hadn't been his intent. But in the height of tourist season, when all kinds of strangers were in town, a little well-placed trepidation was not really a bad thing.

She was driving a black four-door rental. She used the fob to unlock it and he opened the driver's door. She quickly slipped inside. "Thank you for dinner," she said, looking up at him. She extended her hand.

He shook it, somewhat amused. Most of his dates did not end with a handshake. "My pleasure, Erin. Drive safely."

Ivan shoved the remains of his dinner aside. "I'm getting tired of eating sandwiches in crappy hotel rooms," he said.

"Better than sleeping outside," Gasdrig said. It wasn't as bad as Ivan made it out. But then again, he'd never known the hardship that had been a constant in Gasdrig's life for many years. "Stop complaining. Not much choice of rooms in our price range." Soon, they would have more money than they could spend. Assuming they found what they were looking for.

"We searched all day," Ivan said. "Didn't see no signs of the red-haired woman."

"We'll find her. Now shut the damn television off. I need some sleep."

Ivan picked up the remote and angrily flicked the power button.

Gasdrig understood the frustration. The concern that they were wasting time. There was still a lot to do. They would need to work quickly so that when the politicians, the military and the thousands of other people lined the streets, all would be ready.

The fools would be celebrating their country's independence.

It was going to be a celebration, all right. Bubbling up, erupting from the ground like a newly opened geyser. Fireworks that this nation was never going to forget.

# Chapter 3

Erin was happy when her brother-in-law took her presence at the hospital as a welcome chance to grab a shower and food other than what was offered in the hospital cafeteria. It gave her an opportunity to see Morgan alone. She loved Brian and thought he was an awesome husband, but it just wasn't the same when he was around.

And no matter how hard he might try, he probably didn't really trust Erin yet. She'd given him reason over the years. Had caused Morgan heartache, and it was unlikely that he was going to easily let that go.

She'd spent the first fifteen minutes at her sister's bedside telling her all about the day. Morgan had been very pleased at the amount of sales, saying it was one of the best days of the summer yet.

"You must be tired," Morgan said. "Have you even had anything to eat?"

"I had dinner with Marcus Price. Officer Price," she added.

"I know Marcus. Everybody knows Marcus," Morgan said. "How exactly did this come about?"

She told her the story, omitting the part where Marcus had pointed his gun at her. "I thought it might be a nice way to pay back his very timely response to the alarm," she said. "By the way, still need the code to shut it off in the morning when I open up."

Morgan gave it to her and she dutifully committed the four digits to memory. "Thank you," she said. "There will be no more false alarms."

"I imagine Marcus wouldn't mind. Perhaps it would lead to more dinner dates. And perhaps you wouldn't mind that too much."

Erin sighed. "He is terribly handsome."

Morgan smiled. "And very nice. But… Well, let's just say it might be best to be careful."

"You're not suggesting…"

"No. He's a great guy. But he breaks a lot of hearts. Always nicely and in such a way that he's able to stay friends with almost everybody he's ever dated, but he won't ever stay with just one woman. He's not wired that way."

"That's perfect. I'm not interested in anything permanent. And besides, it was one dinner. A friendly gesture."

"He's not the welcoming committee," Morgan said. "Although that would be really good for Knoware if he was. Women would be lined up to move here. Business would be booming."

"I'll let him know you've got his next job picked out for him."

"He's got enough on his plate, with being interim chief."

"He didn't mention that," Erin said.

"Not his style to brag, I suspect."

"That's refreshing. Especially after Albert."

Morgan laughed. "Yes, your Albert was a bit of a blowhard."

"He was never *my Albert*." That implied an intimacy that simply hadn't materialized. Her best friend in Paris had teased her that she was getting picky in her old age. She supposed that was true. It had been easier when she'd been in her early twenties to have a fling of sorts. But in the last couple of years, it had seemed…more important, somehow.

She'd liked Albert but certainly hadn't felt anything more serious. Her friend had thought that she'd owed Albert a debt. After all, he'd been the one who'd introduced her to the owners of Preston's Automobile Exchange. She'd had the credentials for her position, but she suspected it hadn't hurt that he'd purchased an expensive vehicle just six months earlier.

"I suppose not," Morgan said, responding to her *your Albert* denial. "I guess in fact, you and Marcus are somewhat alike. Neither of you wants to commit with your full heart."

"Mommy and Daddy had true love. You've found it with Brian. I think it would be too much to hope that I'd do the same," Erin said. "The law of averages, right? So many marriages end in divorce. Marcus told me his dad had been married four times."

"I don't think I'd ever heard that," Morgan said. "No doubt that probably has something to do with his *like 'em and leave 'em* approach."

"No love 'em and leave 'em?" Erin asked.

"You'd have to ask Marcus," her sister said with a big yawn.

No way. She wasn't having those types of conversations with the handsome police officer. "Listen, we're both tired. I'm going to go."

"You've got your key to the house? I think Brian is intending to come back here tonight and the two of you might miss each other."

"Got my key."

"Have I told you lately how much I appreciate this?" Morgan said. "I feel bad that you had to leave your own work."

She had yet to tell Morgan about what had happened at Preston's Automobile Exchange. It was too raw, too unexpected. "No worries," she said. "And listen, I could do this five summers in a row, not that I think that many babies in that many years is wise, and we'd still never be even."

"There's no score-keeping, Erin. You were my sister. I was responsible for you after Mom and Dad died."

"I didn't make it easy."

"You were young."

"Still making it easy for me," Erin said, "by letting me off the hook."

"If I can keep this baby inside me for another eight weeks because I don't have to worry about the store, we'll be even forever."

Morgan's doctor had felt confident that the baby would fare well if she could get to at least thirty-four weeks. "Eight weeks, hell no, sister. We're going for full-term. We want that baby to cook for the full forty weeks."

"The doctors have said that's unlikely."

"They don't know Morgan Tiddle. When you put your mind to something, there's no stopping you."

"I hope you're right," Morgan said, blinking her eyes. "Nothing has mattered this much to me for a very long time. Maybe ever."

Morgan must be terrified, Erin thought as she drove her rental car to the house. She was not going to give her one more reason to be concerned about anything.

The house was dark and she assumed that Brian was already on his way back to the hospital. She let herself in and went to the kitchen for her last cup of tea of the day. This one was decaffeinated and she carried it up the stairs. She'd washed her face and put on her pajamas when her cell phone dinged with an incoming text from Handsome Officer Price.

Hope your visit with Morgan went well. I really enjoyed dinner.

She debated a response. It had been a really lovely evening, one of the nicest she'd had in a long time. He'd been charming and when he'd walked her to her car, she'd thought it might get awkward. Would he ask her out again? Would he try to kiss her?

As lovely as that sounded, she hadn't come to Knoware for that. She needed to be focused on the store, focused on being there for Morgan.

With that in mind, she wrote Excellent shrimp and grits. Thank you for making my first meal here a good one.

She pressed Send, set her alarm on her phone and

then put it on her bedside table. She slipped underneath the cool sheets and closed her eyes. Tomorrow was Saturday, likely a busy day for the store.

Marcus woke up on Saturday morning and was in the office by six thirty, listening to a shift report from the two officers who were going off duty at seven. There had been a DUI arrest, a bar fight that had ended in an ambulance ride for the person who threw the first punch, and a vehicle accident that had likely totaled two cars, but fortunately, because of seat belts, all four occupants had walked away with minor injuries.

Forty minutes later, after signing some paperwork that would have normally been the chief's responsibility, he was in his car, making his first pass through town. Gertie's was just opening and there were already people going in the door. The windows of Tiddle's were dark. The store wouldn't open for another two hours.

Erin was likely still sleeping.

Perhaps she'd packed in such a hurry that she'd forgotten to include pajamas.

That was such an entertaining thought, especially after seeing her in her little black dress, that he almost missed movement in the corner of his eye. He checked his mirrors, made a quick turn left, went around the block and pulled up in front of two men who were standing in the narrow alley that ran between the buildings across the street from Gertie's Café. There was just enough space for them to stand shoulder to shoulder. They were both smoking and holding coffee cups. Oddly, given that it was a lovely June morning, one was wearing a stocking cap. He looked younger than the other man.

Their intense conversation stopped when they became aware of Marcus's arrival. He looked behind them and didn't see anything that concerned him. He used his mirrors to again check the street. Then he opened his door.

"Morning," he said pleasantly.

"Good morning, Officer," the older man said.

Marcus took a couple steps toward them. "I think it's going to be another nice day."

"Indeed."

Again, it had been the older man who responded. This was what he both loved and hated about tourist season. The summer months attracted all kinds and he'd met some of the most interesting and nicest folks. And then there were always a few that he'd desperately wished had picked another place to vacation. He wasn't sure yet which camp these two fell into.

"Vacationing here in Knoware?" he asked, letting them know that he recognized them as strangers to the community.

"Nearby."

"Where at?" Marcus pressed.

"Brickstone Bungalows," the older man said, after the slightest hesitation.

It was a popular place.

"We heard the fishing is good here." The older man flicked the hand with the cigarette carelessly in the direction of the community pier.

"Make sure you've got a camera with you. You're going to want to show your friends proof," Marcus said with a smile. He'd purposefully addressed his remarks toward the younger man. It seemed odd that he'd not yet said a word.

"We'll do that," the older man said. "But first I think

we'll have some breakfast. The place across the street seems popular."

Was that why they'd been watching? "You won't be disappointed," Marcus said.

"It's been a pleasure, Officer," the older man said, taking a step toward the café. When he saw that the younger man was rooted in his spot, he pulled on the man's sleeve. Still, he didn't budge. Instead, he put one hand in the pocket of his lightweight sweatshirt, holding both his cigarette and coffee cup in the same hand.

And Marcus got a feeling that something was not quite right.

"Come on," the older man said. "I'm hungry."

Marcus could see him tighten his grip. It must have registered, because the younger man let himself be pulled along.

Marcus watched them cross the street. Before entering Gertie's, they tossed their cigarettes into the receptacle filled with sand just for that purpose. And then they entered through the wide door. Through the big windows that ran alongside the front of the restaurant, he could make out their progress as they walked down the aisle and took the last booth. They sat and immediately turned their faces toward the street.

Marcus locked eyes with them. Gave them a nod.

Yeah, he was watching. He wanted them to understand that. Visitors, like Talk and Hat, as he mentally dubbed them, were welcome. But if any came to his town to cause trouble, they quickly discovered that he had very little tolerance for that kind of nonsense.

"I hate cops."

Gasdrig again glanced out the window. The officer who'd approached them this morning had long since gotten into his SUV and driven away. "Keep your voice down," he said. The café was filled with people and there was enough noise that it wasn't likely they'd be overheard. But still, he was frustrated with Ivan. "You gave him a reason to look at us twice. If he'd have seen your gun, there would have been real trouble. You need to be smarter than that."

"I hate cops."

"Yeah, yeah, broken record." Gasdrig reminded himself that he needed Ivan's very unique skill set. He pushed his dirty plate to the side. The cop had been right about one thing—the food had been very good at Gertie's Café. He tossed money down to cover the bill.

"How come you said that we're staying at Brickstone Bungalows?" Ivan asked. "That's not right."

"He caught me by surprise. I certainly wasn't going to tell him the truth, and it was the only place I could remember stopping at to see if they had rooms. He's not going to remember it. Forget about it. Now let's get out of here."

"Where to?"

"To the sporting goods store. I saw one on the out-skirts of this town. Pratt Sports Spot."

"Why the hell are we going there?"

He wasn't going to admit that he had also offered up the fishing information without much thought. "We told the cop that we were going fishing. Hard to do that without a pole." He leaned forward. If they ran into the same cop later, he wanted their story to hold.

"I'm driving," Ivan said.

Gasdrig preferred to drive, but he would give in to the kid on this one. He tossed him the keys.

"What if at the end of the day we're no closer?" Ivan asked.

"That's not an option. She didn't disappear. We just have to look in the right place."

"What if she found it and looked at it?"

"Impossible. The encryption is the best."

"Maybe she turned it over to the cops?" Ivan said, adjusting the stocking cap on his head.

"Then we will retrieve our rightful property from them. You said it just a few minutes ago. You hate cops. A few dead ones in the middle of nowhere, get it, nowhere, is nothing."

# Chapter 4

An hour after watching the strangers walk into Gertie's, Marcus was racing to the far eastern edge of Knoware. A 911 call had come in, stating that a bike rider had been hit by a driver who'd left the scene. When he got close, he saw that the fire department had beaten him there. His friend Blade was bent over a woman lying on the ground. He was immobilizing her arm. Her neck was already in a brace and there was a fair amount of blood on her clothing and in her hair.

Her hair. Oh no. He pushed forward, then stopped so fast that he almost fell over his own two feet. From ten feet away he'd seen the long red-gold hair and it had scared him. But now, close enough that he could see better, he could tell that the texture was different and there were no curls.

"I want to talk to whoever was here first," he said to

the crowd of approximately ten. A man raised his hand and stepped forward.

"I made the 911 call," he said. He was late sixties, maybe early seventies.

"Sir, I'm Officer Price. What's your name?" Marcus asked, pulling out his notebook.

"Maury Clay," he said. "I live just up the road a mile. I came over the hill and saw her on the ground."

"Do you know her?"

Maury shook his head. "No, but she was conscious. Said that she and her family are in the area visiting. She chose to take a bike ride while her husband took their two kids fishing."

"Does her family know that she's been hurt?"

"I let her use my phone to call them. I imagine they're on their way. By the time she finished talking to them, the paramedics had arrived and they wanted us to step back."

"Did you see who hit her?"

Maury shook his head. "She told me that she was on the ground for at least five minutes before I came along. Whoever did it was long gone. Damn cowards. Left her alongside the road like she was some rodent."

Yeah, it was pretty hard to accept that somebody had hit the woman and not realized it. Hopefully she'd gotten a good look. "Thank you, Mr. Clay. For stopping, for helping her, for calling 911. That's all I need right now except your contact information in case I have other questions."

After the man gave it to him, Marcus made his way over to Blade. They were loading the woman into the back of an ambulance. "I need to speak with her," Marcus said.

Blade shook his head. "She's out. Compound fracture of her radius. I had to give her something pretty strong for the pain."

"Did you get her name?"

"Jordan Reese."

"She tell you anything about the person who hit her?"

"Yeah. Black SUV. Man driving. Another person in the front seat but she couldn't tell if it was a man or a woman."

"They didn't stop?"

"She said she didn't think they even slowed down."

Marcus felt the words settle on him. Maury Clay had called them cowards. He had some other ways to describe them. "I'll catch up with her at Bigelow Memorial. Does her family know that's where she's headed?"

"Yeah, I actually spoke to her husband. He's shaken up and he's got a couple little kids to deal with, but he's on his way." Blade stopped walking. Turned to Marcus. "When I was talking to him, for a second, I flashed forward a couple years. I could see me, with the twins, getting a call like that about Daisy. I felt for the man."

"I know. Not that it helps them right now, but we'll get the driver. We'll find him."

"I know you will. I wouldn't want anybody else looking," Blade said. "On a happier note, I met Erin McGarry."

"And?" Marcus asked.

"She seems very nice."

"That's it?" Marcus asked.

"I'm not good at sizing up women," Blade said. "So I had Daisy stop by."

So it hadn't been by chance that Daisy was at Tiddle's. "Did you tell her why she suddenly had to go shopping at Tiddle's?"

"I did. She understood."

"And what was Daisy's opinion?"

"Thumbs-up. And she wants to know where she buys her clothes."

"Oh, I'll make sure and ask her that," Marcus said.

Blade shrugged. "You're the one who will have to deal with Daisy's disappointment if you don't."

Marcus rolled his eyes. "We had a great time last night. At least I thought we did. This morning, in a text, she told me that the shrimp and grits were delicious."

Blade looked at him blankly.

"I'm glad she enjoyed her dinner, but I guess I was hoping for something more," Marcus said. For being a smart guy, Blade could be amazingly dense.

"Maybe you're going to have to work at this one a little harder than most," Blade said, his tone thoughtful.

"You say that like it would be a good thing," Marcus said.

"Might not be a bad thing."

"You got to give me more than that," Marcus said, a little irritated.

"Nope. I do not," Blade said.

They were within earshot of the other members of Blade's team. Marcus pressed his lips together, not willing to give them all something to talk about.

When Erin got the cash register ready, she saw three women standing on the sidewalk, peering into the windows. She hurried toward the front and unlocked the door six minutes early. "Come in, come in," she said, holding the door for them. She flipped the pretty Open sign as she followed them into the store.

They did not look at her oddly or ask about Morgan. That told her that they weren't local. Sure enough, later she heard one of them say, "We need a store like this in Omaha."

Erin smiled. She suspected that somewhere in Omaha, Nebraska, there was a similar store. If not, well then, perhaps that was food for thought. She had no immediate plans after leaving Knoware. Omaha might be as good as the next place. After having been outside the States for most of the last ten years, she felt that it would be good to have USA soil under her feet. She wanted to be closer to her new little niece or nephew. Closer to Morgan and Brian.

Closer to Marcus Price.

She lost her smile. That wouldn't matter. He'd have moved on. They were two rolling stones, rolling in different directions.

One of the women laid a scarf on the counter. "I'll take this."

"Excellent," Erin said, happy to focus on work. And for the next eight hours, she did little else. She'd thought it might be a no-lunch day, but there'd been a brief break in the action shortly after one. She'd put the Be Back Shortly sign in the window and had hurried over to Gertie's Café for a delicious grilled cheese sandwich.

She'd sat at the busy counter, next to a man who appeared to also be eating alone. He was talking with the waitress. Erin had shamelessly listened. That was how one learned things, after all.

"I imagine you heard about that poor woman who

got hit on her bicycle today on the edge of town," the waitress said.

The man nodded. "Bad situation. She's visiting here with her family. The police are all over it," he added in a reassuring tone.

"Was she injured badly?"

"I don't know. Transported by ambulance from the scene. I've got a call in to get an update."

The man must be in some type of role that he believed qualified him for that. By the look on the waitress's face, she wasn't surprised.

"Well, I certainly hope she's okay."

Erin ate her sandwich and silently added an "Amen to that." She had not been hit on her bike, but she had been rushed to a hospital once in a strange place. The memory of that day and the three subsequent awful lonely days in the hospital had barely faded in four years.

She was pushing her plate to the side when the man turned to her. He extended a hand. "I'm Bill Bliss, the mayor of Knoware."

"Erin McGarry," she said with a smile. "I'm Morgan Tiddle's sister."

"I thought that might be the case. I heard that you were on your way. Happy to have you in Knoware. Let us know if we can be helpful."

"Thank you," she said. People here were really nice. She got her check, paid it and slid off her stool. She was three steps from the door when two men walked in. The man in front was older, maybe late fifties. The man behind him was midtwenties. And for just a quick minute, she felt a flare of recognition. But couldn't place them.

Automatically, she stepped to the side so that they wouldn't collide. The older man nodded, swung around to face the younger man, wrapped an arm around his shoulders, and, rather forcibly, she thought, directed him toward the one empty booth.

Erin walked out the door, tidied up Morgan's plant and then used her key to unlock the front door of Tiddle's. She made sure the Open for Business sign was in the window.

"Stay here," Gasdrig ordered Ivan. Then he exited the front of Gertie's in hopes of keeping track of the red-haired woman. It wasn't difficult. She was next door, picking dead leaves off the flowering plant that sat in front of the door. Then she pulled keys from her pocket, unlocked the door and entered. He saw her in the window, changing the sign. He looked at the name written on the glass. Tiddle's Tidbits and Treasures. Based on the display, it was a gift store.

Yes, a gift. They'd hit the mother lode. She was here and by all appearances, wasn't going anywhere. She worked at the store or maybe even owned it.

He reentered Gertie's where Ivan sat aggressively tapping his index finger on the Formica-topped table. "Well?" he demanded.

Gasdrig sat down. He was still very angry with the kid. His reckless actions were going to get them into trouble. "Keep your voice down and order your damn lunch. She works next door. This is going to be easy." *Finally*, he added silently. The morning had been one problem after another. He had not planned on having to drive back to the airport to return the rental vehicle. But there'd been no choice once Ivan had seen the woman on the bike, make the incorrect assumption that it was the redheaded woman they were searching for and crashed into her.

He'd said it was an accident. Gasdrig was not so sure. But that was hardly what was important.

The SUV had escaped significant damage. He doubted he could say the same for the bike rider. But they hadn't stuck around to check. There were no witnesses, nothing to tie them to the crime. But still, he'd wanted to rid them of the vehicle as soon as possible. They'd returned it to the lot, handed it off to an overworked attendant, and then rented a sedan from a different company thirty feet down the line. All of that had eaten up the better part of their morning.

"Did she recognize us?" Ivan asked.

"I don't think so. Our disguises on the plane were good. But still, we don't need her to suddenly get suspicious."

"She didn't have her brown shoulder bag," Ivan said.

"I know. Perhaps too big to carry every day."

"It's at her house," Ivan stated with confidence.

"Or at the store, or in her car, or at her gym," Gasdrig explained.

"I suppose," Ivan acknowledged. The waitress came up with menus and water and both men were silent until she was gone.

"All that means is that even though we've located her, we're going to stick with our plan," Gasdrig said. "We'll hang around town a bit, spend a little time fishing." That meant that the $108 he'd spent on fishing equipment on their way back from the airport car rental would not be all in vain. "If we're lucky, we'll find someone who knows something about our woman that will help us in our hunt. Regardless, this afternoon, we close in."

\* \* \*

It was shortly after 2:00 p.m. that Marcus walked out the door of the police station, toward his SUV. It had been a grim day. After Jordan Reese was taken to the hospital, he'd worked the scene for a bit, making sure that her bike was gathered into evidence and that every bit of the surrounding area was searched for clues. They'd found a small piece of plastic trim that he hoped might be the thing that would link a vehicle to the scene.

Then he'd driven to Bigelow Memorial to get the victim's statement. He'd had to pass some time in the waiting room because she was in surgery getting pins in her broken arm. It had given him the chance to catch up on some emails that the chief would have handled. His phone had rung while he was doing it. His dad. He let it go to voice mail.

He was just about finished when he was notified that Jordan Reese was available to talk to him. "Five minutes," the doctor had said. "We've got her arm in pretty good shape but she's banged up all over."

It had taken him less than that to get everything that she knew. It was pretty much what Blade had already told him. Yes, she had seen the vehicle that hit her. Black SUV with a man driving and someone else in the front seat. It had been hard to tell in her mirror. That had surprised him. "Your mirror?" he'd double checked. Yes, it had come up behind her, she'd explained. There was plenty of space to pass her, but the next thing she knew, she and her bike were flying through the air.

The vision of that, with her hair so like Erin's flying out behind her, had him seething.

He'd pulled up records of every black SUV in a fifty-mile radius and he and the other two officers on days had started knocking on doors, asking people where they were at approximately nine o'clock that morning and also asking to see their vehicle.

Thus far they had nothing.

All in all, Jordan Reese had been lucky. The next person might not be. Marcus intended to have the driver behind bars before that could happen.

A crowd was starting to gather in the harbor. Food Truck Saturday was a big deal. He swore every week there was a new vendor. Had mentioned to the mayor recently that maybe there ought to be a limit on the permits. Bill Bliss had smiled, but in the next breath had been talking about tax revenue and making hay when the sun shone.

Marcus had warned the man, who was months shy of his thirtieth birthday and thus a full half-decade younger than Marcus, that it was useless to update his online profile at least once a month if he was going to talk like he was eighty.

"Will I see you there on Saturday?" Bill had asked.

Marcus had been noncommittal. He had a rare evening off and he didn't necessarily want to spend it surrounded by people. Still, it was a fun event and he liked supporting the town. He suspected that he'd see Blade and Jamie if they weren't pulling shifts.

Off-season, he could make the three-block drive from the police station to the harbor in less than a minute. Today, it would take over ten. Lights and siren would help, but not much. Some wayward pedestrian was likely to get hit by a vehicle moving too quickly to the curb and then there'd be real trouble.

Everybody who came to Knoware spent time at the Knoware Harbor. It was a beautiful place with good sidewalks, lots of grass and towering trees. People with coffee cups in hand or perhaps an ice cream cone would sit a spell on one of the many wooden benches scattered about. The hundred-plus boats regularly anchored in the large half-circle ranged from modest sixteen-foot pleasure crafts to small yachts that could comfortably sleep sixteen. There was a long, wide purpose-built pier installed more than thirty years earlier by people who understood that there would need to be room for those fishing and those simply out for an evening stroll.

Once he was there, he parked and got out. It was three hours yet before the crowds would arrive, but almost every food truck and other assorted vendors, selling jams and chocolates and all other kinds of consumables, were getting set up. He wandered among them, nodding and greeting those he knew. Which was most of them. Because they came back every year.

"Hey José," he said, waving to a man who sold amazing tacos.

"Officer Price," José said, a broad smile on his face. "What's this I hear about you being the top dog?"

"Interim top dog," Marcus said, stepping closer. He drew in an appreciative breath. The meat was already on the grill behind the tent.

"I feel safer than ever," José said. "But you're too early for a taco."

"I'll be back tonight," Marcus said.

"With a pretty lady on your arm?" José said knowingly.

"Not always," Marcus defended himself good-naturedly and kept walking.

It was five minutes later, as he casually inspected the

marina, letting his glance run the length of the shore-line, that he saw Talk and Hat, the two men he'd en-countered that morning across the street from Gertie's and Tiddle's.

Their backs were to him, but the young one still wore his damn stocking cap even though it was at least eighty-five. They'd said they were going fishing. Lots of people did that in Knoware. But for some reason, he felt uneasy.

He watched as the older one cast into the water. His movements seemed awkward, as if he didn't fish all that often. Again, not that unusual in Knoware. Lots of tourists came who hadn't thrown a line in the water for years.

Still.

He had no reason to talk to them again. That did not keep him from heading their direction.

Talk saw him first. And said something to Hat, but Marcus could not make out the words.

"Afternoon," he said. "Catching much?" If they were, it was going to be a waste. They had rods and what ap-peared to be a new bait box with a few plastic lures, but no bucket or cooler to keep their catch. But again, lots of people practiced catch and release.

"Enough," Talk said. Hat stared at the water.

Marcus stood next to them and casually glanced around the harbor. No one said anything. Finally, Talk turned to him. "Lots of activity here today."

"Food Truck Saturday. You plan on sticking around for that?" He didn't want them there. For some crazy reason, he wanted these two to pack up their fishing gear and move on.

Hat leaned forward, looking past Talk, making eye

contact with Marcus. "I heard there was a movie. What is it?"

His voice had a raspy quality that was distinctive. But there was little accent to identify place of origin. "Don't know the movie," Marcus said. That was a lie. It was a romantic comedy that had been big in the theaters six months ago. People would be happy with it. The committee did a good job given that their choices were a bit limited in that they didn't show anything that wasn't G or PG rated.

"I imagine we'll have had enough sun by tonight," Talk said.

Marcus nodded. "Gorgeous day, right? Remember I said you'd do well to have a camera. Well, I got one and am getting a few pictures of that sky." He took his cell phone out of his pocket, walked farther out onto the pier, and snapped away. Coming back, he whistled and held his cell phone in front of him, casual-like, tilted at just the right angle. Snap. Snap.

"Well, gentlemen, I hope you catch the big one." He walked on without stopping. He had places to be, photos to show.

"Fishing is stupid," Ivan said. "We're stupid for fishing. We should hit on her, get the thumb drive and get out of town."

"If you'd have caught a fish, it would have simply been icing on our cake. We learned a great deal this afternoon." It had been easy and painless. They'd taken their places on the pier and he'd struck up conversation with others close by. Those who were visiting were of no interest to him. But he'd found two people who had lived in Knoware all their lives. When he'd asked where one might find a nice gift, they'd both immediately said Tiddle's Tidbits and Treasures. One had been exceedingly happy to chat on at length about the owner, Morgan Tiddle, who was in the hospital trying to avoid early labor, and her sister who had come to watch over the store in her absence. He hadn't offered up the sister's name, but Gasdrig knew it didn't matter. A few taps on his phone had Morgan Tiddle's address. It was likely where she was staying. Ivan had wanted to go there immediately.

"Patience," Gasdrig had said. "It could be many places. On her. In the store. At her sister's house. We don't want to spook her too soon. We certainly don't want to get the authorities involved." Now, after this second interaction with the same police officer, he was more sure of that than ever. There was something that told him that the man was not as stupid as most American law enforcement. "This has been years in the planning. Another day or two will not make the difference."

"I might die of boredom. At least it smells good."

"You're thinking about your damn stomach all the time," grumbled Gasdrig.

Ivan shook his head and a look of speculation entered his eyes. "I was thinking about the redhead. You think she's fiery, like her hair?"

"That's not why we're here," Gasdrig said.

Ivan shrugged. "All I am saying is that if it takes some gentle or not-so-gentle persuasion to get her to reveal the location, it might not be a hardship. And perhaps you are right. A day or two delay will not make a difference. Twenty-four hours with her could be quite… enjoyable."

"Keep your focus where it needs to be," Gasdrig said,

his tone harsh. Years of experience with Ivan told him that the man could be impetuous.

"You're not my father," Ivan said.

"But your father was my friend. Your mother, too."

"Don't talk to me about my mother. She is a whore."

She was not. And she was the reason Ivan had been educated in the States and lived in relative comfort while many in his country suffered greatly. But now was not the time for that debate. Not for the first time, he cursed his reliance on Ivan's bomb-making abilities. "Stay focused. That's all I'm asking."

# Chapter 5

At twenty minutes before four, a woman walked in the front door. She took one look at Erin and put her hand to her mouth. "Oh my God, I'd have known you were Morgan's sister," she exclaimed. "I'm Jo Marie."

"It's a pleasure," Erin said. She walked toward the woman. "And most people don't automatically get that we're sisters. I think it's the hair," she said, pulling at her curly red locks. Morgan had a sweet, very manageable head of thick straight blond hair.

"But your eyes. Just the same." Jo Marie straightened up a stack of unframed prints as they walked back behind the cash register. "How's the day been?"

There were currently five women shoppers in the store. "Like this. There were a couple times I wished for three hands and eyes in the back of my head."

"Shoplifters?" she questioned.

"No, thank goodness. I'm not sure what I'd do about that."

"Call the police. They're a responsive bunch in this town."

Responsive. All kinds of naughty thoughts crossed Erin's tired brain imagining Officer Price being terribly responsive. She was pretty sure that wasn't what Jo Marie meant. "Good to know," she said.

"What's that?" Jo Marie asked, pointing to a wrapped package on the counter behind the cash register.

"Oh, a mistake. Well, not really, but a woman came in and thought she wanted a box of chocolates for a friend who is sick. I had it wrapped up and ready to go when she saw the scarves and decided to go that route."

"I'll get it back on the shelf," Jo Marie promised.

Erin looked out at the street. There were still lots of people on the sidewalk. She glanced right, then left. Saw two men, one older, one younger, walking in the direction of the store. Had they been in earlier? She didn't think so. Then she remembered. She'd seen them at lunch, as they'd jig-jogged past one another.

They'd been shopping. Both carried small bags. They opened the door to her store.

"Good afternoon," she said. "Welcome to Tiddle's Tidbits and Treasures."

The older man nodded, but did not speak. The younger man did not make eye contact.

"Let me know if we can help you find anything," Erin said. She didn't believe in dogging people. Shopping should be fun.

"Now you've got to be tired if you've been here all day," Jo Marie said.

"Perhaps a bit. Fortunately, today went a bit smoother than yesterday."

"What happened yesterday?"

"I started it off with a bang when I set off the security alarm by mistake."

Jo Marie laughed. "Did the police come?"

"Very quickly," Erin said.

"After there were a couple break-ins on the block, Morgan was insistent upon getting an alarm. Have you talked to her today, by the way? How is she?"

"She sent me a text earlier and said she was doing fine."

"Is Brian staying with her?"

"He's there a lot," Erin said. "Devoted husband, that one."

"He is a good one," Jo Marie agreed. "Are you going to Food Truck Saturday?"

"I don't even know what that is, but based on those two simple words—*food truck*—you've got my attention."

"It started a couple years ago and it just keeps getting bigger and bigger. A bunch of food trucks sell food from five to nine, and then there's a starlight movie shown in the park. It attracts so many people that it makes sense for Morgan to keep the store open to nine on Saturdays during the season."

"Well, I'll certainly keep it in mind. If not tonight, then perhaps next week." Two of the women shoppers came up to the counter and purchased candles and lotion. Jo Marie rang up the order and Erin bagged the items. "Thank you," she said to the women.

"Lovely store," one said in return. "We'll be back before we leave town."

As the ladies walked out, the men who'd been browsing followed them out the door without buying anything.

Jo Marie waited until they were gone before turning to Erin. "Win some, lose some. Now I've got this. You need to get going. Morgan is going to be anxious to see you."

That was true. "Okay, I'm gone," she said, smiling. She took a step, stopped. Then came back for the wrapped candy. "I think I'll take this with me to the hospital."

"Morgan does love her chocolate," Jo Marie said.

Erin walked down the hall, got her purse and her keys, and walked out the back door. She took a step, but then stopped short. The two men who had been in her store were standing very close to her car and it appeared they were looking in the windows.

The younger one saw her at that moment and yanked on the arm of the older one. He gave her a little wave. "Is this your car?" he asked.

"Yes."

"It's a nice one."

It was a standard four-door midsize Chevy. A common rental. "Thank you."

"Good on mileage?" he asked.

"It's a rental," she said. "I've only had it a couple days so I can't really say."

"I see. Well, sorry to have bothered you. Nice store you have, by the way."

She smiled. "My sister owns it. She's Morgan Tiddle."

"Real nice. We'll be back."

And they walked away.

* * *

Marcus stood at the far end of the alley, watching Erin and the two strangers have a conversation. He was too far away to hear what they were saying.

It wasn't a long conversation. At least the part he saw. After the men walked away, Erin got in her car. She sat there for a minute before starting the car and driving off.

He'd first seen the men that morning. That was when they'd told him that they were staying at Brickstone Bungalows. When he'd seen them later at the pier, with the frustration of the morning fresh in his mouth, he'd thought of the advice the Homeland Security folks had given officers across the country. *Pay attention to strangers.*

He'd left the two men, driven out to Brickstone Bungalows and shown his cell phone photos of them to Brenda Brickstone, who with her husband, Arty, had run Brickstone Bungalows for twenty-some years. The photos were off-center and the faces a little distorted, but certainly a decent effort.

Brenda had looked at them and shaken her head. He'd pushed her, saying that he was confident that the men were staying there. But Brenda, who was the eyes and ears of the ten-cabin operation, was adamant. Arty had come in the office at that point and while he wasn't as confident, he thought he recalled talking to the older one two nights back about a cabin, but they were full and the men had driven on.

He'd thanked the couple and driven back into Knoware, all the time thinking why the men had lied about where they were staying. And he couldn't come up with any good reasons.

*Pay attention to strangers.* Especially to strangers who had funky stories, he added.

When he'd gotten back into Knoware, he'd parked his SUV, determined to walk off some of his frustration. Then he came upon the exchange in the alley.

And the pit burning in his stomach right now was the surefire knowledge that Erin and the two strangers had arrived at roughly the same time.

Had they arrived together?

Did they know one another?

Were the men watching Tiddle's this morning and using Gertie's as a useful diversion?

Did this have anything to do with Erin's reluctance to impart any specific information about her background?

All he had were questions.


Morgan and Brian were playing cards. Her sister was propped up against her pillows and she looked good. That made Erin immediately relax. "Who's winning?" she asked.

"Your sister is a shark," Brian said. "If this was strip poker, I'd be naked by now."

"I think there's a gown over there you can borrow," Morgan said.

"My important parts might still be showing," Brian said.

"TMI," Erin said, holding up her hand. "Those are images that I don't need in my head."

Morgan patted Brian's hand. "I like all your parts." She smiled at Erin. "Now tell me how the day went."

"Every bit as busy as yesterday. I like Jo Marie, by the way."

"Yeah, she's wonderful. I appreciate her working

tonight so that you can get a few extra hours of sleep. You have to still be suffering from jet lag."

Erin smiled. "Drinking lots of tea, I'll admit." On her way to the hospital, she couldn't help but think of the woman who'd been hit riding her bicycle. If she'd been taken by ambulance, then the injuries had to be somewhat serious. "This is going to sound weird, but I overheard some people at Gertie's Café talking about a woman who was hit by a vehicle this morning while she was riding her bike. A visitor to the area. She was evidently brought to the hospital and I was thinking about how terrible it must be to be on vacation and end up in some strange hospital. I... I brought some chocolate from the store and I thought I might give it to her. But now that I'm here, I don't have any idea how to manage that."

"That's very sweet of you, Erin," Morgan said. "I don't think the hospital will give you any information about her. Privacy laws and such. But if you ask the charge nurse, she might be able to get it to her. I think she has responsibility for a couple units. This isn't that big a hospital, so the woman might even be on one of those units."

"That's a good idea," Erin said.

Brian picked up the cards that were facedown in front of him. "Or you could go to room 207 and hand it off yourself."

Both women looked at him. "And you know this how?" Morgan asked suspiciously.

"Not that tough. I was in the lobby when her husband and two little kids came in. The guy was stressed and the kids were oblivious and thought it would be cool to play in the hospital waterfall. I overheard him asking about where his wife might be and the woman behind the desk gave him the room number."

"Would that be weird if I go to her room?" Erin said.

Morgan shrugged. "Maybe. But also very caring. Take a walk that direction. Peek in and go with your gut. You've always had a good one."

"Again, giving me more credit than I probably deserve." She leaned down and kissed her sister goodbye. "I'll see you tomorrow."

She walked around her sister's bed and gave her brother-in-law a peck on his cheek. Then looked at his cards. "Oh, nines and threes. Pairs. How lovely."

Morgan was laughing as Erin left the room. She took the elevator to the second floor, got off and easily found room 207. The door was open halfway. She stood outside but didn't hear anything. After a minute, she knocked.

"Come in."

She walked in and tentatively peeked her head around the corner. A woman was in bed, watching television. There was no one else in the room.

"Excuse me," she said quickly. "I don't want to bother you."

"Okay," the woman said, not sounding too concerned. Erin understood. People waltzed in and out of hospital rooms with all kinds of purpose. To provide care. To deliver food. To talk about payment plans. To encourage completion of a survey.

"I'm Erin McGarry."

"Jordan Reese," the woman said. She held up her wrist, as if Erin might want to check her name on her wristband.

"I... I heard about what happened to you. About four years ago, I was visiting somewhere and ended up in the hospital." She'd been alone and hadn't spoken the language. And she'd been very sick. "It wasn't great," she said. "Actually, it was a pretty horrible experience." She took a breath. "Anyway, I work in a store that has amazing candy and I brought you some." Erin put the wrapped package on the bedside table.

"Oh my gosh," the woman said. "That's so nice of you. I'm not going to tell my kids," she added with a smile. "And I just have to tell you, I love your hair. I so wish mine would do that." She sat up and used her good arm to run her fingers through her long hair.

She'd been lying back against the pillows, but once she did that, Erin was struck by the similarity in color and length to her own hair. But this woman's was silky and straight. How lovely that would be. "If you only knew the fortune I've spent on straightening products," Erin said.

The woman laughed. "I guess we always want what we don't have."

"True enough. Well, I don't want to intrude, Jordan. I just wanted you to know that there are people here who think what happened to you was so wrong and we're hoping you have a speedy and full recovery."

"Thank you." She looked at the box of candy. Erin had put a discreet sticker on the wrapping paper with the name of the store. "Tiddle's Tidbits and Treasures," the woman read. "When they spring me, I'll make sure I stop by."

"You do that," Erin said. She walked out the door, turned the corner and ran smack-dab into Marcus Price.

* * *

Marcus reached out to steady Erin. "Whoa," he said. What the heck was she doing on this floor? "Lost?" he asked.

She shook her head. "No. You?"

Again, so evasive. He was getting tired of it. "I'm working," he said.

"I was hoping so. Didn't think you wore your uniform on your off-hours."

She said it lightly. Teasingly. Was she trying to throw him off the scent? "I thought Morgan was on the maternity floor," he said.

"She is."

"All still good?"

"Yes. She and Brian were playing poker," she said.

"I've played poker with Brian. He starts to breathe fast when he's got a good hand."

"I think Morgan had that figured out."

"Right. So what are you doing in this area?"

"Visiting someone."

"Who?"

"Jordan Reese. She's the woman who—"

"I know who she is," he interrupted her. "How are you and Jordan Reese connected?"

"We aren't."

"But yet you felt compelled to visit her in the hospital?"

She looked uncomfortable at the question. "I should probably be going."

She still hadn't told him why she'd felt compelled to visit a stranger's room. "Big plans tonight?" he asked, switching tactics.

She shook her head. "No plans tonight."

Was that true? Why did he feel as if he couldn't quite trust anything she said? "You should check out Food Truck Saturday."

"Jo Marie mentioned something about it. It seems to really have a reputation."

"Well-earned. Want to go?" It would give him a chance to question her in a relaxed setting.

"Um…"

She was going to say no. He could tell.

"I think I'll have to take—" She stopped. Her eyes were focused somewhere over his shoulder.

Marcus turned. Brian Tiddle was hurrying their direction.

"Hey, I was hoping I'd catch you," Brian said, looking at Erin. "Morgan forgot to tell you that she'd arranged for somebody to come in and clean the store floors tomorrow morning since you don't open until one on Sunday. She didn't want you to stumble upon them and freak out. We tried your cell, but it went straight to voice mail and she said you sometimes forget to check your messages."

"Guilty," she said. "Thanks for making the effort to catch up. You know Marcus?"

"Of course," Brian said. "How's it going, Marcus?"

"Good," he said. "Morgan doing well, still?"

"Yeah. Having Erin here is allowing her to really rest and forget about the store. That's huge."

"Tell her we're all pulling for her," he said.

"How's the new job going?" Brian asked. He turned to Erin. "Marcus is the newly appointed interim police chief."

"I did hear that," Erin said.

He didn't recall telling her. Had she been talking

about him to somebody else? Maybe her sister? Or maybe the two guys in the alley? "I was just telling Erin about Food Truck Saturday and trying to convince her to go with me." He wasn't above using Brian to twist Erin's arm.

"Yeah, you should definitely go. It's super fun and the food is delicious."

"I…guess I'm just a little tired," she said.

"You've got to eat, right?" Brian asked. "I'm sure Marcus could make it an early night."

"Oh course. Pick you up at six?" Marcus asked, focusing on Erin.

She licked her lips. "Sure. That sounds lovely. I'll see you then." She turned and walked away from the two men.

"Good to see you, Marcus," Brian said. "I'm going to get back to Morgan."

Marcus watched him walk to the elevator. Then he turned and knocked on Jordan Reese's door.

"Come in," she said.

"I'm Officer Price," he said. "We talked this morning."

She smiled. "I remember. Not everything is a blur."

"I thought your husband might be here," Marcus said.

"He was, with the kids, but they were getting restless so I sent them all home. I think they are springing me in the morning so he'll be back to pick me up. I'm going to simply enjoy the quiet tonight."

He saw the familiar wrapping paper from Tiddle's Tidbits and Treasures. "I see you got some chocolates."

"Yes. A woman dropped them by. She was very sweet. Said that there were a lot of people who felt bad about what happened to me."

That was probably true. But not everybody brought candy to a stranger. "This is a pretty friendly place," he said. "I wanted to give you an update on the investigation. Unfortunately, I can't tell you that we've made an arrest. I can tell you that we're continuing to search."

"I appreciate that," she said. "I wish I could be of more help."

"We'll figure it out," Marcus assured her. "One way or another."

*Chapter 6*

Marcus was five minutes early, but Erin was ready. She wore lime-green pants and a silky royal blue sleeveless shirt that billowed in the breeze. She had a white jean jacket hanging over one arm.

She looked summer fresh and…innocent.

But he was too good a cop to be fooled by wrapping paper. Spending the evening together at Food Truck Saturday would hopefully allow him to get past the exterior.

"Nice outfit," he said.

"Thank you."

There was no way he was going to ask her where she bought it. Daisy Savick was just going to have to be disappointed in him. "Hungry?" he asked, as he walked her to his SUV. He opened the door for her.

"Always," she said.

"I'm going to recommend the tacos, but I won't be upset if you go for the pork sandwiches, the corn on the cob or the egg rolls."

"Tacos and egg rolls in the same night. Is this heaven?"

"Well, it ain't Iowa," he said.

"Based on the crowd you told me to expect, it's definitely a case of if you build it, they will come," she said, proving she got the reference. The movie *Field of Dreams* with Kevin Costner was decades old, but he never got tired of watching it.

He continued his drive toward the harbor. "We're going to have to walk a block," he said a few minutes later, pulling into a spot.

"No worries. Tacos *and* egg rolls, remember. Maybe fresh-squeezed lemonade, too," she added as a woman walked past their vehicle carrying a cup.

"If you have indigestion tomorrow, do not blame me," he said.

She patted her flat stomach. "Made of iron. Once, in Poland, I lived on fried pickles, creamed corn and hard-boiled eggs for three days."

"Now it sounds as if you're bragging."

"Never any bragging," she said. "Some lighting of candles in penance, perhaps?"

*Penance.* "So, I've heard you mention Paris and Poland. What is it you do when you're not helping out your sister?" he asked. Talking about work was usually a safe bet.

She got out of his SUV. He joined her on the sidewalk.

"You were saying," he prompted.

She sighed. "Well, let's see. In alpha order, it would be actress, barista, color consultant and dog walker. No

*E*s, *F*s or *G*s. House sitter. Ice cream salesclerk. Journalist. *K* through *O* are yet to come. Process server. Quality control supervisor, roofer, shopper—mystery, that is—teacher, used-car salesperson, veterinarian assistant, water taxi operator, no *X* or *Y*, and finally, zoo attendant."

He had no words. "Wow," he managed. She'd rattled off the whole list without taking a breath. Impressive, but a bit too smooth, too rehearsed. "Maybe chronological would be helpful."

"Sorry. Your mantra may be to never pass by a food truck, mine is that you never voluntarily offer more than one ical at a time."

"Ical?" he repeated.

"Alphabet*ical*. Geograph*ical*. Or chronolog*ical*. One ical. Now I've worked up quite an appetite. Lucky for you, I see at least fourteen food trucks and another half dozen booths."

"Fine." He'd rest, but he wasn't giving up. They continued on. He wasn't surprised to see people sitting and eating everywhere—at tables that were scattered about, on the rock wall that bordered the water, on the ground a bit farther back. She took a few more steps toward the trucks. Stopped short.

"Oh my God," she said, grabbing his arm.

He looked around fast, trying to quickly identify the danger. He saw nothing. "What?" he demanded.

"You said nothing about fried doughnut holes drizzled with caramel and chocolate." She was pointing at a woman's plate. The woman in question smiled, shrugged and took a big bite.

The look on Erin's face was…damn, she was cute. But he wasn't going to get sucked in by a pretty face.

He was still plenty bothered by seeing her brief inter-action with Talk and Hat and her unexplained visit to Jordan Reese. "It was a significant omission," he said.

She gave him a serious look. "Don't let it happen again."

People were giving them a look as they passed by. For every local who was in attendance, they would tell two, who would tell four, who would tell eight. Soon, everyone would think that Marcus Price had a new woman.

And the betting would likely begin. Two weeks. A month. Six weeks. Till Labor Day. It could take many forms. Wagers would be made on how long this one might last.

There was an easy answer. Until he figured out what her story was. And if it had something to do with the strangers who seemed to give him hives. Or with the first hit-and-run in two years.

"The interim chief is getting a few looks," Erin said, almost under her breath.

"They're all jealous," he said. "They want to be walking alongside the woman who is interested in tacos, egg rolls, fresh lemonade and fried doughnut holes."

"Fried doughnut holes with caramel and chocolate," she corrected. "You *are* lucky." She studied the water. "How long is that pier?"

"Almost two hundred yards," he said. "We can walk out there. Only time it gets a little dicey is when the wind is whipping up the water over the sides. Then it can be slick enough that a less-than-careful person might slide right off."

"And have to be fished out of the Pacific."

He'd saved someone who'd done just that the previous summer. "Yeah. But tonight, you're safe."

"I should think there might be no place safer than with the interim chief of police," she said.

He'd like to think so. Liked to think that he and the rest of the Knoware PD kept residents and visitors safe and responded appropriately when things went astray. Which was more often than people realized. Their department had a good track record of proactively responding to information and often prevented situations from getting out of hand. Many times they didn't get credit for their efforts because the information didn't make the twice-weekly newspaper. That didn't bother him. He didn't do it for the public accolades. He took the oath to serve and protect seriously.

Unfortunately, that meant that he was always in cop mode, even on nights like tonight when he wasn't officially on duty. Always watchful.

There was something, or more specifically two someones, he was watching for. Thus far he had not seen Talk and Hat. While he was consumed with wanting to know what the two of them had been chatting about with Erin, he wasn't going to ask. He was not willing to tip his hand that he'd seen the three of them together.

"Tacos first?" Erin asked, interrupting his thoughts.

He turned to her. "You think the egg rolls will feel jilted?"

"Not when I'm done with them," she promised.

"Let's go," he said.

He led her to José's truck and stood in line, five people back. It was not José working the counter, but rather his daughter. They waited their turn, studying the menu sign. When they got to the front, Marcus saw José standing in the back of the truck and waved. The man immediately came forward.

"Officer Price," José said. "Always a pleasure. What can I get you and your…friend?"

"This is Erin McGarry," Marcus said. "She claims to have had some experience with food trucks, but I've told her that she hasn't truly eaten at a great food truck until she's had your tacos."

José beamed and extended a hand. "Ms. McGarry, it's nice to meet you. If you're a pork eater, I'd suggest that. It's a family recipe."

"Sold," Erin said. "With a side of guacamole and chips."

"Same," Marcus said.

In less than three minutes, they had their food and bottled waters and were on their way. He let her take the lead and was a little surprised when she quickly found a spot sitting on the grass. "There are tables," he said.

"No need," she said. "Oh my God," she added, after biting into the taco. "Delicious. I should have gotten a second one."

"Egg rolls," he reminded her. "Doughnuts drizzled with caramel and chocolate."

"Oh, fine. I need to slow down, savor every bite," she said. She set her half-finished taco down. Then leaned back to stare at the blue sky. The band that played for every Food Truck Saturday had started and she was tapping her foot in rhythm to a cover of one of Kenny Chesney's songs.

"You want something stronger than that?" he asked, motioning to her water. "Glass of wine? Beer?"

"I better not," she said. "I think the jet-lag may be

catching up with me. It wouldn't take much for me to fall asleep. And I saw a sign by the park bench that said no overnight sleeping. I wouldn't want to get arrested." She ate a chip with guacamole on it. "You don't happen to carry any Get Out of Jail Free cards?"

"No need. I'll personally vouch for you," he said. "But I would like to circle back to your list of jobs. The alphabetizing was very impressive, but I'm still a little fuzzy."

She shrugged. "What's the one that surprised you the most?"

He considered. "Roofer. I've shingled a few roofs and those packets are heavy."

She nodded. "I was lucky and was part of a crew. The shingles got carried for me, but it was still one of the hardest jobs I ever had. Squatting. Bending. Keeping my damn balance on some pitchy roofs. And it was so hot. Not the best way to spend summer in Costa Rica."

"What took you to Costa Rica?" he asked.

She shrugged. "I don't even remember."

Was that true? Or was that a way to avoid the question? He wanted to press, but held back. "Best job of all?"

"Dog walker, hands down. I had nice customers who had the sweetest dogs. Cleaning up their messes wasn't so great, but that was certainly tolerable in exchange for getting to walk around Paris."

"So that was the Paris job?"

"One of them," she said. She picked up her now-empty paper plate. "What direction are the egg rolls?"

He pointed. He was good at peeling back layers of paint.

She got two egg rolls and an order of fried rice. "My

grandmother in Ireland used to say that my legs were hollow," she explained. "I didn't realize what she meant until I was in my teens. But I'm sure I amused my teachers because I repeated the fact on multiple occasions."

"Where did you grow up?"

"My mother had dual citizenship, here in the States and in Ireland. We divided our time almost evenly until my parents died. My grandparents were all gone by then and so it was just Morgan and me. She was working and living in Chicago and I could have stayed with her after I finished high school, but…" Her voice trailed off. "Chicago is really cold in the winter," she finished.

She was right. And it was a fine reason. But it didn't feel like the truth.

"This is so good," she said, finishing her second eggroll. "And I've reconsidered. Maybe I will have a glass of white wine." She reached for her purse and started to get out money.

"I've got it," he said, standing up.

She shook her head. "I've got it."

She didn't say it harshly, but definitely firmly. Maybe her way of sending a message that this wasn't really a date. "Okay," he said, holding up his hands. "Thirty feet that direction," he said, pointing south.

"Can I get you something?" she said.

She had a twenty in her hand. Wine was five bucks a glass. "Sure. Whatever you're having."

He watched her walk away, saw her standing in line, waiting her turn for wine. The crowd was still peaceful. It was still daylight and on the odd occasions that there was trouble, it didn't usually start until much later, after much more alcohol had been consumed by attendees. He scanned the crowd. Saw Blade and Daisy—they were handing money over to their sixteen-year-old daughters. Once the girls had cash in hand, they couldn't get away from their parents fast enough. Marcus waved and caught Daisy's eye. She grabbed Blade's hand and the two of them walked toward him.

They reached him just as Erin returned with two glasses of wine. "Hi," she said. "I can go back and get a couple more glasses," she added.

Daisy smiled. "No need. I'm off alcohol for quite a few more months." She patted her slightly rounded abdomen. "I'm Daisy Savick, by the way. I was in your store yesterday."

"Me, too," volunteered Blade. "Buying some chocolate for my lovely bride."

"Of course," she said. "I remember you and your friend. I didn't know you knew Marcus."

"Everybody knows Marcus," Blade said easily.

"This is my friend Blade Savick and his lovely wife, Daisy. Blade and I've known each other since we were kids in a sandbox. Daisy, on the other hand, has only been in Knoware for a few months. But long enough," he added, "to be foolish enough to marry this guy and have a baby, no, make that a pair of babies, with him."

"Congratulations," Erin said. She handed one of the glasses to Marcus. "We'll drink in your honor."

"What did you have to eat?" Daisy asked.

"Started with a pork taco and chips and guacamole. Then had egg rolls and fried rice," Erin said. "Dessert is next. Doughnuts drizzled with chocolate and caramel."

Daisy smiled wide. "I've met my new best friend." She turned to Blade. "You know I'm eating for three."

"Really?" he asked, pretending to be confused.

"Is that why there are six quarts of ice cream in our freezer?"

"Six is a pretty reasonable number," Erin said, her tone thoughtful.

Daisy high-fived her.

Marcus felt a pang in his chest. It would be so easy if there was nothing bad about Erin. "We…uh…should probably be moving on. I want Erin to get the full impact of Food Truck Saturday."

"Okay," Blade said, looking a little surprised.

"If I find the doughnuts, I'll report back," Erin said, smiling at Daisy. She didn't see it as odd that he was hustling them along. She didn't know the friendship. Right now, that was the way he wanted it. He wanted to know a lot more about her than she did about him.

Erin walked through the crowd, toward the water. The sidewalks were crowded enough that they were walking single file, with her in the lead. The food had been delicious but she could not shake the feeling that something was off. Maybe it was Marcus's interest in her background. That always put her on edge.

She'd bounced around. A lot. She'd struggled to find something that she could settle into. More so than many, or so it seemed to her. Which made her feel a bit inadequate. So she didn't talk about it much. But when pushed, like she had been tonight, she'd developed the alpha list that generally stopped people from asking much more. She wasn't sure the tactic was going to work with Marcus.

The sidewalk widened and he stepped up to walk next to her once again. "There's your doughnuts," he said. He was pointing off to his left.

"Excellent. If you want to grab a spot at that table that is opening up, I'll stand in line."

He nodded and headed to the area where a family of four were preparing to leave. She got in line, appreciatively drawing in deep breaths of fried dough and cinnamon and sugar.

She was still six back when she realized that one of the men who'd been looking at her rental car was behind her in line. It was the older one. "Oh, hello," she said. "Again," she added, letting him know she remembered him.

"This seems like the place to be, right?" he asked, motioning to the long line.

"We can't all be wrong," she said lightly.

He was looking at her purse. "Is that from your store?"

"My sister's store," she corrected automatically. "She's always had good taste."

"Indeed. Maybe I could get one for my wife. She's crazy about inside pockets, always wants to know how deep they are."

She smiled. The line moved and she used that as an excuse to turn away from him. She stood there another minute before she suddenly bolted from the line. When she got back to Marcus, he was looking at her oddly and she assumed it was because she'd come empty-handed.

"They ran out?" he asked.

"You know, I changed my mind." It was true. After her encounter with the man, she'd lost her appetite. "I hope you're not too disappointed, but I really think I should call it a night."

"You're sure?" he asked. "We're so close."

"Yeah, I'm sure. This has been great. I'm grateful

that I got to see the event. But I think I should be heading home. Get started on that full night's sleep."

She turned and started walking in the direction of their vehicle. Marcus caught up with her in a few steps. Once there, he opened the passenger-side door and waited while she got in. Then he rounded the vehicle, got in and waited for a break in the traffic to pull away.

He never said a word.

She wondered about that. Wondered if he was put off by her sudden need to leave. In her defense, the expectation had been set that it would be an early night. But they'd been having fun. She would've been content to hang out a while longer if that man hadn't been there. Again, she'd been caught up with a general feeling of familiarity and felt even more strongly now than earlier that today was not the first time she'd encountered them. But she couldn't put her finger on it, although it *felt* recent. That unnerved her.

Had it been at Preston's Automobile Exchange? Was it possible that they'd been in the showroom looking for a vehicle? Or there for a more nefarious reason that she'd suspected but never confirmed?

Odd if that was the case that she'd encounter them again in the United States, in Knoware. Perhaps their odd interest in her rental car had spurred the idea that it was over a vehicle that their paths had crossed at some time. Maybe she was connecting dots trying to make a neat and directional line when really, all she had was some random ink blotches on ugly scratch paper that meant nothing. Ugh.

Marcus pulled up in front of Morgan's house. She opened the passenger door and got out. He surprised her when he also got out and walked her to the door.

"Thanks for the invite," she said. "It was fun and now I can join in the conversations about Food Truck Saturday without looking like a fool."

"My pleasure," he said. "Hope it didn't interrupt your sleep schedule too much."

She unlocked the door, but didn't push it open. "I can sleep in tomorrow since I don't have to be there until one. I'll be fine." She shifted. This was always so awkward. She decided to take matters into her own hands. She leaned forward and brushed a quick kiss onto his cheek. "Good night, Marcus."

She opened the door and walked inside, shutting the door tight behind her.

# *Chapter 7*

Her lips had barely brushed his face, but heat had arced from cheek to chest in record time. It had taken a Herculean effort to keep his hands at his sides, to not reach for her, to not pull her into his body and kiss her the way he wanted to.

She'd slipped inside and he'd managed to get off the porch without falling. But truth be told, he was now four blocks away and he still felt a bit wobbly. He gripped the steering wheel a little tighter.

Jamie and Blade would fall down with laughter if he told the truth about this. It had been a little kiss, like one he might have gotten in seventh grade. It was… embarrassing.

And telling, he admitted.

Erin McGarry was getting to him. Like no other woman had gotten to him.

He should go home. It had been a long day. Instead, he drove back to the harbor, parked and walked through the marina again. He did not see Blade or Daisy, but he caught a glimpse of their daughters. They were with a group of high school kids and were headed toward the open area where they showed the movie.

He was looking for Talk and Hat. He took two full passes through the space, but did not see them.

He'd been watching Erin as she'd joined the line for doughnuts. Out of the corner of his eye, he'd seen Talk come around the corner of a tent and head her direction. By the time he'd reached the line, there'd been several other people in line behind Erin but Talk had butted his way in. The people had been too polite to make a fuss or perhaps they'd assumed he was with Erin when the two of them quickly struck up a conversation. It hadn't been long, but once it was finished, she had turned around, waited just a brief time and then exited.

Without her doughnuts. The ones she'd been talking about all night.

Then she'd been all about leaving. Her pace toward the vehicle had been brisk and she'd been quiet, offering no information.

There was some connection between Erin and the strangers. He was confident of it. And that did not make him happy.

He went back to his office, booted up his computer and initiated a background search on Erin McGarry. If she wasn't going to volunteer information, he was going to get it, one way or another.

Erin didn't wake up until almost eleven the next morning. She threw back the sheet and light blanket that had kept her warm during the night and stretched. For the first time in days, she actually felt rested.

She listened to see if she could hear movement in the rest of the house. But it was quiet. Brian had no doubt already left for the hospital. She sat up, swinging her legs over the edge of the bed. She had plenty of time to shower and wash her hair and grab a bite to eat before opening the store at one.

The thought of eating reminded her of her last meal. Delicious, definitely. She could see a repeat visit to Food Truck Saturday in her future. Would Marcus ask her again?

It didn't matter. Even if he did, she was confident that she'd say no. Would not let herself be pushed into accepting a second time.

It wasn't that he wasn't charming. And handsome. And oddly enough, in the past, learning that he was commitment-phobic would have been an attractive bonus. It would have fit her own needs. They could have enjoyed their time together and when it was time to move on, done it quickly and without remorse.

The way she'd done it with Albert and others.

But her gut told her that it wouldn't work that way with Marcus. There was something about him, some-thing she couldn't or wouldn't define, that told her he might be the one who could break her heart.

So she would wander through the next Food Truck Saturday on her own. She was not a stranger to eating by herself. Had done it many meals in many places. Such was the life of a rolling stone. But truth be told, those meals were about sustenance, eating to survive.

Eating with another person was so different. Food was social. And the shared experience of enjoying a meal together was still one of the best ways to spend an hour.

She'd let the stranger steal that joy from her, which was probably stupid. And Marcus had a right to think that she was maybe just a step shy of rude. She hadn't wanted to explain so she'd done the next best thing and awkwardly apologized with the kiss.

But that had backfired on her. His skin had been warm, his scent all male. And it had made her desperately want to invite him inside, to offer explanations and accept forgiveness. But common sense had prevailed and she'd left him on the porch and slipped inside. No one needed to know that then her forward progress had stalled. Thankfully, there existed no incriminating proof that she'd stood by the door, sliding slowly to the floor and staying there long after his footsteps had faded.

She was tired of being alone. That was what had probably led to her dating Albert Peet. He'd lived down the block from her flat and they'd encountered each other at their local patisserie. Interest had been stirred over discussion of tarte tatin and one thing had led to another until Albert proposed seven months later.

It had been unexpected, unwanted, and she'd lost plenty of sleep finding a nice way to tell him just that. He'd taken it badly, had said odd things about everything falling apart, and then had quite literally disappeared. Concerned for his general welfare, she'd called and emailed. All had met with no response.

She'd been grateful to him for his help in securing her position at Preston's Automobile Exchange. When that, too, had ended badly, she'd been in a poor position to argue when her best friend had summarized the situation quite succinctly. *Face it, Erin. The Albert Phase was not one of your better ones.*

She walked downstairs, opened the refrigerator and poured herself a glass of orange juice. Then she popped two pieces of bread into the toaster. While she waited, she wandered over to the bay window in her sister's kitchen. It was another beautiful day. The sky was blue, the clouds scattered and billowy light, and the birds clearly approved because they were out en masse. Tourists should also be out and about, hopefully making for a busy afternoon.

Would Marcus wander by and poke his head in? If not, should she send a quick text, apologizing for her fast exit last night? Knoware was a tourist town. There were strangers everywhere. Would he understand her concern about these two particular strangers or would he think she'd overreacted?

Her toast popped and she slathered on butter and jam. She heard the shower running in the master bath and realized that Brian must be home.

She ate her breakfast and went back upstairs to get ready for work. At twelve thirty she walked down the stairs. She did a quick look around for Brian, but didn't see him. If he was smart, he'd be catching a nap. There was no way that he was getting good sleep at the hospital.

She left via the front door, locking it and pulling it shut behind her. She got in her car and started it.

"Let's do it," Ivan said, his nose pressed up against the window.

"Sit back," Gasdrig ordered. The kid had no damn sense. "We need to see where she's going."

"We need to check the house," Ivan said.

"We wait until there's no one there." They'd done a pass by an hour earlier and the garage door had been up with two cars parked inside. Gasdrig assumed they belonged to the sister and her husband. The redhead's rental car was parked on the street.

"We wait," Gasdrig repeated himself. He knew he was being cautious, perhaps too much so. But he had been surprised last night when he'd seen the red-haired woman and the nosy police officer together. It was one more unpleasant complication, like learning that the gift store had an alarm system and the police response was quick.

He eased the vehicle away from the curb, following the woman from a distance of three blocks. He wasn't going to lose her in Knoware.

She made a left turn and he guessed that she was on her way to the gift store. Sure enough, four minutes later when he rolled by the alley, her rental car was parked in the same spot where it had been yesterday when he and Ivan had looked in the windows, hoping it would be easy and the brown shoulder bag would be tossed on the floor or perhaps the back seat.

No such luck. Car had been spotless with the exception of a small case that likely held sunglasses. She'd exited the store faster than he'd hoped. When he and Ivan had followed the women shoppers out of the store, Erin was engaged in conversation with another clerk. He'd figured they had plenty of time to check her vehicle. But they'd been delayed because just as they'd rounded the corner, a young man had come out of the back door of the restaurant, wearing a white apron. He'd lit up a cigarette and in less than a minute, a beat-up Jeep had pulled into the alley, rolling to a stop in front of him.

Gasdrig had been checking his cell phone and easily switched it to video recording. He captured a nice little business transaction. The man in the apron had passed cash to the driver and in return, the driver had handed over a bag of what Gasdrig assumed was nose candy. The man was standing so that anyone looking out the back of the restaurant would not be able to see the transaction. But Gasdrig and Ivan were at an angle, affording them quite a nice view.

When he'd heard the Jeep shift into gear, he'd focused his camera on the vehicle and its license plate. You never knew when proof of something would come in handy.

He quite frankly didn't care if the two of them shot heroin in the alley; right then he'd simply wanted them gone. Once the vehicle had driven away and the kid had gone back inside Gertie's, they'd approached the car.

Only to be interrupted by the woman. She'd seemed to buy the story that they were looking at her rental because they were anticipating a vehicle purchase.

When he'd seen her at the harbor, she'd been chatting with the cop and then had reached into her purse for money. It dawned on him that perhaps she'd transferred everything from her brown shoulder bag into the brightly colored purse. He wanted to see inside. When she approached the doughnut line, he'd slid in behind her and struck up a conversation about said purse, mentioning a nonexistent wife, hoping that she'd take the hint and open her bag for his inspection.

But she hadn't been inclined. And she'd left the line and the event pretty damn fast after that.

There could be a thousand reasons for that. Most that would make no difference to him and Ivan. But if she'd left because she'd suddenly recognized them from the plane, that changed everything. And what if she'd confessed her concerns to the cop, who'd driven her away? For the tenth time, he checked his mirrors, aware that sometimes the watchers were watched. His cousin had lost his life because he hadn't remembered that basic truth and had been too focused on his prey without realizing that he was under a microscope.

Gasdrig would not make the same mistake. He would be watchful. The time to strike would come. And it would not be in vain.

Marcus slipped into Gertie's for a late lunch on Sunday. He slid onto a stool at the counter. Gertie was at the cash register, less than six feet away. She waved at him and came over once she finished checking out a customer. "Chief," she said.

"Interim," he said.

"The job should be yours," Gertie said.

He shrugged. He didn't want to get a job because somebody was too sick to return to work. "How are you feeling?" he asked.

"I still get tired," she admitted. "Even though I'm working less than half the hours I used to."

"Give yourself a break," he said. "You were shot." And came close to dying, he added silently.

"I know. What's your pleasure today?"

"Turkey special," he said. Nobody did roast turkey, dressing, mashed potatoes and gravy and cranberry sauce like Gertie.

"Got it. Saw you at the harbor last night."

"I didn't see you," he admitted.

"No…"

Her voice trailed off as the dishwasher she'd recently hired walked past, collecting full bus tubs from under the counter. "Sonny," Marcus said, greeting the man. He got a nod in return. The man had been working for Gertie for just a month now and Marcus hadn't heard him say five words. Gertie had a soft spot for lost souls, especially veterans like Sonny who'd returned home without purpose. No doubt it had something to do with her late husband's Vietnam service.

"No surprise," Gertie said when she could step close again. "We were coming from the west as you and Erin McGarry were exiting east." She paused. "Early night."

"Yeah."

She smiled at him. "She seems nice."

"She does," he agreed. He couldn't tell Gertie the truth, that he'd initiated a background check on her.

Gertie studied him. "Holding your cards close, aren't you?" she asked, her tone kind.

"It's probably best for right now," he said.

She patted his hand. "You'll make a good decision, Marcus. You always do. I'll go turn your order in. Missy will bring it out," she added, nodding her head at the server at the other end of the counter. "I'm going home to put my feet up."

A half hour later, Marcus parked his car and went to find his overburdened desk. Sure enough, there were new things to read and sign. He was almost done when his computer dinged. It was a preliminary background check on Erin. International police databases had been checked. There were no outstanding warrants. An arrest three years ago in Brazil got his attention, but when he read the details, it appeared that no charges had ever been filed and she'd been released after three days.

There was information on her work history. Names of employers and dates of employment.

He thought back to the list of jobs she'd so breezily offered the night before. He could make some links. Pagagy Roofing in Costa Rica. That was when she'd been shingling. Tomahawk Small Animals Clinic in London. *V* had been *vet assistant*. There was nothing he could easily tie to dog walking in Paris. That had probably been for cash, or rather euros, and this report likely only picked up wages reported by an employer.

He looked at her most recent workplace: Preston's Automobile Exchange. Likely the job she'd been working at when she'd gotten the call to come help her sister. But wait. He studied the dates. Her employment had ended there a month before she'd come to the States.

He remembered their very first conversation. Maybe not word for word, but definitely the gist of it. He'd complimented her on being willing to drop everything to come help her sister, that it wasn't easy to suddenly interrupt one's work or home life. And he remembered that it had taken her a minute to answer and when she did, she'd said something that he thought was odd at the time. *Indeed. All kinds of interruptions in my life lately.*

He remembered thinking that for just a brief moment, she'd looked sad. He'd thought it was because it had been difficult to leave her old life behind. But maybe he'd been wrong. Maybe there was another reason.

*Please provide additional information on most recent employment at Preston's Automobile Exchange,* he typed. He pressed Send.

# Chapter 8

Erin lit some candles in the store to take away the rather strong smell of ammonia. But the newly cleaned floors looked good. She took a photo and texted it to Morgan. Her sister immediately responded with a smiley face and a short message. Can you bring black sweatpants, gray sweatshirt, more socks and toothpaste when you come tonight?

She wasn't surprised. It was summer and most people weren't wearing sweatshirts, but Morgan was always cold. The hospital probably couldn't keep the place warm enough for her sister.

Of course, she responded. Then she flipped the sign and unlocked the door. Once that happened, she barely had time to take a breath until she relocked the door at five o'clock. In four hours, they'd had the same amount of sales as the entire previous day. Some of that was due to the fact that a man had bought one of the more expensive paintings for his wife but still, she'd been flying around the store.

She'd loved it.

She walked out the back door and drew in a deep breath of warm summer air. Another beautiful day. No wonder people had been out and about. When she drove to her sister's house, she left the driver's-side window down, enjoying the feel of the air in her hair.

Once there, she took a minute to have a cup of tea and a turkey-and-cheese sandwich and then went upstairs to find her sister's things. She stacked them up. It was a pile by the time she finished and she went to get her brown shoulder bag. She took out the shoes and the scarf that still remained inside the bag, but left the two novels. She wouldn't get to them for some time and Morgan might as well enjoy them.

When she got to the hospital, Morgan and Brian were watching television. She leaned in and gave her sister a kiss and then hugged her brother-in-law. "What's new?" she asked brightly.

"He won't play cards," Morgan said.

"I've lost forty-three dollars," Brian said. "And I have to do all the dishes for three months after the baby is born."

Erin winked at her sister. "Speaking of baby?"

"All good still," her sister said. "The doctor was in. According to her, I'm an exemplary patient and if everything continues to look good, I may be able to come home by Tuesday or Wednesday."

"I imagine Brian is sad about having to give up meals in the hospital cafeteria," Erin said.

Brian shrugged. "The meat loaf was pretty good but I'd shy away from the Swiss steak if I was you."

"No worries," Erin said. She pulled the things out of her shoulder bag. "I got your things. And added a couple new books."

Morgan almost purred when she saw them. And she rubbed her hands across her soft sweatshirt. "I'm a happy girl," she said. "How was business?"

"Really good. I sold the painting in the corner, the one on the easel."

"No way. Oh, that's nice. The artist will be thrilled. I get paid, he gets paid. Speaking of which, do you need money? We never talked about what I would pay you for doing this, but I certainly don't expect you to work for free."

Erin waved a hand. "I don't have many expenses right now besides an occasional lunch at Gertie's Café. And that's pretty reasonable."

"Is handsome Marcus Price going to be providing more free dinners?" Morgan asked. "Brian was telling me that he took you to Food Truck Saturday."

"Yeah, what a nice event," she said, not answering the question.

"Nice because you had a hankering for food trucks or nice because you enjoyed being with Marcus?" Morgan pressed.

"You know I love a good food truck."

"Erin," Morgan said, her tone more serious.

Brian stood up. "This sounds like an excellent time for me to get a cup of coffee. Anybody want anything?"

Both Morgan and Erin shook their heads. When he was out of the room, Morgan patted the edge of her bed. "What's the deal?"

Erin moved to the bed and sat. "Well, he's funny and smart and apparently hardworking."

"And super sexy," Morgan added.

"Goes without saying," Erin agreed. "And we have fun when we're together, but there's something weird that I can't put my finger on."

"Weird how?"

Erin shrugged. "There are times when I get the feeling that he's…interrogating me."

"Interrogating. That's a harsh word," Morgan said.

"I know. And maybe I used it because he's a cop and that's what they do. But he's got a lot of questions."

Morgan looked thoughtful. "Maybe he just wants to get to know you?"

She thought about confessing her abrupt departure the evening before after seeing the stranger, but then she'd have to tell Morgan about the two strange men and Morgan would immediately begin to worry. No way. "Perhaps."

Morgan studied her for a moment, but didn't say anything else. Finally, she picked up the television remote. "I've been letting Brian control the television. Let's find a movie, something he'll hate, and make him watch it with us."

Marcus was three hours shy of ending his twelve-hour shift on Sunday when the 911 call came in that a group of teenagers were drag racing on River Road. He knew the road well. It wasn't the first time it had been used for just that purpose.

Serenity was the other officer working and he heard her immediate response that she was en route to the scene. Not sure what she might encounter, he picked up his radio, reported that he was also responding. With both lights and siren going, he covered ground fast. He was in no damn mood for this. He'd already investigated four different automobile accidents that day, one of them a mess that had involved a transport to Bigelow Memorial. He sure as hell didn't need a carload of teenagers who were injured or worse.

He had a pretty good idea of where the kids would be on River Road. He communicated the location to Serenity, arranging that they approach the scene from opposite directions. He was thirty seconds ahead of Serenity. There were eight cars and probably twenty kids. When they saw him, they scrambled toward their vehicles.

"Everybody stop," he yelled. "Put your hands in the air where I can see them."

Fortunately, they all did as ordered. He scanned the crowd and didn't see any weapons. A couple of them were holding cans of beer.

He recognized at least half of them and thought they were likely old enough to buy the beer legally. But they were damn fools to be drinking and racing. "Who wants to tell me what's going on?"

Nobody responded. Serenity pulled up behind the group. He waited until she got out of the car before repeating his question.

"I'll ask it just once more. What's going on?"

"We weren't hurting anyone." It was a voice from the back of the group. Marcus moved to his left so that he could make eye contact. He remembered a time when he, Blade and Jamie had done something very similarly stupid on this same stretch of road. They'd likely thought the same thing. But he and his friends had been younger than this group, who looked to be in their early twenties, definitely old enough to know better. "You're lucky you haven't hurt anyone yet," he said. "Now I'm Officer Price and this is Officer Jones. She and I are going to need to see identification from all of you and if one of these vehicles belongs to you, we're going to want to know that, too."

He and Serenity began working the scene. It took a while. Information had to be recorded. Everybody got a field sobriety test and for those unfortunate few who'd been observed with a beer can in their hands, they took Breathalyzers at the scene. None of them tested over the legal limit, which made him very happy. Two of the females were minors, just sixteen, which didn't sit well. What the hell were they doing with a group of people who were mostly six or seven years older? They had to call their parents and arrange to be picked up. There was some additional drama when all that happened. Both girls had cried, one mom had been pretty angry and the other one's dad had seemed to think it wasn't any big deal. In fact, he'd said that he'd hoped that Dawson would be the arresting officer. When Marcus asked why, he said that he lived down the street from him.

All of it had Marcus thinking about what kind of parent he'd be as he finally drove away from the scene. When his next immediate thought was wondering what kind of parent Erin McGarry might make, he almost crashed his car.

Maybe he was light-headed? He was certainly hungry. The turkey lunch had been delicious, but that was many hours ago. He was thirty minutes shy from ending his shift but there was more paperwork to do. He got in line at a local drive-through and ordered a burger and fries. Maybe not the best choice, but he was tired and hungry and when they asked if he wanted a drink, *chocolate shake* was his first thought. "Iced tea," he said instead.

He got his food, took it back to his desk, and settled in behind his computer. Ninety minutes later, he pushed his chair away. He tossed his garbage into a bag in their small break area, checked in via radio with the two officers who were patrolling and in person with the additional two administrative staff who would work the overnight shift, and left the building.

He was looking forward to a shower and a minimum of eight hours of sleep.

But still, on his way home, he took the time to swing by Erin's home away from home. Her rental car was not on the street. She must still be at the hospital.

It was getting dark. She'd likely be heading home soon.

"That was the best movie ever, sister," Erin said, standing up and stretching.

"Best two movies ever," grumbled Brian good-naturedly. "It was from the goodness of my heart that I agreed to a second one, but now I'm thoroughly depressed. That's why guys don't like romantic movies. All it does is prove to us is that we'll never measure up to these guys."

"*These guys* are actors, playing a part, written and directed by others," Morgan said. "You're perfect. Not lacking in any way." She paused, holding her index finger up in the air. "But if you learned anything from that bathtub scene, so much the better."

"Again, TMI," Erin said. "I'll see you tomorrow,

Morgan." She turned to Brian. "Are you spending the night here or coming back to the house?"

"I'll be along in an hour or so," he said. "Want me to walk you to your car?"

She shook her head. "I walked Paris in the dark. I think I can handle Knoware."

"Still, be careful," Morgan said.

"Of course." Erin waved as she walked from the room. The hospital was very quiet on a Sunday night. There were two employees at the nurses' station, both looking at computers. There were no visitors in the waiting area. Perhaps other units were busier, but this one looked tucked in for the night. She took the empty elevator to the first floor, waved at the security guard behind the desk, and walked out the revolving door.

She walked across the parking lot. Now, about every third space was empty. It hadn't been that way when she'd arrived. All of the close spots had been taken, but she'd been happy enough to park at the end of the fourth row because there was a nice big tree there and it would shade her car from the late-afternoon sun.

She hadn't anticipated staying this late, but one movie had led into another and she'd enjoyed the time. They'd ordered a pizza and pretended that the sodas they were drinking had rum in them. It had been fun to torture Brian, who would have wanted to watch baseball if given the choice, but then again, he'd do just about anything to make Morgan smile.

That was what she wanted. A guy who would do anything to make her smile.

She saw her car and pushed the remote. The lights blinked on.

She heard a noise to her right, turned her head to

look, and was shoved hard to the ground from behind. Instinctively she braced herself, feeling the rough pavement dig into her hands. Her elbows gave out and she caught herself just in time to avoid a full face-plant. Instead, her cheeks grazed the ground.

She lifted herself to all fours. She needed to get up, fight, run. Something. But before she could do any of that, her assailant ripped her bag off her shoulder, wrenching her left arm in the process. She sucked in a breath of air and screamed.

Marcus was a block from his house when the call came over the radio. Heard the code, translated it and had his car turned around before the transmission ended.

Assault and theft of property. Parking lot of Bigelow Memorial Hospital. Medical and police response needed.

When he arrived, a fire truck was already in the lot. He saw the back of Blade. He was squatting on the ground. As he approached, Blade turned. "She's okay," he said.

And Marcus's heart rate shot up. He'd been right. There'd never been a time when he'd wanted to be more wrong.

Erin was sitting up, her back braced against the fender of a car. She gave him a wobbly smile, but when he got three steps closer, there was enough light from the surrounding vehicles that he could see that her eyes were laced with pain and her face, her beautiful face, was dirty and blood-streaked.

Marcus dropped to his knees. "Is he right? Are you okay?" He wanted to touch her, but was afraid.

She nodded. "Your friend thinks I may have a dislocated shoulder. I'm trying to argue the point, but every time I move, I forget what I was saying."

He looked at said shoulder and it was obvious that something wasn't right. He turned to stare at Blade. "She needs a doctor."

"Yeah. Well, good thing we're in a hospital parking lot."

If Blade was trying to ease the tension, it wasn't going to work.

"Is Jamie working?" Marcus asked. If he wasn't, he was calling him in.

"Yes," Blade said. He was cleaning the dirt off Erin's face with wipes. "I've already texted him. He'll be waiting for us. An ambulance team would generally transport, but given our proximity, I've got permission from my chief to deliver her inside."

"I'll do it," Marcus said.

Blade just shook his head. Marcus stood down. Blade was the medical response and he needed to let him do his job.

"That lovely woman helped me," Erin interjected, nodding in the direction of an older woman standing off to the side.

He would talk to her. But first, he wanted any information Erin could provide. "What happened?" Marcus asked gently, hardly able to watch Blade clean her up. It killed him that she'd been facedown in the dirt, so to speak, while her attacker had loomed over her.

"Somebody pushed me down and stole my bag."

"What kind of bag?"

"A shoulder bag. A brown leather shoulder bag. Big. Kind of beat up. I use it when I'm traveling. I brought some things to Morgan tonight so I had it instead of a purse."

It was easy to recall the brightly colored purse she'd had last night. He could easily see her fishing inside for money to buy the wine. "So this bag was much bigger than a purse?"

"Yes. But if you like, you can call it a purse. I'm not the fashion police."

She was trying to make a joke. He was pretty confident the thief had assumed the bag was her purse. He'd refer to it as the latter to avoid confusion. "You said somebody. Male or female?"

"Male."

"Did you see him?"

"No. I mean, I saw the back of him." She stopped. "I guess I can't say a hundred percent that it was a male but the push on my back was strong and—" she closed her eyes for a moment before opening them again "—the hand on my back felt large. It looked like a guy from the back. Broad shoulders, narrower hips. Ran fast."

"Okay," he said. "One guy. You didn't see anybody else."

She shook her head.

"After you got pushed down, what happened?" He was trying very hard to remain calm, but he wanted to rip somebody apart. It didn't matter that he still had questions about Erin, about her past, about her connection to Talk and Hat.

He couldn't stand this.

"I tried to catch myself and I sort of did. At least I didn't break my nose. Anyway, I was trying to get up when he yanked the bag off my shoulder. I think that's what pulled it out of place. Let's just say I saw a few stars," she said, clearly trying to put a brave front on it.

He'd seen dislocated shoulders make big strong cops cry like babies.

"By the time I turned my head, he was running away."

"What was he wearing?" Marcus asked. He realized that Dawson, who was on duty, had arrived and was standing behind him. If he thought it was odd that off-duty Marcus was at the scene and already jumping into investigation mode, he wisely said nothing.

"Dark pants. Dark shirt, long-sleeved. Maybe a hoodie," she said.

It was too warm to be wearing a hoodie, which told Marcus that this had been planned. Maybe not with Erin as the victim, but the perp had dressed for business.

"You think you can stand up, walk with me into the emergency room?" Blade asked.

"I'll give it the old college try," Erin said.

Marcus watched as she got to her feet. He was grateful to see that she was steady.

"Can we have a minute?" Marcus asked Blade.

"Yeah. Hang on to her good arm," his friend replied. Then he walked away, taking Dawson with him.

"What?" she asked, offering him a sweet smile.

"I'm going to find who did this. I promise you. And you're going to be okay. Jamie Weathers is the best emergency physician this side of the Colorado River. Hell, this side of the Missouri River. He'll fix you up. But don't leave the hospital until you hear from me. You understand?"

"I got it," she said. "I'm going to be fine. It's all going to be fine. And the robber is going to be sorely disappointed. I had my phone in one pocket and my driver's license and extra cash in another. My keys were in my hand. All he got was an empty, rather beat-up, old leather shoulder bag."

"You want me to let Brian and Morgan know?"

"Oh, God no. Please don't do that." She looked panicked. "Morgan can't have stress right now. I'm grateful that her room is on the other side of the building. Otherwise, she could be watching this spectacle."

They would want to know. But it was her decision. And she was in pain. "Okay," he said, giving in easily.

"Thank you," she said.

"Go get fixed up. I'll talk to you soon."

She nodded.

"And Erin," he added.

"Yeah."

"I'm really glad that you're okay."

# Chapter 9

Once Blade and Erin entered the hospital, Marcus turned and looked for Dawson. Before he spoke to the witness, he wanted to get the other officer started on something. He found him, with his flashlight, scanning the bushes at the edge of the parking lot. "Anything?" he asked.

"Nope."

"Okay. I need you to go inside and find somebody in Security. This hospital has a number of cameras in the parking lot. Let's see if they picked up anything."

Then Marcus headed toward the witness. "Thank you for staying," he said. "I'm Officer Marcus Price. Can I have your name?"

"Holly Andrews. I knew your mom," she added.

That took him aback. The woman did not look familiar, but then his mom had lots of friends those years that he'd been away. "How?"

"I was her dental hygienist. She was one of my favorite patients. She used to talk about you when you were living and working in Los Angeles. I was so sorry to hear about her cancer."

"Thank you. I miss her," he admitted. Thinking about his mom made him think about the voice mails that remained unopened on his phone. He needed to listen to them. But first he needed to find the person who had done this. "Can you tell me what happened tonight?" he asked.

"Well, I don't know how much help I'll be. My husband is in the hospital. He has pneumonia."

"I'm sorry."

"He's turning a corner for the better," she said. "Anyway, I was in my car, driving out of the parking lot when I saw someone running across the parking lot. I didn't think that much about it. People jog everywhere these days. But then as I was pulling around the corner, I saw that poor woman on the ground. I stopped and she told me that her bag had been stolen. I could tell that she was hurt. I made the 911 call and sat with Erin until help came."

"Thank you for doing that," he said. "You called her Erin. Do you know her?"

"No. She told me her name. I know her sister just from visiting the store."

"Can you describe the person you saw running across the parking lot?"

"He was running pretty fast," she said. "Dark clothes."

"Confident it was a man?" he asked.

She tilted her head to the side. "Yeah. Moved like a guy. A young guy."

"Hair color? Skin color?"

She shook her head. "I think he might have been wearing a hooded sweatshirt. I saw him from the side, then the back. I never saw his face."

Marcus gave the woman one of his business cards. "If you think of anything else, please call me."

She nodded and put the card in her purse. As she walked away, Marcus realized that Blade was walking back toward him.

"I safely handed her off," Blade said, before Marcus could ask. "She's going to be fine," he added.

"It's just…"

"I know. I thought you were off duty at seven."

"I worked late and was on my way home when I heard the call."

"How did you know it was her?" Blade asked.

Marcus turned to his friend. "I don't know. I just did."

"Right." His friend stared at his shoes. "Last night was weird. It was like you couldn't wait to get her away from Daisy and me. And then I saw the two of you high-tailing it out of the harbor not long after that."

"I told you about the credible threat."

"Did something happen?"

"No. I'm just saying that it's a good time to be care-ful."

"What? Wait. You think she's a terrorist?" Blade asked with a frown.

"No. I don't know. I don't know what to think. But I saw her talking to two guys in town who arrived about the same time she did and quite frankly, they give me the creeps for some reason. Last night, when she was in line to get the doughnuts, one of them slipped in line behind her and they had some conversation. She left the line before getting her doughnuts and couldn't wait to get home."

"Did you ask her about that?"

"No. I didn't want to tip my hand. I did initiate a background check on her."

"And?"

"Fine so far, but still waiting for some additional information."

"Do you think it's possible that you're being too much of a cop?" Blade asked.

"Quite possibly, but asking me to stop is the equivalent of asking me to stop breathing. You should expect limited success."

"Now what?" Blade asked.

"Now, being a cop comes in handy. I'm going to find the bastard who did this."

"Good luck."

"I don't need luck. He might need some when I'm through with him."

He watched Blade climb back into the fire truck and then he walked inside the hospital to find out what Dawson had discovered on the security cameras. The officer had found the Security Department supervisor and they were watching the parking lot feed as he approached.

"Here's the victim leaving the hospital," Dawson said.

Marcus watched as Erin walked through the revolving door and stepped into the night. She had the brown shoulder bag tucked close to her left side and her keys were in her right hand.

"Here's where we pick her up as she gets closer to her vehicle," the supervisor said, switching to another camera.

Marcus watched as she took a couple steps before her assailant came into the shot. His throat tightened as Erin was pushed from behind. Like she'd said, she'd tried to catch herself, but her arms had buckled. She'd been pushing herself up when the perp had bent over her to tear away the shoulder bag.

Then the bad guy had exited stage left. As Erin and the witness had said, moving fast. And while he also couldn't see the individual's face, he concurred with Erin's and the witness's belief that it was likely a young man.

Purse snatchings happened. In Los Angeles, they'd barely warranted a report. In Knoware, they were more unusual, but not unheard of. Like any community, there was a mental list of the usual suspects, the few who immediately came to mind when a crime of this nature occurred. He considered them and none matched up to what he was seeing.

"Remind you of anyone?" he asked Dawson.

The officer shook his head. "Lots of visitors this time of year," he said.

Crime did go up in the summer. It was part of being a tourist community. *Pay attention to strangers.* That's what he'd been told to do. No worries. Everybody was going to get a look now.

"Thank you," he said to the security supervisor. He and Dawson left the office. He knew the hospital like the back of his hand. A quick left, then a long hallway, then a right and he'd be smack-dab in the emergency room. He could check on Erin. Make sure Jamie thought she was really okay.

Dr. Jamie Weathers would likely close the door in his face with something pithy like *you do your job and let me do mine.* And he wouldn't be wrong. His immediate task was to find the person who'd done this. He veered toward the hospital entrance and into the parking lot. "Let's start a perimeter search," he said. They knew the direction the thief had run. They would start with streets and alleys and move into the front and backyards of private residences if necessary.

He and Dawson retrieved powerful flashlights from their vehicles. Both gloved up. If they got lucky enough that the idiot had left fingerprints, they weren't going to screw that up.

He was in his second alley, looking into his fifth garbage can, when he found the brown bag. He didn't touch anything. Instead, he let Dawson know what was going on and then contacted his office. Any officer could collect evidence, but they had an evidence technician who was really an expert. She was on call. Maybe wouldn't be crazy about being called out on a Sunday night at nearly ten o'clock, but quite frankly, Marcus didn't care.

While he waited for the tech to show, he called Erin's cell. He half expected it to go to voice mail so he was surprised when she answered it.

"Hi, Marcus."

"Hey," he said. "How's it going?"

"Dr. Jamie Weathers is a bad man, a very bad man, and truly gifted."

"Huh."

"Those were the simultaneous thoughts I was having as he *popped*, his word not mine, my shoulder back into place. I may never be able to pop popcorn again. I may be scarred for life."

Marcus laughed and felt a certain pressure release in his chest. "Where are you right now?"

"Waiting for a prescription. Then I can go home."

"Okay. There's a lobby on the first floor of the hospital, near the waterfall. Sit there and wait for me. I shouldn't be long."

"Do…do we know who did this?"

"No. But I found your purse."

"Where?"

"In a garbage can about two blocks away."

"Oh, man," she said, her voice sad. "I know I said it was beat-up, but I loved that bag. I've had it forever."

"You can have it back, after we're done with it."

"It's been in a garbage can," she said.

"I know." He'd buy her a new purse. A new bag, whatever she called it. Ten new bags.

"An evidence tech is on her way to work the scene. She'll be responsible for evidence retrieval."

"I've seen this on television."

"I imagine you have. Everybody is now an expert on crime scene analysis. Unfortunately, many of the bad guys also watch television. They don't leave as many clues as they used to. The smart ones, anyway."

"Right. Oh, I have to go. The nurse is back. Thanks for calling, Marcus."

"No problem. Wait in the lobby."


When Marcus got off the phone, Dawson was already talking to the homeowner, Ray Raymond. No, he hadn't heard or seen anything, and did the police really need to take his garbage can?

The evidence tech pulled up to the scene and Marcus stepped away from the conversation so that he could bring her up to speed. When he finished, he saw that

Dawson had finished with the homeowner and had searched the rest of the alley for additional clues.

"I got nothing," he told Marcus. "Might be better to do it in daylight."

"Yeah," Marcus said. He would be back. Bigclow Memorial was in the middle of residential housing. He'd canvass the area to see if any home security system might have picked up anything that was useful. "I'm going to take off. See you tomorrow."

Dawson shuffled awkwardly on his feet. "I heard that you were at Food Truck Saturday with the…victim," he said.

"That's right." If Dawson was going to lecture him on getting personally involved in a case, he'd picked the wrong time to do it.

"I'm sorry this happened," he said. "Had to be tough for you. If it was my girlfriend, I don't think I'd handle it well."

His instinct was to protest that Erin wasn't his girlfriend. But since he had no idea how to explain what she was to him, he said nothing.

"You're doing a good job as interim chief," Dawson said. "Lots of us think it would be good if you had the job permanently. Not that we wish the chief any ill will. But maybe it's time."

"Things generally work out the way they're supposed to," Marcus said. "But I appreciate you saying that."

"No problem. Good night, Chief," Dawson said.

"Good night." For the second time that night, Marcus headed toward the hospital's front door.

Erin walked into the empty and dimly lit hospital lobby. Off to her right was the same security guard she'd waved to almost an hour ago when she'd been leaving the first time. He was staring at a computer screen, occasionally answering a telephone. To her left was a closed coffee shop. There was a television screen hanging on the wall in the far corner, on mute, showing some kind of car race. She watched for a minute, somewhat mesmerized by the vehicles going around in a circle.

She took a seat wishing desperately for a cup of tea. Silly as it was, it would go a long way to making her feel safe and whole again. She was sure of it. When she got home, the kettle was going on.

This was really nothing, she told herself. So many people endured significantly worse on a regular basis. She needed to suck it up, buttercup. But that was easier said than done, she admitted.

*I'm really glad that you're okay.* That was what Marcus had said. In a way that had made her forget all about the pain in her shoulder.

Maybe he said that to all crime victims?

She didn't think so.

She saw him stride through the front door and she summoned up a smile. "My car is here," she said when he got close. "But the *good* Dr. Weathers gave me a nice pain pill after the *bad* Dr. Weathers tortured me. I don't think I can drive home."

"Don't worry about it. You can get your car tomorrow. I'll drive you home tonight," he said, sitting in the chair next to her.

"That's awfully nice of you."

"Ask around. I'm an awfully nice guy." He studied her face.

"I had this same look when I was ten and went over my bike's handlebars. It healed pretty well then."

"It'll heal just fine," he assured her.

"What happens next? With the investigation, I mean?" She certainly didn't want him thinking that she was asking anything of a more personal nature. Even if she had been obsessing over it. One little pain pill wasn't going to make her completely lose her grasp on protecting her inner thoughts. She was made of sterner stuff than that.

"We've already got the security tapes from the hospital of the parking lot. Doesn't give us much more than what you saw, but still, good to have. We're retrieving the purse as we speak. Tomorrow, in the light of day, we'll re-canvass the area, see if we missed anything tonight. We'll also attempt to retrieve any residential security video that might be helpful."

"Wow. All for an old leather shoulder bag."

Marcus shook his head. "He assaulted you. Pushed you to the ground. Injured you. Could have much more seriously injured you."

"Scared me," she admitted. She was too tired to be really brave.

He put his hand on her knee and she felt the warmth travel up her leg. "For that alone, he's going to have to pay a big price."

Dr. Weathers had been wrong. He'd said that she'd soon feel very relaxed. Marcus's touch made her feel rather... Hoping for composure, she glanced away, catching the car race in the corner of her eye. Yup. That was it. She felt rather revved up. "I should be getting home," she said.

"Of course." He stood and held out a hand.

She took it with her own. And didn't let go until they

got to his SUV. He opened the door and waited while she slid in. Then he gently closed the door.

When he got in, he turned to her. "Still okay?"

"Yes. That's the last time you get to ask me that," she said gently.

He shook his head. "Nope."

She yawned. Widely. "Sorry," she said once her mouth was closed. "One shouldn't race when one is almost asleep."

"Race?"

"Never mind." She yawned again.

He smiled. "You'll be in bed in ten minutes."

"Less if you use lights and siren," she said.

"You want that?"

"Good grief, no. I've been enough of a spectacle tonight."

"Hardly your doing." He started the vehicle and drove out of the parking lot. When he got to Morgan's house, he turned to her. "Pretty dark inside. Brian coming home tonight?"

"Probably not. He spends many of the nights at the hospital. There's a recliner in Morgan's room."

He tapped his index finger on the steering wheel. "You feel okay about being alone in the house?"

She'd been living alone for the last ten years. In places much scarier than Knoware. "Of course."

He nodded.

"Is there a reason I shouldn't?" she asked, getting a bad feeling. There had been nothing in her bag to tie her to Morgan's house.

"No," he said, shaking his head. "I just wanted to make sure."

"I'm going to close my eyes and the world is going

to fade away very quickly," she said, reaching for the handle on her door. He was out his own side quickly and reaching a hand toward her as she swung her legs toward the ground. Then he took the house keys from her and unlocked the door.

She turned to him. "Thanks for the ride," she said, determined to keep it light. The pain pill was making her emotional. Or at least she was going to blame it on that.

"You wouldn't mind if I came in for just a minute to look around, would you?" he asked.

She motioned him forward and waited while he checked every room on the first and second levels and finally the basement. "I'm getting a bad feeling," she said when he was done.

"It's just me being me," he said. "I don't have any reason to believe that you weren't a random victim." He studied her. "Do you have any reason to believe differently?"

"Of course not. I don't even know anybody in this town. How could anybody be upset with me?"

He seemed to hesitate before smiling. "That's what I thought. Do you need any help getting ready for bed?"

If she'd been revved up before, she was now a driver on the last leg of the course. Full throttle ahead. She might spontaneously combust and he hadn't even touched her. "Uh...no."

He stared at her. "There's something here, isn't there?" he said. "Between us. Something different."

Her throat felt tight. "Different how?" she managed.

"Something different than what I've experienced before," he said, his voice soft.

"Yeah. That's what I thought you meant. Same," she admitted.

"I thought so," he said. He didn't say it as if he was happy or sad, just accepting.

"What now?" she asked.

He reached out and with two fingers, gently tipped her chin up. Then every bit as gently, he kissed her.

He didn't linger. Drew back with a soft sigh. "Lock the door after me and go to bed, Erin." Then he walked out the door.

# *Chapter 10*

On Monday morning, when Marcus walked into Gertie's, Blade and Jamie were already in a booth. "Good morning," he said.

"You look like hell," Jamie said. "And I have the medical degree that says I'm qualified to say that."

Marcus smiled at Cheryl, who had brought him a cup of tea. When she was away from the table, he turned to Jamie. "Your opinion, as always, is highly valued."

"I don't think he means that," Blade said, not looking up from his coffee. "How is Erin doing after last night?"

"Physically, I think she's fine," Marcus said.

"Of course," Jamie said smugly. "I patched her up."

"She's referring to you as the bad Dr. Weathers," Marcus said.

"That's going to make it harder to step up when she gets tired of you," Jamie said. "Oh, wait. What's the statute of limitations on *dibs*?"

"It hasn't run out yet," Marcus said, his tone hard. He leaned forward, lowered his voice. "I spent the night in my SUV outside Erin's house."

"What did you expect to happen?" Jamie asked, all teasing gone from his voice.

"I don't know," Marcus said.

Blade turned to Jamie. "He ran a background check on her." His tone was crystal clear. It said *our friend has gone round the bend*.

Jamie cocked his head. "You don't do that with every woman you date, do you?"

Marcus didn't even bother to answer. Cheryl delivered their food. He cut into his omelet and chewed. He was hungry and tired and mixed up inside. He and Erin had both admitted that there was *something different* going on between the two of them. Throughout the long night, to keep his mind busy and to stay awake, he'd added and discarded various descriptors until he'd narrowed the list to one.

Substantial.

As long as he was stuck on *S*, he'd add Sweet—the kiss. Sexy—her, at all times in all ways. Scary—because for the first time in a long time, maybe ever, he felt out of control.

If there was anyone he could tell that, it would be his best friends. But he stayed silent. Another *S* word.

"Do you have the results of said background check?" Jamie pressed, not put off by Marcus's lack of response to his other question.

"Preliminary," Marcus said. "Nothing that is terribly unusual."

"Somewhat unusual?" Jamie prodded, picking up on the word choice.

"She was unexpectedly called upon to come to her sister's aid. I assumed she would have left a job. But the report showed that she left that job a month ago."

"So?" Jamie asked. "People leave jobs all the time."

"People do. But most of the time, people leave jobs for other jobs," Marcus said.

"Maybe the place closed down. Maybe they laid off a bunch of people," Blade said.

"All that is possible. That's why I'm getting more information," Marcus said.

"How much will be enough?" Jamie asked, pushing his empty plate to the side.

"What do you mean?"

"How much will be enough?" Jamie repeated his question. "At what point will you have convinced yourself of a reason that she's not the one?"

"What?" Marcus was genuinely confused.

Jamie sighed. "We've been friends for a very long time. Our friendship is one of the most important things in my life. Tell me that you'll remember that when I say this."

"Yes, fine." Marcus waved his hand, impatient with his friend.

"You welcome the reasons why a relationship won't work. It *confirms* for you that you're not built to have a serious ongoing commitment with a woman. I imagine it has something to do with your father's...history."

It wasn't a gut punch, but still, his breath seemed to come hard. "I didn't realize your specialty was psychiatry," Marcus said.

Jamie said nothing. The two men stared at each other. Blade was sliding the salt shaker from hand to hand, his head bowed. Marcus grabbed the salt shaker. "You agree?" he demanded.

"Come on, Marcus, don't do this," Blade said, looking up. "We're not the enemy."

It was two against one, hardly a fair fight. But then again, his friends wouldn't fight fair. Not if they were trying to help. He felt the pressure in his chest ease.

"I'm sorry," Marcus said, looking at them both.

"No problem," Jamie said easily. "You don't talk about your dad. So that means we don't talk about your dad. But he's somewhere in the mix in this."

Right now more than ever. Again, if there was anybody that he was going to tell about the calls, it would be his two best friends. But he wasn't ready to do that yet. He needed some time. And maybe a large bottle of very good whiskey. He threw some money down to cover the check and slid out of the booth.

"We're okay?" Jamie asked.

Marcus smiled. "Hell, yes. But you're buying your own breakfasts." On his way out of Gertie's, he dialed Erin's number.

"Hello," she said.

"Good morning. Sleep okay?"

"Yeah. Great."

"How's the shoulder?"

"Feels as if it might have been dislocated sometime in the recent past."

"Erin," he said.

"It's fine. Listen, I can't talk. I have to get ready for work."

What was this? Didn't women always want to talk about relationships and all the things that went into

# Get ready to relax and indulge with your **FREE BOOKS** and more!

## Claim up to FOUR NEW BOOKS & TWO MYSTERY GIFTS – absolutely FREE!

Dear Reader,

We both know life can be difficult at times. That's why it's important to treat yourself so you can relax and recharge once in a while.

And I'd like to help you do this by sending you this amazing offer of up to FOUR brand new full length FREE BOOKS that WE pay for.

**This is everything I have ready to send to you right now:**

Try **Harlequin® Romantic Suspense** books featuring heart-racing page-turners with unexpected plot twists and irresistible chemistry that will keep you guessing to the very end.

Try **Harlequin Intrigue® Larger-Print** books featuring action-packed stories that will keep you on the edge of your seat. Solve the crime and deliver justice at all costs.
Or **TRY BOTH!**

All we ask in return is that you answer 4 simple questions on the attached Treat Yourself survey. You'll get **Two Free Books** and **Two Mystery Gifts** from each series you try, *altogether worth over $20*! Who could pass up a deal like that?

Sincerely,

*Pam Powers*

Harlequin Reader Service

# Treat Yourself to Free Books and Free Gifts.

## Answer 4 fun questions and get rewarded.

▼ **DETACH AND MAIL CARD TODAY!** ▼

| | YES | NO |
|---|---|---|
| 1. I LOVE reading a good book. | 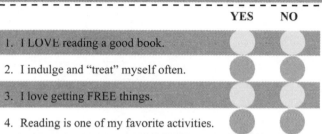 | |
| 2. I indulge and "treat" myself often. | | |
| 3. I love getting FREE things. | | |
| 4. Reading is one of my favorite activities. | | |

### TREAT YOURSELF • Pick your 2 Free Books...

Yes! Please send me my Free Books from each series I select and Free Mystery Gifts. I understand that I am under no obligation to buy anything, as explained on the back of this card.

Which do you prefer?

☐ **Harlequin® Romantic Suspense** 240/340 HDL GRCZ
☐ **Harlequin Intrigue® Larger-Print** 199/399 HDL GRCZ
☐ **Try Both** 240/340 & 199/399 HDL GRDD

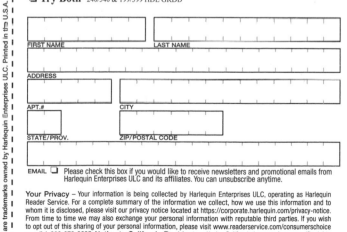

FIRST NAME                    LAST NAME

ADDRESS

APT.#                         CITY

STATE/PROV.                   ZIP/POSTAL CODE

EMAIL ☐   Please check this box if you would like to receive newsletters and promotional emails from Harlequin Enterprises ULC and its affiliates. You can unsubscribe anytime.

HI/HRS-520-TY22

one? They'd kissed. Twice. Didn't she want to dissect that? Analyze it?

Acknowledge it?

Because he desperately wanted to know what she was thinking.

He was not, however, the begging type. "I thought you might have Jo Marie take your shift."

"There's no need. I am perfectly capable. My shower is running."

"Okay. Well, if you need—"

"Marcus," she interrupted. "I told Brian this morning what happened. I was afraid that he might hear about it at work. I'm learning what a small town Knoware really is. We agreed not to tell Morgan at this time. She likely won't hear about it since her contact with the outside world is much more limited and neither of us wants to cause her any worry."

"I'm glad you told him." He'd left his watch over the house this morning when Brian had pulled into the driveway about seven.

"I wanted you to know in case you saw him at city hall. Didn't want to make things awkward between the two of you."

"Appreciate the heads-up. We should have a report later today from the lab if any useful information is recovered from the evidence at the scene. Also, do you need a ride to retrieve your car?"

"Brian is taking me. Got to go. Goodbye."

She hung up before he could say anything. Shaking his head, he used his phone to check his email for the third time to see if there was any update to the background check. There was not.

He got in his SUV. He desperately needed a nap. But

in the light of day, he wanted to see the alley where her purse had been recovered. He headed that direction.

The alley was empty of people. He parked at one end and walked it on foot, looking for anything that they might have missed the night before. When he got to the space where the purse had been tossed, there was a circle of dirt or rust, or some combination, on the pavement, where the garbage can in question had likely stood for some time. It and its contents would hopefully yield some info.

It would be too much to hope for that the perp had cut his hand on the metal lid and there'd be blood to tie him to the crime. But maybe they'd get some fibers or hair or skin cells.

He walked the entire length of the alley, finding nothing. Then he started knocking on doors. An older woman, still in her robe, answered the first knock.

"Yes," she said.

"I'm Officer Price of the Knoware Police Department," he said. He handed her a card and waited while she looked at it.

"I've seen you around town," she said. "What can I do for you?"

"Last night, a woman's purse was stolen in the hospital parking lot. It was recovered from the garbage can behind the house across the alley from yours. I'm wondering if you saw anything or have any security cameras that might have captured anything?"

She shook her head. "I was home all night, but I'm sorry, I didn't see or hear anything. I don't have any cameras. You should ask the Swanhills next door," she said, pointing to the left. "They have a dog who hears everything. And barks at it," she added, rolling her eyes.

"Thank you," Marcus said. He left and immediately walked to the Cape Cod house to his right. He rang the doorbell and barking commenced. Yippy. A man, maybe early seventies, opened the interior door and sure enough, a little dog with hair in its eyes was frantically circling the man's heels, barking up a storm. A screen door still separated them, but did nothing to mitigate the noise.

The man eyed the uniform first. "Judy, be quiet."

His dog was named Judy. For some reason that struck Marcus as funny and he had to work to keep a smile off his face.

Judy, however, was a good listener and thankfully shut up. Marcus had had nowhere near enough sleep to tolerate that kind of barking for long.

"Did that woman next door complain again?" the man asked. "She hates animals. I swear she does."

"No complaints, sir. I'm Marcus Price with the Knoware Police Department. Are you Mr. Swanhill?"

"Yes."

"May I have a minute of your time?"

The man opened the screen door, which set Judy off again, and it was another thirty seconds before Mr. Swanhill had her calmed down. No wonder the neighbor complained. It was an ear-piercing bark.

Judy had a blanket in the living room and headed for that. Marcus remained standing until Mr. Swanhill motioned for him to have a seat. "Thank you, sir. I'm here because last night a woman had her purse stolen in the hospital parking lot a little after nine o'clock. The thief ran through the alley behind your house and tossed the purse into the garbage can of the neighbor whose house backs up to the alley on the other side."

"Ray and Paula. That's who lives there. We've been friends for a long time."

"Right. We spoke with Ray last night after we found the purse in his garbage can. My question for you is whether you saw anything last night or whether you might have a security camera that would have captured a portion of the alley."

"No camera. But Judy did get awfully upset about something about that time last night. I was eating my ice cream. I figured it was some squirrel in the backyard. I finally let her out because I was afraid that she was going to wake up my wife, who was already in bed. I went out with her and looked up and down the alley. I didn't see anybody by the garbage cans, but there was somebody at the far end dressed in dark clothes getting into a car."

"The car was parked in the alley?" Marcus asked, trying to clarify.

"Nope. On Webster Street. It had pulled up at the end of the alley. The individual on foot got in the passenger side. They drove off and Judy finally stopped barking. My ice cream was near melted by the time I got back to it."

"Could you describe the man on foot or the driver of the vehicle?"

"Nothing more than I've already told you about the man on foot. Didn't see the driver at all. He was driving a light-colored sedan if that's helpful."

"Anything is helpful," Marcus said.

"I hope the lady with the purse wasn't hurt."

"She's going to be fine," Marcus said. He stood up. Judy lifted her head. "Thank you, Mr. Swanhill. If you think of anything else, you have my card."

He left quickly and he could hear Judy all the way to his SUV.

There had been at least two people. The thief and the driver. And a description of the car.

They were getting closer.

Four hours later, after some much-needed sleep, Marcus was ready to face the remainder of the day. He stood in his kitchen, eating a turkey-and-avocado sandwich and drinking a glass of milk. His cell phone rang. He didn't recognize the number, but he answered it.

"Hello."

"Marcus, it's Brian Tiddle."

Marcus put his milk down. Brian sounded stressed. "What's up?" Marcus asked.

"I need some assistance. At my house. I think somebody broke in."

"Where's Erin?" Marcus asked, grabbing his keys.

"At the store."

"Okay." Marcus took a breath. "Why do you think somebody broke in?"

"There's a broken window and…" Brian trailed off. "And I can see some damage inside. It had to have happened this morning."

Indeed. He'd been parked outside the house all night. "Why do you say that?"

"I spent the night at the hospital. Got home about seven this morning. Needed to shower and shave before I had a video conference call. Once the call was done, I drove Erin to the hospital to pick up her car. I went to my office for a couple hours and was going to join Morgan for lunch. On the way, I swung by the house to get a clean shirt in case I decided to spend the night at the hospital again. I saw the window and given what happened to Erin last night, I thought I should call you versus 911."

"I'll be there in five minutes. Don't touch anything and don't go inside. And call Erin at the store. Make sure she's okay."

"Should I tell her what's happened?"

Marcus pulled out of his garage. "Not yet. Just make sure she's okay."

Brian was leaning against the mailbox at the curb when Marcus pulled up. "You think this has anything to do with what happened to Erin last night?" he asked by way of greeting Marcus.

"I don't know," Marcus said. But the thought had been pounding in his head pretty much the entire drive. Was it just a coincidence? That was always a possibility, but it just didn't feel right. No. The two events were related. "Did you talk to Erin?"

"Yeah. I told her I was just checking to make sure she still felt good. She said she did and that the store was pretty busy."

That was one worry put to bed. "I'm going inside. I want you to stay out here. Can I have your key to the front door?" Marcus said, pulling on gloves.

Brian handed it to him. He unlocked the front door, pushed it open with his foot and went inside. He pulled his weapon. He didn't really think anybody was still inside, but he'd been a cop for a long time and he didn't believe in being careless.

The place was a stark contrast to what he'd seen last night when he'd searched the house after bringing Erin home. It had been pretty well tossed. In the kitchen, drawers and cupboards were open and the contents haphazardly tossed on the counter or floor. Fortunately, most of the dishes were still whole with just a few exceptions. The living room cushions were off but not cut open. Everything was out of the entertainment center and off the built-in bookshelves in the corner.

Room by room, he went. Then upstairs. In Erin's room, the disarray and damage was more extensive. The mattress had been flipped and sliced open. Same with the box springs. Everything was out of the drawers and the closet. The furniture had been moved away from the wall.

He finished his inspections of the upstairs and then went to the basement. More of the same. He walked out, his phone to his ear, as he called it in. Once he was finished, he approached Brian. "Good news is that there's nobody inside," Marcus said. "Bad news is that you've got a mess. Once we have an evidence tech do their thing, we're going to need you to take a look and tell us if anything is missing."

"This kind of stuff doesn't happen in Knoware," Brian said.

"Stuff happens," Marcus said. "Everywhere. But you're right in that the burglaries that we generally see in Knoware, it's a fairly quick in and out, taking electronics, prescription meds, cash. The easy stuff. We don't see this kind of destruction."

"It seems personal," Brian said. "I'm a city accountant. Morgan runs a gift shop. I don't understand what kind of beef somebody would have with us." He pushed dirt around with the toe of his dress shoes. "This has something to do with Erin," he said, his tone full of dread.

Marcus studied him. He got a feeling that Brian was waging an internal war. He wanted somebody to blame, but he felt guilty pointing the finger at his sister-in-law.

"Tell me about Erin," Marcus said.

Brian shrugged. "She's great. I mean, she's fun and friendly and she's always been very nice to me."

"But…"

"I wasn't happy with her when she caused Morgan to worry."

"Why would Morgan worry?"

"Because Erin was…unsettled. She never had a job for very long, she never lived in the same place for very long. Morgan used to say that her sister was searching. I'd asked for what, but Morgan either wouldn't or couldn't say. She got thrown in jail once, in South America."

"Do you know why?"

"Yeah. She stepped in when she saw a man beating his wife. She tried to help. He was somewhat influential in the community and she got arrested. She was released, but I got to tell you, that was a bad three days at our house. I thought Morgan was going to lose it. It's hard sometimes for me to forgive Erin for that."

"She was probably doing the right thing," Marcus said.

"Yeah. I know."

"What was she doing when Morgan needed her to come watch over the store?"

"Working at a car dealership in Paris. She said that she could get a leave of absence."

If the background check had been correct, she'd lied about her employment status in Paris. Maybe that meant nothing. Marcus couldn't press for more information without running the risk of showing that he already knew more than he should. He certainly wasn't ready to admit that he had his own doubts about Erin.

His team arrived just then and he brought them up to speed. It was another hour before they were finished and Brian had finally gotten inside to see the damage. When he finally returned to the kitchen, Marcus gave him a minute to find a glass on the countertop, thoroughly wash it and then get a drink of water from the faucet.

"Are you missing anything?" Marcus asked.

"Yeah. About three hundred dollars that we always keep in cash in one of the laundry room cupboards. Nothing else that jumped out at me. Was…was all this for a lousy couple hundred bucks?"

Marcus shrugged. "I don't know. But I will. We're going to find out who did this. We've got a fairly narrow window that the crime occurred in. Maybe one of your neighbors saw something. We'll talk to them all."

"I should get to the hospital. Morgan is going to be wondering where I am."

"Are you going to tell her about this?"

Brian shook his head. "No way. She can be mad at me later if she somehow hears about it. I just got to find a way to get it all cleaned up before she gets released. We have a lady who comes in and cleans for us every couple of weeks. Maybe she can get a few friends to help her."

"That's a good idea. What about Erin? Are you telling her?"

"I think I better," Brian said. "I mean, she's going to see it when she comes home this evening."

"I can swing by the store and tell her," Marcus said. "That way you can get to the hospital."

"Thank you," Brian said. "That would help a lot." He took three steps toward his car. Then turned back to Marcus. "Her room was the worst. Did you notice that?"

"Yeah," said Marcus.

"What do you think that means?" Brian asked.

"I have no idea."

Marcus parked in front of Tiddle's and sat in his vehicle for a minute. Trauma was cumulative. She'd been physically attacked and robbed last night and now her home away from home had been ransacked. He wasn't looking forward to giving her the news.

He was just about to open his car door when his cell phone rang. It was a strange number, but he answered it. The only calls he was avoiding were from his father. "Hello."

"Is this Officer Marcus Price?"

"Yes."

"This is Special Agent Pierre Sargeant of the FBI. I work out of the Seattle field office."

He did not regularly get calls from the FBI. "What can I do for you?" Marcus asked.

"I want to know why you're doing a background check on Erin McGarry."

If Marcus hadn't already been sitting down, he might have needed to grab a chair. "How do you know that?"

"We've been monitoring the hits on databases that contain Ms. McGarry's information. We got your name from the investigator that you were using. He was interviewed this morning and he said that you had particular interest in her employment at Preston's Automobile Exchange."

"What business is it of the FBI who I do a background check on?"

Special Agent Sargeant sighed. Loudly. "Listen, I think we're all on the same side here. I understand that she's living and working in your community. Would you have an hour this afternoon that we could meet? I'd be happy to come to you."

"Sure. Can you be here by three?"

Marcus gave him the address and ended the call. The FBI was coming to see him about Erin. What the hell was going on?

Should he wait to see her until he'd had that conversation? No, he could not. What if she decided to run back to her sister's house for something? What if some well-meaning neighbor stopped in the store and told her about the police activity at the house? Right now, Serenity was knocking on doors in the neighborhood, trying to figure out if anybody had seen anything.

Plus, most importantly, he'd told Brian that he'd tell her, and he would.

He opened his door and walked inside the store. She was behind the cash register helping a customer. She looked beautiful, so perfectly at home in a store of pretty things. As she chatted with the customer, she brushed back a strand of hair and the bracelets on her arm jingled. He knew little about what colors were best for redheads, but her green dress with a wide leather belt looked perfect.

She wore more makeup than before and he suspected it was an attempt to cover the scratches on her face. It did the trick for the most part, although they were still there, a reminder that someone had gotten way too close to her.

He pretended to look at the artwork on the wall. But all he could think about was kissing her again.

The customer left the store. He knew he needed to be quick. There was no telling when the next shopper would open the door. "Hey," he said, walking to the front.

"Can I help you find something, sir?" she asked innocently.

"Not today. How are you?"

"I'm just fine. You're the second person to ask me that."

He knew who had been the first. "I asked Brian to do that."

"Why? And where did you see Brian?" she asked, looking very confused.

"Listen, something has happened. Brian and Morgan are fine, but the house was broken into this morning. It's been tossed pretty good. Brian had run home for something, saw the broken window, and given what had happened last night to you, called me first."

She said nothing. He could almost see the wheels churning. "This has something to do with me," she said, her tone flat. "I'm the reason this happened."

"Are you?" he asked. Did she know something? If she did, it was high time for her to come clean with the details.

"I must be. Brian thinks so. You hear what happened and you have him call and check on me. So you must think so."

She was smart. "I had him call because I was concerned. Not because I had any strong feeling that it was related to you." He paused. "But when I walked through the house, the damage in your room was the most extensive."

She came out from behind the cash register, walked to the front of the store, put the Closed sign in the window and shut off the lights. "I need to go there. I need to see it."

"We've not officially released the scene. Maybe by tomorrow. But I can escort you in."

"I just need a few things and then I'm going to find a hotel. Can you recommend somewhere?"

"Most places are full right now. This is the busiest time of the year."

"Brian can sleep at the hospital," she said, talking fast, as if she was trying to quickly get it sorted out in her head. "He does that most nights anyway. Morgan likes having..." Her voice trailed off. "Is Brian telling Morgan?"

"I don't think he intends to. But you'll probably want to talk to him about that."

"Morgan is looking forward to coming home in a day or two."

"Brian was talking about hiring some folks to come in and put the house back in order."

She started pacing. Up one aisle, down the next. "What if this is because of me? I can't bring trouble into Morgan's life right now. She can't have the stress of that. I'm going next door."

"What?" he said, struggling to keep up.

"I'm going next door to Gertie's. She knows everybody. She can find me a place that has a vacancy." She stopped pacing as quickly as she'd started. "I should go talk to Brian."

"Let's get back to whether there is any reason, any at all, that somebody would be targeting you," he asked, trying one more time.

"No," she said.

"And nothing else unusual has happened to you since you arrived in Knoware?"

"Well, besides last night?"

They weren't getting anywhere fast. "Yes. Look, it's really important—"

"Listen," she interrupted. "I really need to talk with Brian. I have to make sure that he and I are on the same page, that one of us doesn't slip up with Morgan. She can't be thinking about this."

"Morgan is probably tougher than you're giving her credit for," he suggested gently.

"She's plenty tough, but her doctor said to limit the stress and that's what I intend to do."

There wasn't much else he could ask her about without tipping his hand. He did not intend to do that until he had more information. Maybe his visitor from the FBI would provide that. "Brian was on his way to the hospital."

Erin fished out her cell phone from a drawer beneath the cash register. She dialed and waited. She must have gotten voice mail because she said, "Brian, it's Erin. I've talked to Marcus Price. Call me back as soon as you can."

"I can drive you to the house, help you get what you need," Marcus said when she'd finished her call.

"I have my car." She walked to the back room, retrieved her purse from a drawer and tossed her cell phone inside it, set the alarm, and led him out the back door. He stood there while she locked it.

"I'm sorry about this, Erin. We're going to find out who took your purse last night and who broke into the house this morning. Then we'll have some answers."

"I hope so," she said, getting into her car. "I really hope so."

# *Chapter 11*

At the house, Erin got out of her car. Marcus had followed her from the store and parked right behind her. She'd been expecting the yellow police tape—had seen plenty of crime shows on television. But it was still rather startling to see it blocking access to the front door.

Her cell phone rang. It was Brian. "Hey, thanks for calling," she said. "Are you with Morgan?"

"At the hospital but in the coffee shop."

"Marcus said that he didn't think you were planning to say anything to Morgan about the house."

"Right. I don't feel great about that, but I'd feel less great about seeing her get upset and worried."

"Agree. Lesser of two evils," she said. "Once the police let us back in, I can clean everything up."

"I've got a call out to a lady who cleans for us. You have the store to worry about. That's enough."

"Do you think the store could be a target?" she asked.

"I don't know. I've been thinking about it. I'm going to ask Marcus to have the overnight patrols beefed up. Plus we have the security alarm. I'm damn glad your sister convinced me to have that installed."

"Me, too. Listen, Brian. I'm sorry about this. If this has anything to do with me, I'm sorry."

"It's not you. I had some time to think about this on the drive to the hospital. How could it be you? You just arrived in Knoware days ago. What's happened is just a crazy coincidence."

"Still, I'm going to find someplace else to stay." Marcus had joined her on the sidewalk and wasn't even pretending to not listen to her side of the conversation.

"That's not necessary. In fact, it's weird. What's Morgan going to think?"

"We'll tell her that I didn't want her to have the worry and stress over entertaining a houseguest when she comes home from the hospital."

"I'm not sure she's going to buy that," Brian said.

"We'll think of something," she said. "Listen, I'm here at the house. Marcus is going to let me in and I'm going to grab a few things that I'll need."

"Okay. I'll talk to you later."

Erin put her cell phone back in her purse. "Ready," she said, looking at Marcus.

He said nothing but led her to the front door. He took her keys and unlocked it. "Please don't touch anything," he said.

Erin wandered from room to room on the first floor. It was hard to believe that when she'd left the property just hours ago, it had been neat and clean. Normal.

*A new normal.* When she'd lost her job unexpectedly, that was what her friend Alisa had said. *You have a new normal.*

The hell with that. She wasn't getting used to this anytime soon. "I'm ready to go upstairs."

Her room was indeed a mess. She barely looked at it. "Can I take these clothes?" she asked, motioning to the items that were on the floor.

He nodded and she began picking them up. "I could really use my brown bag," she said. She glanced over at the suitcase she'd brought from Paris. The lining had been slashed in multiple places and it looked like somebody had kicked in the hard plastic side. It wasn't going to do her much good.

"I can carry things," Marcus said. "You have a lot of clothes here," he said, looking around. "Did you travel with all these?"

"I shipped some of them. They arrived the same day I did. I only traveled with that suitcase and my brown shoulder bag."

She'd wash everything she was taking with her tonight once she landed somewhere.

*Especially these*, she thought as she picked up her bras and panties from the floor and shoved them in between shirts and jeans. When she was done, they both had a big armful of clothing. She could barely see around it. "That's good," she said, looking around the room. It looked better now that the clothes were off the floor.

"Now what?" he asked as they walked downstairs.

"I'm going to dump this in my rental car and go back to work. The store has been closed for almost an hour."

"Planning to sleep in your car?" he asked.

She hoped not. But it wouldn't be the first time.

Sometimes a rolling stone didn't come to rest in a bed. "I'll work on that this afternoon."

They put the items in her trunk and she got into her car. She looked up at Marcus, who stood by her door. "Thank you for making the effort to tell me and to come here with me. I'm not sure I'd have wanted to be alone when I saw this."

"You're welcome," he said, looking very serious. "You know that you can ask me for help. On anything," he added.

It seemed like an odd thing for him to say. "Of course," she said. "Well, I guess I'll see you later."

She closed her door and drove off, noting in her rearview mirror that Marcus still stood in the street, watching her.

Her underwear was like everything else she wore—colorful. Yellows and blues and greens. As he returned to his office for his afternoon meeting, he suspected that the FBI wasn't going to be interested in that.

At five minutes before three, Special Agent Pierre Sargeant arrived. He was early forties, lean and pale. He needed to get outside more. Marcus kept those thoughts to himself as he led him back to the chief's office. He motioned for him to have a seat at the table in the corner. "Coffee or tea, Special Agent Sargeant?" he asked.

"Pierre is fine. Or SA Sargeant if you feel the need. And coffee sounds good."

Marcus poured that and a cup of tea for himself. He took the chair across the table.

"Thank you for seeing me." The SA's tone was easy, relaxed.

Marcus was strung tight. "I didn't think I had much

choice. And I was pretty curious. I don't think I've ever had a background check generate FBI interest before."

"You do a lot of foreign background checks?"

Marcus shook his head.

"Then my first question is, why Ms. McGarry?"

Marcus was used to asking the questions. He didn't much care for being on the other side of the fence. "Ms. McGarry arrived in Knoware at or about the same time that we were advised that there was a credible threat of terrorism on United States soil. We were advised to be mindful of strangers." That was enough to tell him.

"No other reason?"

Marcus was getting a bad feeling. He shook his head.

"Prior to Ms. McGarry coming to this area, she was living and working in Paris, France. She worked for a car dealership. Preston's Automobile Exchange. Does any of that mean anything to you?"

"No, but it's not new information, either. I saw it on the report. Ms. McGarry had identified herself, in conversation, that she'd been living and working in France prior to coming to Knoware to manage her sister's gift store."

"Preston's Automobile Exchange has been on our radar for some time."

"I'm not sure I understand. Unless they've got a US location." The FBI investigated domestically, not internationally.

"It's a joint operation with French authorities. Ms. McGarry is not the only American citizen who warrants watching in this particular circumstance."

"So you *are* watching Erin McGarry?" This was bad, very bad.

"Yes."

"Why?"

"Because Preston's Automobile Exchange is very likely an intermediary in what is turning out to be a relatively complex supply chain linking fundamentalist terror groups with weaponry and currency. In addition to the owner, an Albert Peet, a man Ms. McGarry was romantically linked to and likely was responsible for her employment at Preston's, is being surveilled."

*Romantically linked to.* Hard not to let that phrase reverberate in his head, drowning out the rest of the message. But whether Erin had a lover or was in love was not the real issue. "Beyond her association with Peet, what other proof is there that Erin McGarry is part of something that warrants this kind of surveillance?"

"Her employment at Preston's ended abruptly. We ascertained through a friend of hers in Paris that she was surprised and unhappy about this. That changed our mind that she might be a willing participant. After several more weeks of monitoring and no contact between her and Albert Peet, we were just about to approach her to ask for her assistance, when she suddenly had contact with Peet and then left Paris for the United States."

"Her sister lives in Knoware and she's hospitalized awaiting the birth of a child. Erin is watching over her sister's gift store."

"It hardly appears that she could have engineered that," Pierre said—somewhat grudgingly, Marcus thought.

"Pretty confident she didn't," he said.

The agent considered Marcus. "This is a summer vacation community, right?"

"Yes."

"So you've got a lot of strangers in town. But you

decide you need a background check on Ms. McGarry. Somehow that doesn't sound exactly right to me."

So SA Sargeant wasn't a dummy. They were on the same side. And perhaps the man could be helpful to Marcus. "She arrived at roughly the same time as two other individuals. I can't put my finger on exactly why, but these two make my eye twitch." A solid law enforcement officer would understand that one didn't ignore those intuitions. "Maybe it's more than a decade of police work, maybe it's because they don't fit the mold of our typical tourist, or maybe I'm seeing cobwebs in the corners when there are no spiders. Whatever the reason, when I saw the three of them interact—just briefly, mind you, but nevertheless—that was enough for me to initiate a background check on Ms. McGarry. I got the preliminary results, was interested because there was a gap between her last employment in Paris and coming to Knoware, so I asked my contact to get me additional information."

"Tell me about these two men," the agent said, taking out a notebook.

"I don't know much. I've seen them on four occasions. The first time, this past Saturday, across the street from a local restaurant and from Tiddle's, the gift shop that Ms. McGarry is running. We had a brief conversation. The second time was four or five hours later, they were fishing on the Knoware pier. That was not unexpected—they'd indicated that was their plan when we first spoke. The third time, not long after our interaction at the pier, in the alley behind Tiddle's, having a conversation with Ms. McGarry. The fourth time, which was Saturday night, at a local festival held in our harbor. One of them stood in line behind Ms. McGarry and had a brief conversation with her."

"What are their names?"

"I don't know. I didn't push them for any information. I call them Talk and Hat because the older one does all the talking and the younger one is wearing a wool stocking hat in the middle of summer."

"Where are they staying?"

"Don't know that, either. But I know where they aren't staying. They said they were guests of Brickstone Bungalows. I managed to get a couple cell phone photos of them, which I showed the proprietors, and they are not renting space to them."

"Odd to lie about where you're staying," the agent mused.

"I thought so."

"Can you share those photos with me?"

Marcus didn't see why not. He pulled out his cell phone, made sure he had the correct number for SA Sargeant and sent them that direction. "I did not see them around town yesterday or today. Perhaps they've moved on. Probably didn't have anything to do with Erin McGarry." Was that true or just wishful thinking?

"Did you ask Ms. McGarry about the two men?"

"No," said Marcus.

"That's good," the agent said.

Not sure what he meant by that. "There's something you probably don't know," Marcus said. "Ms. McGarry was attacked last night in the parking lot of the hospital after visiting her sister. She was pushed down and her purse was stolen. It was recovered in a trash can several blocks away. The lone perpetrator has not been apprehended. We have subsequently learned that he was picked up by someone in a light-colored sedan."

"Interesting."

"Ms. McGarry is fine," Marcus said, in a tone that said he was confident the agent really didn't care. "However, she's a little spooked because earlier today, the home of her brother-in-law and sister, where she is staying, was broken into and pretty much trashed."

SA Sargeant put his pen down. "A message?"

"Seems like it. But it's not an obvious one. At least to me."

"To her?" the agent asked.

"I don't think so," Marcus said. He wouldn't stake his life on it, but he was pretty confident that she was as perplexed as the rest of them. "We've done a couple things socially." The agent was going to learn this relatively quickly if he started asking around town about Erin. "I think she trusts me."

"Maybe we can use that," the agent mused.

Marcus was about to say, to set the agent straight, that he wasn't anybody's puppet, when there was a sharp knock on the door. It opened before he could even ask who it was.

It was Serenity. Wide-eyed. Marcus thought she'd perhaps learned something in her house-to-house inquiry about the break-in, but her reaction was pretty exaggerated. It was something else.

"I'm sorry," she said, looking at SA Sargeant. "I didn't realize there was someone here."

"What's wrong?" Marcus asked, already pushing back his chair.

Serenity motioned for him to come close. As Marcus got closer, he saw that she was shaking. "My twenty-year-old sister is home from college and she cleans rooms at Pinetree Paradise. She was attacked. In one of the rooms." Serenity swallowed. "Almost raped."

He'd met Serenity's sister at a picnic that Chief Ralley had hosted. She'd been sweet. Marcus put his arm around his young officer. He looked over his shoulder. "We're done here," he said.

SA Sargeant shrugged, but he got up and left.

"Is she injured otherwise?"

"Knot on the back of her head. He had ripped her pants down when she thought she heard the door open. She thought help had come. But before she could turn her head, he was off of her and she got hit with something hard enough to knock her out. When she woke up, she was alone and called me."

"Can she describe her attacker?"

Serenity shook her head. "He came at her from behind. Pushed her facedown."

It sounded hasty, not well planned. There would be other evidence. They would find the bastard. "We'll get him."

# Chapter 12

Gasdrig considered killing Ivan. He deserved it. He was risking everything.

"I was angry. I needed to blow off some steam," Ivan said, his face turned away from Gasdrig as he drove them away from Pinetree Paradise.

"When you need to blow off steam," Gasdrig said, irritated at the odd American phrase, "then run a couple miles. What you did was stupid and risky and…wrong." Gasdrig had daughters. He'd easily kill a man who'd done what Ivan had done.

Two things stopped him. He needed him. But as importantly, how could he face Ivan's mother afterward? He'd loved Maret long before she'd married another. That act and the child she had with her new husband less than a year later had sent both their lives in a different direction. But love did not die easily.

"You don't understand," whined Ivan. "We've come up empty. It was no longer in the brown bag and not at her house. We're running out of places and time."

"I understand perfectly. But I have not done anything to complicate our lives. Now we have no place to stay. Plus, we're no longer free to move around. We must stay out of sight in the event that somebody saw you or a camera picked you up somewhere." It would make it much harder to watch Erin McGarry, but he did have an idea about that.

"There were no cameras," Ivan said. "The place is a dump."

"You don't know that. The police may be very attentive to this."

"Like I've said before, all cops are stupid." Ivan rolled down his window and spit.

Gasdrig decided to save his breath. He needed to think. They'd been watching the redheaded woman yesterday when she'd left her store, went home, and then less than an hour later, had left the house with the brown bag over her shoulder. They'd had to curtail any approach at the time because a neighbor had been outside, watering flowers.

They'd followed the woman to the hospital parking lot, but again, there'd been too many people around. *We wait.* That was what he'd told Ivan. And he'd been confident that it had been worth it when she'd left hours later, after the sun had set and the parking lot had been quiet.

Ivan had been quick about it, just as Gasdrig had instructed. The bag had been theirs, but despair had quickly followed when it became evident that the thumb drive they needed was no longer in it. Ivan had wanted to go back and force the woman to tell him where it was, but by that time, there were people gathering.

They'd intended to hit the house during the night. Had parked several blocks away and come in on foot only to see the cop parked outside. He was not going to kill a cop unless he had to. They'd returned home, pledging that tomorrow would be the day.

It had ended up being pathetically easily to get inside the house. A broken window, a turned bolt lock. Child's play. But their search had revealed nothing except to convince them that it was not in the house.

He'd known that Ivan was frustrated. Had left him alone just long enough to take a shower, but that was enough time for him to attack the cleaning woman in a nearby room. They'd gotten out of there fast enough, he thought, but now what? He couldn't drive around indefinitely.

He slowed to take the corner. The gravel road was rough and the ditches on both sides were deep. To his right he saw a small house that needed paint and a yard that was more weeds than grass. An old woman was in the yard, sitting on a lawn chair. There was just the one chair. And one old truck parked in the carport.

He made the turn into the long lane that led up to the house. Ivan was looking at him.

"What is this?" Young Ivan asked.

"Home," Gasdrig said. "Our new home."

Marcus worked the scene at Pinetree Paradise. The property was about fifteen minutes outside of Knoware. Thus far, they'd interviewed the day manager, seven other guests who were at the property at the time of the attack, and two of the other young women who cleaned rooms. Everybody had been nice, concerned and pretty unhelpful. They hadn't seen anything suspicious, hadn't heard anything that made them come out of their rooms.

The manager had confirmed that he had twenty-eight other guests who were not at the property. That didn't surprise Marcus. It wasn't the kind of place anybody would hang around during the day. The rooms were clean, but the carpeting was old, and heavy drapes made the area seem dark and small. There was no green space or even a pool.

He got information out of the registration system. Guest names. Make and model of vehicle and license number. Dates of stay. He was especially interested in anyone who had checked out that day, but there was nobody. He told the day manager that he'd be back later to talk to the night manager and left his business card with everybody he spoke to with instructions to contact him if they thought of anything else that would be helpful.

Serenity's sister was still at the hospital, but she was going to be fine. Relatively speaking, of course. How could anyone ever be fine after that experience? She had a mild a concussion, but they weren't going to keep her overnight.

"Take a day," he'd told Serenity earlier. She'd argued, saying that there were still a few people who lived on Brian Tiddle's street that she had been unable to talk to. Given that those she had talked to had not had anything helpful, he wasn't holding out hope.

"Who will work my shift?" she'd asked.

"I'll take care of that," he'd told her. What he'd meant was that he would. Right now her attention needed to be with her sister. Plus, selfishly, he wanted to be the one to run this guy to ground, wanted to be the one to look him in the eye and tell him that it was over, that he was going to jail. Would rot there if Marcus had anything to say about it.

He was getting into his SUV when his phone rang. It was Dawson. "Marcus Price," he said.

"Good and bad news."

Better than all bad news. "I'll take the good news first," Marcus said.

"There was blood on some of the glass we recovered from the Tiddle break-in."

Marcus thumped his hand on the steering wheel. "Yes. Now the bad news."

"Nothing from the bag or the garbage can."

They still had the hospital security video. It wasn't conclusive, but it was something. "Thanks for letting me know. I'm headed back."

"How's Serenity and her sister?"

"Coping," Marcus said.

He had no more than hung up the phone when it rang again. Jamie's name came up on the caller ID.

"Yeah," Marcus said.

"I had thirty seconds and I wanted to call and… I guess apologize. I'm sorry if I came on a little strong this morning. It's just that I think you really like this woman and from my brief but intense interaction with her, I'd say she might be a keeper. I don't want you to walk away from something that could be very good. I care about you too much for that."

"I know that," Marcus said. It touched him that Jamie had been concerned enough to call. He, Jamie and Blade didn't often say it to one another, but they were his brothers in every way that mattered. "It's been a weird day. Brian Tiddle's house was tossed this morning.

Nobody there so nobody hurt. Lots of damage. Some money taken."

"That seems like a weird coincidence," Jamie said.

"Given that the damage in Erin's room was the worst, I think it's not a coincidence," Marcus said. "An FBI agent came to see me earlier today. About Erin."

"Why?"

He filled Jamie in on the conversation.

"What do you think the agent meant when he said that they might be able to use your relationship with Erin?" Jamie asked.

"I don't know. But I suspect I'll find out. I don't think I've heard the last from him."

"Are you going to tell Erin?"

Marcus shook his head. "I really can't do that." He would never intentionally jeopardize an ongoing investigation.

"That's tough," Jamie said. "You're not going to feel good about not being truthful."

That was true, but he wasn't sure he had a whole lot of choices right now. Speaking of choices, he wondered where Erin had landed in terms of finding a place to stay. Maybe Brian had convinced her to remain at the house. It was likely she was back at the store.

"Your thirty-second break is over," Marcus said.

"Talk soon," Jamie said, and disconnected.

He drove directly to Tiddle's Tidbits and Treasures. Inside, he saw several customers. He immediately recognized one. It was Jordan Reese, the woman who'd been hit on the bicycle. He'd left her a voice mail yesterday, letting her know that while he didn't have good news that the driver had been identified, he wanted her to know that they were still working on it. He walked toward her.

"Ms. Reese?" he said.

"Officer Price," she said, her tone quiet in deference to the other shoppers. "I didn't expect to see you here."

"One of my favorite stores for gift buying," he said easily.

"It is beautiful. I decided that I had to have more chocolate and now that I've seen these scarves, one of those is coming home with me, too."

"I'm glad to see you out of the hospital."

"Thank you. I appreciated your voice mail. We'll be leaving the area within a couple days, but you've got my cell phone if you need me."

"I do." He turned to see if Erin was still busy with her customer.

"I think your granddaughter would love this one," Erin was saying as she pulled a necklace out of a glass case. "It's perfect for a high school senior."

The woman examined the piece and looked at the price tag. "The other one is more expensive," she said.

"It is," Erin agreed.

"I appreciate you not trying to get me to buy the most expensive one," the woman said.

Erin just smiled.

"I'll take it. Can you wrap it up?"

"Absolutely," Erin said.

He was sure she'd seen him, but she gave absolutely no indication that she did. When the customer was finished, he turned back to Jordan Reese. "You're next."

She walked up to the counter and Erin's smile could hardly have been wider. "I am so glad to see you."

"I told you I'd stop in," Jordan said. "Beautiful store."

"I'll pass that on to my sister. How are you feeling?"

"Really well, thank you. My bruises are a lovely shade of purple."

"Stylish," Erin said. The two women laughed.

Seeing them together like this hit Marcus hard. Their hair, while different, was still very much alike. Jordan was taller by a couple inches, but other than that, their builds very similar. Age had to be within a couple years.

And given what had happened to Erin in the last twenty-four hours, he was suddenly very confident that the attack on Jordan had been aimed at Erin. It was a case of mistaken identity that had sadly swept up Jordan Reese in their little melodrama.

Should he tell either woman? He discounted telling Jordan immediately. It wouldn't make her feel any better. Right now, she didn't think she'd been targeted for any reason, just thought it was the work of a careless and uncaring driver.

The decision whether to tell Erin was significantly more difficult. She was going to feel responsible for Jordan's injuries and that would be hard on her. But to not know was to deprive her of all the reasons why she needed to be forthcoming with everything she knew.

Deprive her of the reasons to be extra careful.

That could have disastrous results.

Erin and Jordan finished their conversation and Jordan left with her items and a quick wave in Marcus's direction. He approached the cash register before any of the other three customers in the store could.

"How's it going?" he asked.

"Fine. Good to see Jordan Reese up and about."

"Yeah. I was wondering what you'd settled on in terms of a place to stay," he said, keeping his voice low.

"I'm working on it," she said.

"You've called a couple places," he pushed.

"Four," she said, frustration in her tone. "You were right. I got some names from Gertie, but those places were booked up." She shrugged. "I can always sleep in my car. I've done it before."

"You're not doing that." That would mean that he'd have to watch over her there and his limited sleeping time would become even more limited.

"I'll figure something out."

"Stay at my house," he said.

She drew back. "What?"

A woman was approaching the cash register. Marcus stepped to the side and pretended to look at the books by local authors that the store featured. From the corner of his eye, he watched Erin as she counted back the woman's change, got lost midway through and had to start over.

He'd startled her. Shaken her up a bit.

He wasn't going to simply let her dismiss the offer. It made sense. He had a big house. Everybody in town knew it was his house and most would be reluctant to approach it with bad intent. He could sleep in his own bed. The reasons were mounting up.

The customer left and Erin turned to him, her chin set. Marcus had a feeling he better start talking fast because she wasn't convinced.

"It's really the only solution that makes sense. I live alone—you won't be inconveniencing anyone. I have plenty of space, so you can have your pick of bedrooms." He stopped. That sounded a little suggestive. "Pick of guest rooms," he corrected.

"I get it. But it's not necessary. I'll find something."

"You're running out of time. Aren't you headed over to the hospital tonight?"

"Yeah."

"You're not going to have any time to look. How about you just spend tonight and you can resume your search tomorrow."

"You're sure?" she asked.

Marcus spent about three seconds wondering what SA Sargeant might think of the fact that Erin was now staying with Marcus. It didn't exactly scream impartial observer, but then again, he was long past the point of impartiality. "Positive." He wrote the address on the back of one of his business cards. "Call me when you're leaving the hospital so I know when to expect you. And Erin, be careful in that parking lot."

She nodded. "Thank you. I think."

He smiled. "Happy to do it. You've had a streak of bad luck. I think it's time for something simple and good to happen for you."

*Simple and good.* Her habit of coping via word association made her think *tasty* and that made her feel hot and bothered since it all revolved around Marcus. She eyed the business card where he'd left his home address. Just days ago, he'd left his cell number in the same way. And now she was moving in.

Was it any wonder that she felt a bit discombobulated?

She locked up the store, attempting to identify next steps. She had clothes and a toothbrush and other necessities in her trunk. She was grateful that Marcus had allowed her to get her things earlier.

Now, how exactly did she intend to tell Morgan about

this sudden change in events? The truth wasn't an option. But her sister was smart. Had always been able to see through any pretext that Erin might have spun. Had been able to quickly drill down into the core of any issue. On most days, Erin appreciated her sister's skill. Today, it was just another complication.

She walked out the back entrance of the store, looking both ways before she pulled the door shut behind her and locked it. Then she quickly walked to her car, got in and locked the doors. Then she checked all her mirrors.

Nothing alarming, but still, her heart was pumping. She hadn't mentioned it to Marcus, but the visit from Jordan Reese had shaken her. Seeing the woman upright, walking and talking, had made her realize that someone might have easily mistaken Jordan for her. Without the attack in the parking lot or today's break-in, she'd have been able to discount it. But now it seemed more than a possibility that Jordan had taken a blow meant for her.

It made her feel sick.

And frightened.

It was one of the reasons that she'd given in rather easily to Marcus's offer to spend at least tonight at his house. He was a cop. An interim chief. She should be safe there. Tomorrow, she would start calling places in the morning and wouldn't stop until she found a new temporary home.

She went to the bank, dropped off the deposit, and then drove to the hospital. She circled the lot four times until she saw a car in the front row leaving. She slipped into the spot and walked quickly inside.

"Hey," she said, once she reached her sister's room. She walked over to the bed, kissed Morgan on the cheek and smiled at her brother-in-law, who didn't seem able to meet her gaze. She got a bad feeling.

"How are you doing?" she asked Morgan.

"Good. I'm going home tomorrow."

"Great." Was that why Brian was acting oddly? Was he afraid that he wasn't going to have the house cleaned up? If they both worked several hours tonight, she was sure they could manage it. "You must be excited."

"Yes." Her sister stared at her. Intensely.

"What? I don't have spinach in my teeth, do I?" she asked, remembering the soup she'd eaten for lunch.

Brian stood up. "I told her. I told her about you getting your purse stolen last night and about the break-in at the house."

"He is bad at keeping secrets from me," Morgan said.

"We didn't want you to worry," Erin said. She understood why Brian had caved. Someday she hoped to find a guy who couldn't lie to her.

"Of course I'm worried. And mad as hell. Not at either of you, but at whoever is responsible for this. But you two need to remember that I'm not spun sugar. I don't need to be coddled."

"This is somehow about me," Erin said.

"That's ridiculous," Morgan said. "Why would you even think that?"

"The guy in the parking lot. Then the break-in, with the most damage in my room. It adds up."

"You've only been in town for days. It's much more likely to have something to do with Brian or me. Letters just went out under his signature for people who were delinquent on their water bills. Maybe somebody got angry. Or maybe somebody bought something in my shop that they later thought was junk and they got ripped off."

"That would never happen," Erin said.

"You don't know that," Morgan said.

She wasn't going to win this argument and Morgan's cheeks were getting pink. Her blood pressure was likely going up by the second. "It doesn't matter who the target was. What I'm going to focus on is just keeping one another safe."

"How do think you'll manage that?" Morgan asked.

"I'm moving out, that's one thing."

"Where are you going?" Morgan asked.

"I don't exactly have a place. But I will."

"That's not what I heard," Morgan said.

Now Erin was really confused. "I'm not sure—"

"I called Marcus Price. I wanted to arrange extra security for the store. I figured he'd be the best place to start. Sure enough, there is a small security company in Knoware that can do it. I guess the guys who own it are retired officers of the Los Angeles Police Department."

"He mentioned them when we went to dinner. Jim and Tyson, I believe."

"That's right. You'll meet Jim tomorrow. I've already sent a text to Jo Marie telling her about the house and that we've obtained extra security for the store just in case. She was all for it."

It probably was a good idea. Especially if she was right that she was the target. She was spending most of her time at the store.

"Marcus said that he's offered to let you stay at his house," Morgan said.

"That's true. And I have accepted for tonight. But I'm going to find someplace of my own tomorrow."

"No. I want you to stay with Marcus. He can protect you."

"But…" She sent a pleading look in Brian's direction. Maybe he could step in here and help her.

"I agree with Morgan," he said. "I think it's the best place for you."

They were ganging up on her.

"We trust Marcus. I won't worry about you there," Morgan said.

Her sister was playing dirty. But Erin couldn't call her on it because quite frankly, she'd do whatever would put her sister's mind and body to rest so that the baby could continue to grow.

Even if her own body and mind would be moving at warp speed. After the kiss that she and Marcus had shared last night and the subsequent discussion that *this is different*, there was no denying that there was an attraction.

They were both consenting adults. What was the worst thing that could happen?

She could have her heart broken when Marcus decided it was time to move on.

"Erin," her sister said. Her eyes were filled with pleading. Her right hand rested lightly on her abdomen.

Erin smiled at her sister. "I'll do it."

# Chapter 13

Marcus pulled into the parking lot of the Pinetree Paradise at seven thirty. By this time of night, guests were returning to the hotel, tired from a long day of activity. The parking lot had significantly more vehicles than it had earlier in the day. In fact, he saw only a couple open spaces. He parked in a no-parking area near the garbage dumpsters.

He walked into the office, waited while the desk clerk finished giving a guest some clean towels and then stepped up. "I'm Officer Marcus Price. I need to talk to your night manager. She's expecting me."

Dot Mobly was fifty, give or take, with short graying hair and a no-nonsense demeanor that probably served her well with difficult guests. She shook his hand with a firm grip. "I was sick to hear what had happened to Faith Jones," she said.

She sounded truthful and Marcus got the impression that it wasn't just company-speak. "She's a brave young woman," he said.

"I spoke with her earlier to express our outrage and concern."

That might help the young woman. Them identifying and finding the attacker might help more. "From the day manager, I got a listing of all your current guests," he said, producing the printed copy. "Have you had anyone else check out or check in since noon today?"

"No."

"Then this list should still be good," he said. "I talked to these guests this morning." He pointed at the names that had a check mark next to them. "I'm going to want to try to reach everybody else tonight. I'm going to knock on doors. If I don't get an answer, I'd like you to open those doors for me." She could refuse. It would complicate things, but he'd still be able to make it happen.

"I've spoken to the owners. We are to cooperate in any way with the investigation." She looked around. "I realize this isn't a five-star place, but we've still got standards. I'd like to do more around here, you know, but I'm just the manager, I don't control the budget."

"I get it," he said. "Let's go." He had a lot of people to talk to before Erin would get done at the hospital.

It took him an hour to get through twelve rooms, which held a total of twenty guests. Nobody raised any flags. Some had heard about the attack upon their return as they'd visited the snack machines and the ice machine and encountered other guests. Most had not and were visibly shocked to hear the news. He asked everybody what time they'd left the hotel that morning, where they'd gone, what route they'd taken to get there and to name anyone who might be able to verify the information. Then, if their vehicle information was on his list, he'd verified it. For the few that it was not, he'd had them supply it. More than one person had to walk to the parking lot to get the make and model and license plate number from their rental vehicle.

It was edging into twilight as he reviewed the list of remaining four rooms where somebody had not answered his knock. He would go back, knock again, but if nobody answered, it was time for Dot Mobly to do her thing.

The first two rooms didn't offer anything unusual. They were rented by two married couples, Bob and BethAnn Ricket and Anthony and Sela Drake. Both had clothes hanging in the closet and toiletries and cosmetics in the bathroom.

The third room had a do not disturb sign hanging on the door. Marcus ignored it and for a second time that night, knocked hard. When nobody answered, he motioned for Dot Mobly to open it. The two standard-size beds had not been made. Used towels were thrown on the floor.

"The cleaning staff doesn't come in if there is a do not disturb sign on the door," Dot said quickly, as if she was afraid that Marcus would think she rented rooms like this.

He wasn't concerned about that. What bothered him was that there were no suitcases, no clothes in the closet and nothing in the bathroom with the exception of some opened beer cans on the counter. He didn't touch anything.

"Tell me about the people who rented this space," he said.

Dot looked at the list. "Michael Stone and Don Burtiss. They checked in last Thursday." She tapped the edge of the master key against the printed list. "I remember these two. I checked them in. They arrived quite late. They paid in cash for one night, but then came in the next day and paid for a whole week."

"Do you still request identification if they pay in cash?"

"Definitely," she said. "The older guy, Michael Stone, had the money and showed me his ID. He was nice enough. I don't remember the younger one saying much."

Marcus felt a chill run down his back. Older. Younger. Talker. Non-talker.

"Do you recall, did the younger one wear a wool stocking cap?" he asked.

Concern flared in her eyes. "Yes, I think he did."

Talk and Hat. He pulled out his cell phone and thumbed through his photos. Found the one he was looking for. "Is this the two men?"

Dot Mobly studied the picture. "Yes."

"You're sure?" Marcus quizzed, feeling for the first time like he maybe wasn't trying to put a square peg in a round hole.

Dot Mobly nodded confidently.

Good enough. Talk and Hat had real names. Michael Stone and Don Burtiss. He liked Talk and Hat better. So they'd booked it out of Pinetree Paradise before they'd anticipated leaving. There could be lots of legitimate, non-concerning reasons for that. But Dot had said they checked in on Thursday and by Friday, had made a commitment for a longer stay. That was proof that they'd lied to him on Saturday morning when he'd seen them across the street from Tiddle's and Gertie's.

He wasn't inclined to give them the benefit of the doubt.

Especially given that they seemed to have an interest in Erin, and the figure that he'd seen on the security camera footage at the hospital could definitely have been that of Hat. Maybe it was Talk waiting in the sedan at the end of the alley.

He looked back at his list. Make and model and license plate were listed. A Ford Explorer.

Definitely not a sedan. Wouldn't be mistaken for a sedan. "How do you get the information about their vehicles?"

"We ask them. And then just like you did earlier, if they don't know, the registrar is supposed to send them back to the parking lot to get the information. Then we give them a tag to put in their window to show that they can legitimately park here."

"Supposed to?" Marcus repeated, homing in on the word choice.

"Sometimes, if the line is backed up, people at the desk can get sloppy. The guest will usually say that they'll come back with the information. They never do, of course. But as you can tell, we get it with most because we're insistent at check-in."

"You got it with these two," he said, grateful for that. It might be helpful.

"I think that's maybe why I remember these two so well. Not only did I check them in, but I had to correct their information."

"Explain that to me," Marcus said.

"The guy who paid walked out and got his vehicle information. And I didn't think too much about it. But later, in the middle of the night, I took a walk around the parking lot."

"In the middle of the night, you walk around the parking lot?" Marcus asked. Erin's incident in a parking lot was fresh in his mind, as was the attack on Serenity's sister. There were lights, but not that many.

"Yeah. You might have noticed, we don't have any extra parking. And we get people who leave their vehicle here while they carpool with friends to go to Weston's."

He knew Weston's. They rented kayaks and offered both day and night trips that included camping.

"They're real strict about parking, too, because they don't have enough. So anyway, when it's nice out and both we and Weston's are busy, I don't like being a sap. So I patrol the lot and make sure that every car has a parking tag in the window. If it doesn't, then I check the license plate against what I have in the computer system. Most of the time, it is as simple as the people forgot to stick the tag in the window even though we tell them six times to do just that. But if the information doesn't match, I get the vehicle towed."

"In the middle of the night?"

"Yeah. Savick's Garage runs a twenty-four-hour towing service in season. I get a discounted rate at night."

Savick's Garage was owned by Blade's parents. They did excellent work. All of the police vehicles were serviced there. "Tell me what you corrected," he said, going back to her original statement.

"I saw an SUV that didn't have a tag. I remembered that the two guys that had just checked in that night had been driving a Ford Explorer. I checked the license plate. But it didn't match. I thought maybe I put it in the system wrong so I went back to the paper copy that the guests fills out. I had put it in just like he'd written it. But then I realized that he'd mixed up the last four numbers. I fixed it in the system."

"Just to verify, what I'm looking at right here is correct, you visually confirmed that by looking at the license plate?" Marcus asked.

"Yes."

"Did that make you suspicious?" Marcus asked. "That you had to correct transposed numbers?"

She shook her head. "It happens. You'd be surprised at how often."

Maybe. But again, Talk and Hat got no favors. "You don't happen to make a photocopy of the identification that guests show you?" If they'd lied to him about where they were staying, maybe they'd lied to her about their names.

She shook her head.

"Video of Thursday night when they checked in?"

"Sorry. We have video, but it records over itself every other night." She waited, as if expecting that he had more questions.

He was thinking.

"You want to check the last room on the list?" she prodded.

She probably needed to get back to the office. "Yeah. Let's do that. But do me a favor. Don't clean this room. Keep everybody out of it. Can you manage that?"

"Yes. I'll disable the key card that the occupants had. If they come back, they'll need to come to the office to get in. I can also disable the master key that the maids use to avoid any possibility of someone getting inside by mistake."

"Excellent." Five minutes later, after discovering nothing unusual in the fourth and final guest room, he was in his SUV, on his way back to his house. The witness who had seen the man running down the alley had been confident it was a sedan. Was it possible that Talk and Hat had two vehicles? He didn't think so. Dot at Pinetree Paradise was an eagle eye who would have spotted the extra vehicle in the lot. But maybe they'd switched out the vehicle?

Maybe because it had been damaged when they'd used it to run Jordan Reese off the road.

It made sense. The two men had checked in on Thursday night. He'd seen them in Knoware early Saturday morning and later that day, Jordan Reese, who bore an amazing resemblance to Erin, had been hit. By a dark-colored SUV.

Had Michael Stone rented the Ford Explorer on Thursday and then had to suddenly return it on Saturday after the hit-and-run? He picked up his cell and dialed his office.

"Hey, Marcus. What's up?"

It was Dawson. That surprised him. The officer should be out on patrol. "What's going on?" he asked, not wanting to jump on the man.

"I was just about to call you. Had something unexpected happen. My right rear tire got slashed when I stopped home earlier for my meal break."

"Slashed," Marcus repeated, making sure he'd heard correctly.

"Oh, yeah. Three cuts."

Vandalizing a police vehicle was gutsy and stupid. "You see anything?"

"No. I talked to my neighbors and they're clueless."

That reminded Marcus of the guy he'd met. "I met one of your neighbors. His daughter was part of a group of drag racers out on River Road. He specifically mentioned you."

"I know who you're talking about," Dawson said. "He already called me to see if I could somehow *fix* all this."

"So maybe his daughter is mad at the police or she told her friends that she lives nearby an officer. Might be petty revenge."

"I'll check it out. I'm getting the tire replaced right now at Savick's Garage. Was there something you needed?"

"I need you to run a plate for me." He rattled off the information. "I think it might be a rental. I want to know who rented it on Thursday night of this past week and where the vehicle is right now."

"Got it."

"Thank you." He hung up and tossed his cell phone onto the passenger seat. Seconds later, it rang again. He saw the display and reached to snatch it up.

"Erin?" he answered.

"You wanted me to call when I was leaving the hospital," she said.

She was coming. Even though she'd agreed to it earlier, he hadn't been absolutely confident. "Right," he said.

"I'm in my car, headed your direction."

"Great. See you in ten." He hung up and pressed down on the accelerator.

He beat her there. Earlier, before he'd gone to Pinetree Paradise, he'd swung home for fifteen minutes to make sure the place was picked up and to put away the groceries that he'd stopped for. Now he looked around his house, wondering what she was going to think of the place. It certainly wasn't the first time he had a female visitor, not the first time a female visitor had spent the night.

*This is different.* That was why he was nervous.

He checked his refrigerator. For the third time. He was ready to feed an army. Eggs, milk, bread, yogurt, all kinds of fruit. He made a killer French toast with blueberry sauce. Maybe that could be breakfast.

Was he nesting? Pre-nesting?

He needed to calm the hell down. When Morgan Tiddle had called him earlier, he'd been between a rock and a hard place for sure. He'd wanted to be truthful and factual, but he could hear Erin's warning that her sister should not be worried ringing in his ears. It had helped that Morgan hadn't seemed that upset but, rather, just focused on how exactly the Knoware Police Department was going to keep her family, her home and her business safe.

Patrols on their street and a watchful eye on the downtown was one thing. Even security within her store was a relatively easy ask. But when it got to the subject of him offering Erin a place to stay, he hadn't been sure what he expected. But he'd appreciated the quick "that's perfect" she'd offered. He'd been a little sneaky when he'd volunteered that he wasn't confident that Erin intended to take him up on the offer.

"I'll convince her," Morgan had said. And it appeared she had.

He stood at the window and within minutes, he saw

the headlights of an approaching car. Erin parked. She walked toward his house, backpack over her shoulder.

He opened the door before she could ring the bell. "Hi," he said.

She stood in the doorway. "Are you sure this is okay?"

"Positive," he said, reaching for her hand. He guided her into the house. It was a warm summer evening and her skin held the heat.

"Wow, this is beautiful," she said, almost in a reverent voice. "I don't know what I was expecting, but it wasn't this."

He loved his house. Had spent most every free moment the last two years working on it. The hundred-year-old brick two-story had needed work when he'd bought it. Now the walls were all freshly painted, the wood floors refinished, and there were new blinds and curtains in every room.

"Want the grand tour?" he asked.

"Definitely."

"Downstairs there's a living room, family room, dining room, kitchen, guest bath and laundry." He led the way. When they got to the kitchen, she stopped walking.

"Wow," she said. "You said that you liked to cook," she accused, looking at the six-burner stove. "You did not say that you were a professional chef."

"Amateur all the way," he said. "But it's a good way to spend a couple free hours."

"Some of the apartments that I've lived in during the last few years have been smaller than this kitchen."

Perhaps the Paris one? When she'd been romantically linked to Albert Peet.

He had so many questions. But tonight, for a few

minutes, he simply wanted to let his head rest. It had been a day. And she was here. Safe.

"I, too, had a pretty small apartment when I lived in Los Angeles. When I moved here, I started looking for a big house. I've been able to do most of the work myself although I did have help with the kitchen."

She sat on one of the stools in front of his quartz countertop. "I always wondered what kind of house I'd buy if I ever got settled in one place. Now that I've seen this, I think my standards were low."

It made him absurdly happy that she liked it. He opened the refrigerator door and pulled out the tray of cheese and crackers that he'd prepared earlier after putting away the groceries. "Glass of wine?" he said.

"Sure."

He poured them both a glass of pinot noir and led her into the living room. He took a chair. She took the couch. He put the cheese and crackers on the coffee table where she could easily reach them. "How was Morgan?" he asked.

"Good. Coming home tomorrow. I know the two of you spoke. Thanks for helping her with security at the store. Anything that relieves her worry is something I support."

"I don't want worry, but I also think it's good that she knows what's been happening. It may make her more aware."

She sipped her wine. "It certainly did me. I practically parked in the hospital lobby. I wasn't taking any chances of a lonely walk across the lot tonight."

"Smart," he said. He pushed the cheese and crackers in her direction and she helped herself. "We did get a witness statement today that might be helpful." He told her about Judy, the barking dog, and the neighbor seeing somebody get picked up at the end of the alley. "So it appears as if your attacker might have had an accomplice," he finished.

She considered that. "Two people, not one."

"Apparently."

"Hmm," she said thoughtfully.

"What?" he demanded.

"It's probably nothing, but last week, I had a couple odd run-ins with two men."

Should he tell her that he was pretty confident who she was describing? No. He needed to hear it from her. "Describe odd," he said as nonchalantly as he could muster.

"I first saw them in Gertie's. They were coming in for lunch as I was leaving. We literally sidestepped around each other. Then later they came into the store. They didn't buy anything or say anything before leaving pretty abruptly. I left for the hospital shortly after that and I saw them in the alley, looking at my car."

"Why were they looking at your car?" he asked, careful to repeat her words and not put his own spin on it.

"They said they were in the market for a new car and they liked it. I think they might have asked about mileage and I told them it was a rental and that I didn't have much experience with it."

"That was the whole conversation?" Marcus asked.

"I think so."

When he'd happened to see Erin, Hat and Talk standing around her car, he'd assumed that he'd seen part of the bigger conversation. Based on what she was describing, perhaps he'd witnessed the entirety. "Did you see them after that?" he asked.

"That night at Food Truck Saturday. I was in line to get the doughnuts when I realized that the older gentleman was standing behind me in line. He commented on my purse, asked if I'd gotten it in the store. He said he might be interested in one for his wife."

"Did he come back to the store to pick one up?" Marcus asked.

She shook her head. "I didn't really expect him. I think he was just making conversation."

"But as I remember, you quickly left the line."

"I did. But I don't even really know why. He gave me the creeps, okay? I feel bad saying that because he didn't do anything to me, but I just didn't have a good feeling."

"And you don't know these two men? Never seen them before?" he asked.

She hesitated. For the tiniest moment. "No," she said.

He was pretty sure she was lying. But she looked tired and vulnerable and while he wanted to push her, he also wanted to cut her all the slack in the world. It was just twenty-four hours ago that she'd been sitting on the ground in the hospital parking lot, her shoulder yanked out of place. He could still see the pavement scrapings on her cheeks. "Can you think of anything else that might be important?" he asked gently.

"No. I'm not sure any of this is important."

"You'd be surprised what can be important," he said.

"I suppose." She'd finished her glass of wine.

"More?" he asked, picking up the bottle.

"Just a little," she said. "I'm not much of a drinker, but this wine is very nice."

"It's not French," he said pointedly.

"Nothing better than a pinot noir from Oregon,"

she said, not taking the bait. "Other than assisting my brother-in-law, how was your day?"

He couldn't tell her about the FBI visit. "The sister of one of our police officers got attacked today in a hotel room. Her summer job is cleaning rooms."

"Oh, no," Erin said. "Is she…hurt badly?"

"Fortunately, before the man could rape her, there was some type of interruption. She got a knock on the head, but no other physical injuries."

"How old?"

"Twenty."

"She had to have been so frightened."

"I think a lot of people will be frightened when they hear about the story."

"I'm guessing that Knoware doesn't have a lot of sexual assaults," Erin said.

"That are reported," he said grimly.

"If Morgan hears about it, she's going to be even more grateful to you for offering me a safe place. How much free chocolate can you eat in a year?"

"That chocolate? A lot." He settled back in his chair. He was tired. He'd spent the previous night in his car watching over Erin. He'd caught a few hours of sleep this morning, but it had been a very full day.

As weary as he was, however, there was something very nice about sharing an evening glass of wine with Erin, talking about their day, the good stuff, the bad stuff. Just being there for each other.

Yet neither of them seemed inclined to want to talk about last night's conversation. *Something different.* He'd said it. She'd agreed. And she'd certainly responded to his kiss.

He desperately wanted to kiss her again.

"What are you thinking about?" she asked, her tone teasing. "You're looking awfully serious. Contemplating bars of chocolate?"

He shook his head. He'd never been a chicken. "Thinking about how I'd really like to kiss you again."

"Oh." She set down her glass of wine.

Great. Now she was about to make a break for the door.

"I… I think I'd like that, too," she said. But she did not move.

He wasn't waiting for an engraved invitation. He moved from his chair to the couch in three big steps and sank in next to her. Then she was in his arms and the world was as it should be. She tasted of wine and cheese and all sorts of other goodness. Her lips were soft and the perfume that she'd likely dabbed behind her ears was light and fragrant, perfectly matching a summer night.

"I love kissing you," he said between long, succulent feasts.

She pulled at his T-shirt, freeing it from his jeans. Then slipped her warm hands inside, resting them on his lower back. Heat streaked upward. Downward. Pretty much everywhere. He tried to keep his head clear, which was hellishly hard to do when he was turned on. He could not, no, definitely could not, take her to bed tonight. Too many unanswered questions.

For the first time in his life, he anticipated saying *the hell with it*.

And then she pulled back.

Looked him in the eye.

"It's late. I think it might be best if I turned in for the night."

What? No. Dumb idea. The arguments were on the tip of his tongue. Instead, he slowly slid away from her, to the far end of the couch. He waited for her to say that it had been a mistake.

Instead, he got a smile. "I like kissing you, too," she said.

He felt his gut relax. The questions were still there. But he was confident of one thing. This really was different. "Your room is at the top of the stairs. There's a connecting bath."

"Thank you." She stood and picked up her backpack.

He felt off-center. Not able to have the control that generally came so naturally to him. She'd opened up about the two men, had given him a perfectly good explanation.

The question that nagged at him was *why now?*

Was it possible that somebody had seen and reported back to her that SA Sargeant had been in Marcus's office? Did she know the FBI was watching her? Did she somehow know that Marcus had done a background check on her? Maybe the FBI weren't the only ones watching activity on the various databases. Things like that could be monitored from a world away.

He watched her walk upstairs and enter the guest room. Then he picked up their wineglasses and headed to the kitchen. He was halfway there when his cell rang. He looked at the display. Dawson must have something for him.

"Marcus Price," he answered.

"I tracked the Ford Explorer to a rental facility at the Seattle airport," Dawson said. "It was rented on Thursday night for three days, but returned Saturday morning."

The day that Jordan Reese had been hit by a dark SUV. "Where is the vehicle right now?"

"Portland, Oregon," Dawson said. "It got rented again on Sunday. Not expected to be returned until next Saturday."

"When the vehicle was returned on Saturday, was there any damage to it?"

"Nothing noted in the intake inspection report."

Damn. "Who rented the vehicle on Thursday night?"

"A Scott Einstein."

No. Dot Mobly said the room had been rented by Michael Stone. That she'd seen his driver's license.

And surely the car rental company had gotten a copy of the renter's license. Every time he'd ever rented a car, he'd had to show his driver's license. "Did you happen to ask for a copy of Scott Einstein's driver's license?"

"I asked them to email me a copy. I haven't gotten it yet."

"Okay, that's good," Marcus said. "Thanks for the call, Dawson. Did your tire get fixed?"

"Yeah. I'm on my way to talk to my neighbor and his daughter."

"Let me know if you need anything from me," Marcus said.

"Will do." Dawson hung up.

Marcus stared at the empty wineglasses that he'd set on the kitchen counter. Maybe he was barking up the wrong tree. But he didn't think so. Talk and Hat were the men staying at the Pinetree Paradise. Dot Mobly gave him a visual verification. She'd also been confident that she had the license information for their Ford Explorer correct. That vehicle had then been returned to the car rental company by a Scott Einstein.

He was pretty confident that what he was going to ultimately discover was that both Scott Einstein and Michael Stone were aliases.

This was getting more complicated by the minute.

He picked up his phone and dialed Dawson.

"Yeah, Chief," the man said.

"Is the number for the car rental place handy?"

"Yeah. It's right here. Do you need me to call them?"

"No. I'll take this one from here. I appreciate everything you've done so far."

Dawson rattled off the number and Marcus wrote it down. It was his next call. He asked to speak to the manager on duty.

When he explained to the man who he was and what he wanted, there was some resistance. "But Officer," the man said. "That vehicle isn't scheduled to be back here until next Saturday."

"I know that. But I have a reason to believe that it was involved in the commission of a serious crime and I need it examined now. So, here's what I need you to do. I need you to contact the current driver, explain that you need to trade out his current rental with another one just like it. The new vehicle will be delivered to him and his existing vehicle will be taken back."

"But—"

"You don't have to do all that. I'm going to have an officer from the Seattle Police Department come by and pick up the replacement vehicle. You tell him where he needs to take the SUV." He was going to have to call in a favor with somebody at the Seattle Police Department, but there were a couple officers there who owed him one. "Once he or she delivers the replacement vehicle, he or she will take temporary custody of the Ford

Explorer on behalf of the Knoware Police Department. The vehicle will be returned to you, you have my word, just as soon as we're done with it."

"This is crazy," the manager said.

As good a word as any.

Erin undressed for bed, thinking that life was certainly strange, even for a rolling stone. Less than a week ago, she'd still been in Paris, eating tubs of ice cream, and now she was a crime statistic, hiding away in hopes of keeping the rest of her family safe. It sounded like a bad movie, one that went right to cable as they say.

Was it simply about money? They'd gotten three hundred from the house. Was it because of her? Or had she been targeted because of her relationship with Brian and Morgan, and this was really about them?

When Morgan had offered that up, Erin had been tempted to remind her about Jordan Reese. Morgan had never seen the woman, didn't know that there was a resemblance between her and Erin. If she had, maybe she'd have been even quicker to accept Erin's theory.

And unfortunately, that's all it was. Theory. No proof. Perhaps the best thing she could do was get a good night's sleep. Had she been in a hotel or still at the house, she'd have been a wreck, listening for every odd sound. But here, she felt safe. She felt confident that Marcus could and would protect her.

She'd felt much less confident of her own abilities to resist Marcus. Truth be told, it had taken everything she had to put the brakes on downstairs. Had been reckless when she'd put her hands on his bare skin, but she'd simply had to touch him. Her body had been screaming for it.

And it would have been so easy to fall…into bed… in love. It had been the second one that had stopped her. What had it been that her sister had suggested that first time they'd discussed it? That Marcus might be a love 'em and leave 'em kind of guy. Now that she knew a bit more about his relationship with his father, she understood.

But still, rejection was rejection. And another one might break her.

And she wasn't feeling all that resilient these days. A rolling stone should be hard and weathered and capable of doing more damage to other things than to itself. But she was feeling none of that right now. She was feeling soft and malleable.

It had been sweet that he fixed a snack and offered her wine. And it truly had been a good way to end a very long day. She'd tipped her glass back and relaxed, thinking that he'd decided against revisiting the conversation from the previous night. But she'd been lulled into a false sense of security.

She'd even felt comfortable discussing her suspicions about the two men. He'd listened intently, certainly hadn't dismissed her speculations. She'd been grateful for that. She supposed that experienced cops, especially ones like Marcus who had worked in big urban environments like Los Angeles, had heard everything over the years. Nothing much could surprise them.

She felt bad that she hadn't been all the way truthful when he'd asked if she'd ever seen them before. But there wasn't an easy answer to that question. It *felt* as if she had, but since she couldn't place where or when, she thought it was better not to speculate.

She climbed into bed and gave the very lovely guest

bedroom one final look. It was lucky his house was still standing. After all, when he'd offered up that he wanted to kiss her, she'd gone up in flames. And she had suddenly been unable to move.

Thank God he'd not suffered from the same problem.

While it had lasted, it had been good. Very, very good. She ran her tongue around her mouth and let out a satisfied sigh. She could still taste him.

Hopefully, by tomorrow her head would feel less muddled. *Something different* didn't mean that it was going anywhere.

But, she reasoned as she closed her eyes, it also didn't mean that it wasn't.

# Chapter 14

She smelled bacon. One of the very best smells in the world. She stretched and blinked and threw back the covers. Checked the time on her phone. Six fifteen. Her alarm was set for six thirty so it had yet to ring.

Much better to be awakened this way, she thought.

She used the bathroom and then opened her bedroom door. She was still in her pajamas, but they were a cotton shirt and shorts, nothing risqué about them. She walked down the stairs and into the kitchen.

Marcus was behind the counter, cutting up a bowl of fresh fruit. The knife was clicking along at a pretty good clip.

"Good morning," she said. "It's awfully early to be so industrious."

He shrugged. "Hot tea?"

"Sounds delicious."

He poured her a cup from a pot that he had steeping.

"You're not having any?" she asked.

"I've already had a whole pot. I got an early morning call. About five."

"Police business."

"Yeah. Another business got broken into. Remember when I told you that both Gertie's and Feisty Pete's had been robbed in the last few months?"

"I do. Where did this happen?"

"Two blocks down from Tiddle's. It's a craft store. Maybe you've seen places like it. People come in and they can make pottery, or paint vases or other items, or take a cross-stitching class."

"Do you know what cross-stitching is?" she asked.

"No. But I know that people like to do it. They always look busy. I guess it's a good tourist activity, especially when it's rainy outside."

"What happened?"

"Similar to the other break-ins. They approached through a rear door. No vandalism, but they got away with about five hundred dollars."

"You think it was the same person who did all three robberies?"

"I don't know. But I think there's a likelihood. What I am bothered about is that one of my officers had his tires slashed last night. His vehicle was incapacitated for more than an hour, which meant that we had fewer patrols on the street than usual. That seems suspect to me. I had an idea of who might have been responsible for the tire slashing but Dawson, he's the officer, had a discussion with the people and he's pretty confident that they're innocent. So basically, we don't know who slashed the tires and we don't know who robbed the craft store and we don't have a clue whether it was the same person."

"It's no wonder that your chopping has a bit of an edge to it," she said, looking at his knife. She took a sip of her tea. "Oh, this is good."

"Thanks. My friends give me a hard time about being a tea drinker."

"Too civilized for them," she said, sitting down at the table with her drink.

"I never developed a taste for coffee even though my mom drank a pot of it every morning."

"Was your dad a coffee drinker, too?"

His eyes clouded over. "I was pretty young when my parents divorced. I don't really remember. As a young adult, when I would meet my dad for the occasional dinner, his beverage of choice was gin and tonic. Generally at least two. Sometimes three."

She wasn't sure what to say about that.

He also seemed to want to move on. "I have lots of choices for breakfast," he said. "Fruits. Eggs. I can make French toast. With blueberry sauce. And real maple syrup."

When she and Albert had been dating, she'd never spent the night at his house so there'd been no mornings where she'd awakened to somebody actually wanting to do something special for her. Her throat felt tight and it was hard to swallow. "Nice," she managed.

She sipped her tea. She needed to get a grip. To not make this bigger than what it was. "Whatever you're having is fine," she said. "I basically will eat anything that someone puts in front of me. It's a delight not to have to cook my own meal. What can I do to help?"

He shook his head. "Sit. This one is on me."

"But—"

"You can do breakfast tomorrow."

She wouldn't be here for breakfast tomorrow. She couldn't possibly consider staying with him for more than the one night that she'd promised her sister yesterday. "I should find a place," she said.

"There's no need. You weren't comfortable last night?" he asked.

"Of course I was. But maybe we're making too big a deal out of all of this. Bags get stolen. Houses get broken into. It doesn't mean the world is crumbling down around me. Of course, then there is Jordan Reese."

They were both standing at the counter. So still. He stared at her. "What are you saying, Erin?"

"You had to have noticed the resemblance between Jordan Reese and me. Don't you think, given what else has happened, that maybe, just maybe, somebody thought it was me?"

He said nothing.

She waited, hoping that he was going to tell her that she was crazy, that she was making connections that a logical person wouldn't reach.

"I think you might be right," he said.

It seemed hard to breathe. "Please tell me that the woman who was attacked at the motel, that she doesn't resemble me in some way."

He shook his head. "No. Short dark hair. Different build."

"Oh, thank God." She took a sip of her tea and realized that she was shaking.

"Hey," he said, coming close. He wrapped his arms around her and she took the heat, the comfort, the safety that he offered. She sank into his embrace. His skin was shower-fresh and the scent eased her tight lungs.

"I'm sorry," she said, her voice muffled against his shoulder. If she turned her head, she'd be able to…yes, nibble at his neck. It was gentle, just a scrape of her teeth, but still, it was intimate and bold and sent a rush through her body.

And his body, his whole body, responded.

"Erin," he said, as if her name was squeezed from his lungs.

She widened her stance, spreading her legs so he could press against her. He wanted her. She didn't have to guess about that.

His hands cupped her face and his tongue was in her mouth. She ached, literally ached, with the need. "I want—"

She heard a buzz behind her and realized it was her cell. She stepped back to look at the text message. "Oh no," she said.

Marcus looked over Erin's shoulder and tried to focus his eyes. Evidently lust was not a vision enhancer, probably had something to do with dilated blood vessels or something like that. He blinked twice and read. Our lady unable to help put the house back in order. I'll take care of it today. Morgan expecting to get sprung late afternoon. It was from Brian Tiddle.

She was thumbing through her contacts. She dialed. "Jo Marie, I'm sorry to be calling so early, but I wondered if there was any way you could work at the store today. If you could do just the first half of the day, that would even be incredibly helpful." She listened. "Thank you so much. I really appreciate it. And I know you're aware of the extra security. They will be there today."

She hung up and turned to face him. "Sorry. Probably bad form to transact business after...that."

*That* could be rekindled without much effort. But he had a feeling her head was now miles away. But he wasn't quite ready to let it go. "What were you going to say?"

"Sorry?" she said, as if she didn't understand the question.

"You said 'I want.' But you didn't finish the sentence. What do you want, Erin?"

She looked slightly panicked. For a brief moment, he felt bad, but got past it. This was too important. She was too important.

"I don't know. I don't remember."

This time he was confident she was lying. But whatever they'd had, it was gone for the moment. Her head was thinking about her brother-in-law and how she was going to help him. "I saw the message from Brian. You're headed over to the house."

"Yes. There's no way he can tackle that by himself. Every room has to be touched."

"I think I can get a few hours of personal time this morning. How about I make a couple calls and see if I can get us a few more hands."

She tilted her head and looked at him with questioning eyes. It dawned on him that while Erin had enjoyed great freedom in the last ten years, she might not have encountered all that many people she could trust. *She can trust me*, he told himself. Yeah, he was keeping some things from her, but just temporarily. He'd get it sorted out.

"It's no problem," he added before she could refuse.

"That would be incredibly helpful," she said. "And would mean a lot to Brian and Morgan. To me," she added softly, as if she was hesitant to add the weight of debt to their relationship. "I suppose we should get going."

God, she was beautiful. And so sexy. He lifted a hand, trailed it down her arm. "Eat something first," he said.

Brian was already there and had made good progress in the master bedroom and bath. He greeted Marcus warmly, thanking him for volunteering some time to help. Marcus waved it away. Erin wondered if Brian could see a difference in her relationship with Marcus. She felt as if she were wearing a sign that said, *Hey, we were making out and it was amazing.* She thought it was lucky that it was Brian and not Morgan who'd been there to meet them. She wouldn't be able to fool her sister.

"I'll take the kitchen," Marcus said. "I've asked a couple friends to help, too. I hope that's okay."

"More than okay," Brian said. "If I can have things looking normal when Morgan gets back here later today, I am going to be a happy man."

"I'll take the family room," Erin said. Ten minutes later, she was putting DVDs back into the television console when she heard car doors slam. She looked out the window. It was Daisy and Blade Savick, the couple she'd met at Food Truck Saturday. They were joined by Dr. Jamie Weathers.

She got to the front door just as Marcus was opening it.

"Hi, Erin," Daisy said, as if it was absolutely normal

to be doing this on a Tuesday morning. She was carrying a tray of muffins that looked delicious.

Erin felt…overwhelmed. She guessed that was the only word for it. Rolling stones didn't tend to gather a posse of people willing to drop everything to help. "Those are beautiful," Erin said, motioning to the muffins. "And unexpected. All of you," she said, waving her hand. "Unexpected. But so very appreciated." She wasn't a hundred percent successful in keeping the emotion out of her voice.

"We're happy to be here," Blade said.

"But you all have jobs," she said.

"And we work hard. But fortunately for us, we're all in situations where when we need a few hours of personal time to help out a friend, we can usually get it," Dr. Weathers said. "Of course, I'll probably need to pony up some more chocolate."

"It's on the house," Erin said. "Stop at the store anytime. As much as you want."

Daisy put a fist in the air. "Yes, chocolate."

"How's the shoulder, Erin?" Dr. Weathers asked.

"Good. Very little soreness. Thank you again, Dr. Weathers."

"Outside of the hospital, I'm Jamie," he said.

That felt too weird. She looked at Marcus.

"He probably won't even answer to Dr. Weathers," Marcus said. "Which at times has made Blade and me doubt that he is actually a doctor."

Jamie gave him a look. "How about I break your arm and then we see if I can fix it. That ought to prove it once and for all."

"Stop," she said, laughing. "The breaking of arms is

just a bit too close to you-know-what," she said, pointing to her shoulder.

"Point made," Marcus said. "Now give them a job to do," he added, looking at Erin.

It felt super weird to be giving them a task, but that was what they'd volunteered for. Ten minutes later, Blade and Daisy were in the basement, straightening that up. Jamie had joined Marcus in the kitchen. She'd returned to the family room.

It was amazing that Marcus and his friends were here to help. Now she was confident that the house would be put back together before Morgan was released. Nobody was likely to soon forget that an intruder had been in the home, but it sure made it easier to get past it when it wasn't staring you in the face.

She had all the books back on their shelves when Marcus came into the room carrying a tray. On it were two cups and two plates, both with muffins. She liked the look of that, but liked looking at him even more. He was handsome in his police uniform, but in dark jeans and a polo shirt, he was pure sexy male.

"I thought it might be time for a break," he said. "Tea for us and coffee for the rest of the group."

"I can't believe your friends are doing this," she said. She sat on the couch and took a bite of muffin. "As good as they looked," she said.

"Yeah, it's kind of a weird situation. Blade was married years ago to a woman named Sheila. Her family owns the Knoware Bakery. I wouldn't say that she and Daisy are friends, but they're friendly because of their shared interest in Blade's daughter. Daisy makes a point of supporting the business and has even thrown some business from Pratt Sports Spot their direction."

"It hardly seems possible that Daisy has only been in Knoware for a few months. You all seem so comfortable with one another."

Marcus nodded. "I guess that just means that it's right, you know, between her and Blade."

Erin sipped her tea. "What would you and Jamie have done if it hadn't been right? Would you have interfered? Tried to protect your friend from making a mistake?"

Marcus shook his head, suddenly looking serious. "I don't think that would have ever been necessary. But no, I don't think I would say anything. I tried that once with my dad. It's one of the reasons why we don't have much of a relationship now."

"What happened?" Erin asked.

"It was his third marriage. His second wife wasn't that bad. I mean, I was angry that he and my mom split, but the woman he married was actually okay. She wasn't the horrible stepmother from fairy tales. I didn't see my dad all that often, but when I did, she was always nice to me. And they were married pretty much through my grade school and high school years. I thought they were happy. Then suddenly they're living apart and headed for divorce. Later I found out that my dad had an affair with a director in one of his companies. It evidently hadn't been his first affair."

"So he doesn't make good choices," Erin said.

"Apparently not. But this director woman convinced him that they should get married practically before the ink on the divorce paperwork had a chance to dry. I wasn't invited to the wedding, even though by this time I was in college and living in California. When I finally met her some months later, I thought she was superficial and her interest in my dad was heavily influenced by his bank account. I told my dad that."

"How did that go?"

"Not well. As a young person, I thought it was because my dad was an idiot. As I matured, I was able to reason out that it might have been that I'd had the gall to publicly call out something that my dad probably realized but didn't want to admit."

"The third marriage didn't last long," Erin said knowingly.

"Less than two years. The haggling over community property lasted three times that. My dad did manage to stay single during that time. Not sure how because by this time, our sporadic visits had become even more so. A few years ago he married his fourth wife. I've never met her."

"I'm sorry," Erin said.

"I don't care if I ever meet her."

"No. I'm sorry that you and your dad were estranged. I'm sorry that he wasn't there for you when you needed a dad. I'm sorry that you never felt his love."

Marcus looked down at his tea. "Yeah, about that. I don't usually talk about my dad, but he's on my mind. He's been trying to contact me for about the last week. He's left a bunch of messages."

"Saying?"

"I don't know. I don't listen to them." He shrugged. "Do I really need to know that he's getting divorced again? Or that that has already happened, and he wants me to meet wife number five?"

He'd been so hurt. "It might be something important." To suddenly reach out after years of no contact.

To try multiple times. "I could listen to them for you," she offered.

He stared at her. "You're a nice person, you know that?"

She waved a hand.

"No. I mean it. Like the other day in the store, you had a chance to sell that grandmother a more expensive necklace. But you gently directed her to the less expensive."

"It just seemed the right thing to do."

"I should call my father back. That would be the right thing to do," he added softly. "Be the bigger person. Yada, yada."

She smiled. "Yada, yada," she repeated. "Go ahead, listen," she said, pointing to the cell phone in his shirt pocket.

Marcus looked over his shoulder. Even though there were a lot of people in the house, nobody was paying any attention to them. Erin was right. It was wrong to simply ignore the voice mails. And it didn't seem to be working, anyway. Five were stacked up. His dad wasn't giving up.

Marcus pulled his phone, got to his voice mail and listened to the messages in the order in which they'd been received. The first two were simple requests to return the call. The third was more direct. "Marcus, I really need to speak with you. Please call me back. Please."

He could not remember his dad ever pleading with him. Ever. He'd been a little kid when his dad had left. Nobody pleaded with a little kid. And then when he'd been growing up, when it had been wife number two, the visits had usually been short. The longest he remembered ever staying was two weeks one summer, when he was about fourteen. By then, their relationship was loosely formed. His dad worked during the day. His dad, stepmom and Marcus would have dinner together at night, generally at the country club. His dad would order for himself and his stepmom. And then it would freak him out when the server would say, "And what will your son be having?"

He didn't really think of himself as Theodore Price's son. He supposed it was easier for others since the physical resemblance between the two of them was pretty strong.

Anyway, he supposed they talked during dinner, but quite honestly, couldn't really remember any of the conversations. After dinner, it was back to the house where he'd gone to his bedroom to watch television.

He visited his dad when his mom told him he had to. The visits were uneventful. There was never yelling or fighting or any of the other emotions that he later saw in his daily life as a cop. Or heard about from some of his coworkers.

His dad would ask about school, then later, it was work. They both liked sports so that was always safe. Never politics. Never religion. As an adult, Marcus had had similar conversations with the person who delivered his mail.

His dad had been angry the day he'd voiced his opinion about wife number three. And there'd been no contact for over a year. Never another overnight visit. But finally his dad had reached out with a dinner invitation. It had been just him. Conversation had been stilted with no talk of anything of real importance.

They'd had no contact at all once he'd moved back to Knoware over two years ago. Not even when his mother had died.

He listened to the fourth message. "Call me, Marcus. There's important information you need to know."

He couldn't imagine what his father needed to tell him that he'd be interested in.

He listened to the fifth message that had just come in the morning. "This is the last time I'm going to call. I'll assume you're just not interested. Goodbye, Marcus."

"He said goodbye," Marcus said, putting his phone down. "On the last message only."

"What else?" she asked gently.

"That he wasn't going to call again if I didn't return the message. Problem solved," Marcus said brightly.

She shook her head.

"Killjoy," he said. "I'll call him later."

"I think you should do it right now," she said.

"He'll be at work."

She said nothing. But he knew that he'd be disappointing her if he didn't call. "I'll do it from my car." He walked out the front door.

She watched from the window. Knew that it wasn't any of her business, but she was concerned. Marcus had hardened his heart to his father. Had told himself that it didn't matter what the man did. But it couldn't be that simple.

He sat in the driver's seat, phone up to his ear. He said little, but she got the feeling that the call had been answered.

It was less than a three-minute conversation. She expected the door to open when she saw Marcus put the phone down. Instead, he bent forward and put his head down on his steering wheel.

And she was pretty sure she could see his shoulders shaking, convulsing really.

Whatever the man had said, it had made him cry.

# Chapter 15

She could wait inside for him.

No she couldn't, she decided. She hurried out the door and down the sidewalk. Walked to the passenger door and softly knocked on the window.

His head jerked up and he brushed away tears that had run down his face. She heard the door lock spring open and she hurried to open the door. She slid in. "What?" she asked. "What can I do?"

He didn't answer. But he did pull her close and then he rested his face in the crook of her neck. Finally, he lifted his head. "He's dying."

"He's sick," she said.

"He's been sick. For most of the last two years. Now he's dying. Hospice has already been called."

"Oh, Marcus," she said. All the memories of her parents' deaths came rushing back to her. "I'm so sorry."

"Melanoma. Stupid skin cancer. Who the hell dies from skin cancer?"

People did. All the time. "I'm sorry," she repeated.

"I told him that he needs to fight it. That's what people do. Blade Savick's dad has pancreatic cancer and he's fighting it with everything he has."

"Then he tells me that he's been fighting it. For two years. And that he's lost the battle. He wants me to come see him. Today or tomorrow."

No wonder the emotions had burst forth. He'd had no time to process. The news had come and now immediate action was expected. "There's got to be a lot of flights between Seattle and Los Angeles every day."

"Yeah." He looked her in the eye. "Come with me."

Her mouth opened, but no sound came out. How could she say no? But she had a responsibility to Morgan. "I... I don't know if I can. The store."

"Will you try?" he asked.

She would. She would do most anything to take away the pain in his eyes. She leaned in and softly kissed him on the edge of his mouth. "I will."

"I hate to leave you here, but I need to get back to my office, get things in order for me to be gone," he said.

"I'll tell your friends what's going on," she said.

He nodded. "I'll be in touch. Maybe we could fly out tonight, see him first thing in the morning. Be back by late afternoon."

"We'll make it work," she assured him. She opened her door. "I'm glad you called him, Marcus. It's better to know."

"He's only fifty-eight. Too damned young to die. It never dawned on me that was why he was calling."

Erin went back inside with a heavy heart. It was so

hard to lose a parent and there were always regrets. But at least when her parents had died, those regrets had been few. Yes, she could have been a better daughter. Yes, she could have argued less, been a better student and caused them less worry. There were always things. But for Marcus, he had to be regretting a relationship that never happened. Regretting the lack of love. Regretting a lost opportunity.

Daisy and Blade were still in the basement. She went there first.

"What do you think?" Daisy asked, hands on her hips.

It looked really good. "I have to admit that I haven't spent a lot of time down here, but I have a feeling it is now neater and cleaner than it was before the break-in."

"Excellent," Daisy said. "I need a snack."

"Of course you do," Blade said.

"Was that sarcasm?" she asked, picking up a wrench. "I have a pretty good throwing arm, you know."

"I'm sure you do. But the babies shouldn't see their parents fighting," Blade said.

"Pretty sure their eyes aren't open yet," Daisy responded.

"Our babies will be highly intuitive," Blade said. "Come on. Let's go get you something to eat."

Marcus had been right. They were a really good match. She smiled but evidently it didn't fool them.

"Is everything okay, Erin?" Blade asked, obviously pretty intuitive himself.

"Marcus got some bad news," she said. "His dad is sick. Very sick. Dying, actually. He wants Marcus to come to California either today or tomorrow."

"Damn," Blade said. "Where's Marcus now?"

"He left. Needed to get a couple things done at his work before he goes."

"He shouldn't go by himself," Daisy said, looking at Blade.

"I can probably get the time," he said.

"He asked me to go," Erin admitted. "I want to, but I'm not sure, with the store and everything."

"There's someone who works part-time, right?" Daisy asked.

"Jo Marie. She's covering my shift right now. But I was to relieve her later today. I wouldn't feel right asking her to work all day and then all day tomorrow."

Daisy and Blade looked at each other. "Are you thinking what I'm thinking?" Daisy asked.

"Sophie and Raven," they said at the same time.

"We each have a sixteen-year-old daughter," Daisy explained. "They are both very responsible and hardworking. Could they help out?"

Were these people for real? Was there any amount of help that they weren't willing to offer? It was overwhelming for somebody who'd had very few people to rely upon for the last ten years. "That's more than I could ask."

"They would love it. I know they would," Daisy said. "And they would love knowing that you were with Marcus, who is one of their favorites. They wouldn't want him to face this alone."

She really didn't need time to mull it over. She was confident that Morgan would be okay with it. "My sister hired extra security for the store after the break-in here. Some guys that Marcus knows. Jim and Tyson."

"I know them," Blade said. "I like them and Marcus said they were good cops. That makes this an even better solution."

"Then thank you," she said. "I'll let him know. I think he'll be happy."

"We'll fill Jamie in," Blade said. "Now let's go upstairs. My wife turns into a very angry woman when she's hungry. You may have heard the term *hangry*. You really don't want to see it come to life."

Marcus half expected that there would be a message from SA Sargeant, but there wasn't. He suspected, based on the man's parting comments, that it was a temporary reprieve.

Serenity was back at work and reported that her sister was doing well. She'd not yet returned to work, but planned to by the end of the week. That was good news. Serenity had finished her interviews with the rest of the Tiddle neighbors. Nobody had seen anything and no security cameras had caught any additional footage. But they had blood which meant they had DNA. They would solve this one.

He used his computer to look up flights from Seattle to Los Angeles. There were seats on a direct flight leaving at four ten this afternoon. The question was whether he needed one or two tickets.

He dialed Erin.

"Hi, Marcus," she said.

It was weird, but just hearing her voice calmed him. That had never happened before with any woman. "How's the cleaning up going?" he asked.

"We're making great progress. I told your friends what is going on with you. They are very concerned. I imagine you'll get a few calls once they leave here."

He wasn't sure he was yet ready to talk about his feelings about the news. Wasn't sure he understood them himself. Had been surprised and a little embarrassed, truth be told, that he'd hung up from the brief conversation with his father and started to cry.

He wasn't sure of the last time he'd shed tears. Years and years ago. And why the hell was he crying over a man who was basically a stranger? *I'm sorry that you never felt his love.* That was what Erin had said. Perhaps that was the reason. He'd been crying because a man who should have loved him was now dying. Had he been hanging on to the possibility of that love all these years? Never really acknowledging the need. Certainly, never verbalizing it.

Only to rather quickly realize that the opportunity was now gone.

He couldn't dwell on that now. Could not let it consume him. He had a task to accomplish. *Go see your dying father.*

He needed to put a check mark by the item on his to-do list.

"I'm getting ready to book a ticket. I need to know if you're able to come?" he asked, focusing on the small tasks that needed to be accomplished in order for the larger task to be completed.

"I can," she said. "Daisy and Blade have offered up their daughters to watch over the store in my absence."

"That's a great solution," Marcus said, absurdly happy that she'd be by his side. "Sophie and Raven are both fantastic girls and really responsible. Did you let Blade and Daisy know about the security at the store?"

"I did. I think they appreciated it."

"Do you want me to pick you up at the store or at the house?" he asked.

"The store. I'm going to meet the two girls there in just a little while, show them the ropes."

"Okay. I'll be there by one. That will give us enough time to drive to the airport. I'll get rooms for us, too, at a hotel."

"Great," she said.

"We'll be back in Knoware by early evening tomorrow."

"Okay. I'll see you soon." She put her phone in her pocket and went to find Brian to tell him the plan. He could fill Morgan in.

An hour later, she'd said goodbye to Blade, Daisy and Jamie. Brian had also left for the hospital. Now the only thing to do was pack for the trip. Most of her clothes were still in her trunk. As was the backpack that she'd borrowed from her sister and used last night to carry in some clothes to Marcus's house. She'd thrown it back in the trunk this morning, thinking she'd return it.

She opened the front door. She looked both directions and studied her vehicle before venturing forth. Good to be careful, she told herself. But there was nothing to make her nervous. It made her realize that it had been more than two days since she'd seen the two men from Food Truck Saturday. They were likely home with their families by now.

She opened her trunk and in less than five minutes, had the backpack ready to go. Then she remembered that her passport was at the store. While she could fly with just her driver's license since it was a domestic trip, she always preferred to have her passport on her when traveling. She made a mental note to grab it when she was at the store.

She couldn't help wondering about Marcus's dad. Felt bad, of course, that the man was sick. Didn't wish that on anybody. She was glad that Marcus was going to see him. There were so many regrets already, it would have been senseless to add the regret that he didn't see him one last time when he had the chance.

When she arrived at the store, her parking spot behind the store was open, but instead she took one on the street. If Marcus picked her up here, it would mean leaving her vehicle overnight. She felt that it would be safer on the main drag, rather than in an alley. She went inside and headed toward Jo Marie. She quickly brought her up to speed.

"I would have stayed," Jo Marie said when she finished, "but I do appreciate not having to. My granddaughter is coming over tonight and I would have hated to miss that."

"I just really appreciate your flexibility in covering this morning," Erin said.

"Of course," Jo Marie said. "That's what we do in this town. We help each other."

What was it Marcus had said? That it was time for something simple and good to happen to her. Well, he'd been right. Knoware had happened.

"I'm going to introduce myself to Jim," Erin said. She approached the man in black dress pants and a black untucked shirt. He was near the door, watching both the street and the store.

"Hi, Jim. I'm Erin McGarry. Thank you for being here."

"Happy to help. I just had a brief conversation with

Marcus so I'm aware that you'll be leaving in a little while and Blade Savick's daughters will be covering the store. Don't spend a minute worrying about them. My partner and I have this covered."

"It may be nothing," she said.

"Well, that's the best of all worlds, right? Being over-prepared for something that never happens."

"You're right. Anyway, while you're here, please help yourself to coffee or tea from the back room and all the chocolate you want."

"If I ate all the chocolate I wanted, I wouldn't be able to fit through the door. That's one of the bad parts of retirement. I no longer have to worry about meeting the required physical testing."

He looked plenty fit to her. She felt very safe with him in the vicinity. "Did Marcus give you my cell number?" she asked.

"He did. Already in my phone."

"Okay. I'll leave you to it." She saw boxes in the hallway outside the back room that must have arrived just that day. She walked back, got a knife from the drawer and opened them.

It was a collection of angels, all different sizes. They were made of stone and would be perfect for a garden or large planter. She went to the computer, looked at the inventory sheet and saw that Morgan had already set a retail price for each piece. She got busy tagging the items. She could get these on the shelf before she left.

She was halfway done when Jo Marie came back. "Oh, those are as cute as I thought they were going to be," she said, looking at the angels. "They're going to fly off the shelf."

"Well, they do have wings," Erin said.

"Sophie and Raven are here. They're so excited about this that they're practically flying."

She walked to the front part of the store to meet the girls. "Hi, I'm Erin. I can't tell you how much I appreciate this."

Forty minutes later, she got a text from Marcus that he was on his way to pick her up. "Any more questions?" she asked Raven and Sophie.

"I think we got it," Raven said.

She was confident they did. They knew how to run the cash register and the credit card machine, and she'd walked every aisle of the store with them, giving them information that she thought would be helpful. She had introduced them to Jim. They were not expected to do a bank deposit; they could simply leave the money in the back room. Then she showed them how to set the security alarm when they left and how to turn it off when they came in the following day.

It had been absurdly easy to kill the woman, Gasdrig thought. But he would have appreciated a better-stocked pantry. She ate too many canned vegetables and instead of boxed macaroni and cheese, he'd have appreciated some fresh fruit. She'd have been dead soon even if he and Ivan had not hurried along the process.

He liked being in a house better than a hotel. Liked the solitude. Unfortunately, it seemed to affect Ivan just the opposite. The kid was jumping with anxiety.

"We are wasting time," Ivan said.

"We are lying low," Gasdrig explained. "After you poured gasoline on a fire."

"Stop throwing the maid in my face," Ivan exploded. "It's done. We move on."

And they would have to. While Ivan grated on his nerves, Gasdrig knew that he was right. Time was running short. The thumb drive had not been in the brown shoulder bag, nor anywhere at the house. They'd not yet searched her vehicle, but they'd visually inspected it. The logical place was the gift store, but given the security alarm, it was dangerous to attempt that.

Unless they struck while the store was open.

There were two of them. If she was working alone, it would likely not be all that difficult for one of them to distract her for a period of time while the other searched. They would do that today. It was a risk for Ivan and maybe even for himself to be in public if anyone had seen what happened at the hotel, but that likely couldn't be helped. The boy was going to have to give up his stocking cap and they would wear the disguises that they'd used on the plane. Once they'd retrieved the thumb drive, they'd get out of this stupid little town. They would do what they'd been called to do, what they'd been chosen for. What they would be celebrated for.

"Listen up," he said to Ivan. "Here's the plan."

Erin waved goodbye to Sophie and Raven and got into Marcus's SUV. "Hi," she said, brushing her hair back from her face. It was barely midday and she felt as if she'd been awake for about fifteen hours. She was practically panting because she'd seen him pull up in front of the store and was almost out the front door when she had remembered her passport. She'd run to the back room and grabbed the manila envelope that she'd put it in. Now she folded the envelope and stuffed it in her backpack.

"Hi yourself," he said, waiting for her to buckle up. Once she was secure, he pulled away from the curb. "Thanks for coming."

"I'm happy to do it. Your dad knows we're coming, right?"

"He does. I sent him a text and he responded with a thumbs-up emoji. I guess I never saw him as an emoji kind of guy. He was a suit-and-tie guy usually. Sometimes a golf-shirt guy, but only on the country club golf course. He always got his shoes shined. I think he thought there were two kinds of people in the world—those who shined their shoes and those who didn't. 'It says a lot about a man.' I remember him telling me that once."

She looked down at her bone-colored sandals. They were clean but definitely not shiny. "I left my patent leather in Paris," she said.

He smiled at her. "Frankly, Scarlett, I don't give a damn."

He seemed relaxed. That made her happy. "Did you get everything done at work that needed your attention?"

"I hope so," he said, his eyes on the road. "I imagine it will be waiting for me when I get back."

For the first time, she heard something in his tone, something that hadn't been there a minute before. But she reasoned, he had a right to be stressed. He was doing two jobs in the height of the summer season.

They got to the airport with time to spare. The lines for security moved pretty quickly. When she got close, she pulled her passport from the manilla envelope. That was when she noticed the thumb drive that she'd also put in there and remembered that she'd never gone back to see what was on it. No time for that now. She left the thumb drive inside the envelope and put it back into her backpack.

Once she was on her way to the gate, she bought a couple magazines and some caramel popcorn at one of the shops. She loitered on her way back to the waiting area where Marcus sat because she wanted a chance to call Morgan.

"Hi," she said when her sister answered.

"Where are you?" Morgan asked.

"At the airport, about to board a plane. Are you still getting released?"

"Yes, yes, yes. I'm so happy. Not that everyone here wasn't wonderful, but I cannot wait to sleep in my own bed."

And thanks to Marcus and his friends, said bed was put back together, with sheets freshly washed. "I'm so glad for you."

"I was sorry to hear the news about Marcus's dad. How's he doing?"

"Okay, so far. Or he's an exceptionally good liar."

"I doubt that," Morgan said, laughing. "Well, he is a cop. Lying is probably a required course. You know, so they can tell somebody that they have a tremendous amount of evidence proving someone is guilty of a crime when they really have nothing and they're just hoping for a confession. That happens all the time on television."

"And we both know nothing is ever made up there."

"That's right. Listen, I've got to go. Be safe and hurry back."

"I will. Talk to you tomorrow."

She walked back to the waiting area just as they were starting to load the plane. Fifteen minutes later, they were in the air. "Hassle-free trip so far," she said. It was a smaller plane, just two seats to a side, with probably thirty rows. "The last plane I was on was huge. One of those where there are three rows on both sides with five seats in the middle."

"Where were you?"

"Near the middle of the plane. In one of the three-row sections."

Marcus looked around. "I'm surprised to see a few empty seats. Most of the flights I've been on recently have been pretty full."

Yeah, her flight from Paris had definitely been full. She hadn't seen an empty seat. Fortunately, she'd had the aisle seat and the two guys next to her hadn't... Oh my, she thought, sitting up so straight it was like someone had shoved a rod up her spine. She'd been thinking that they hadn't been up and down much when it hit her.

The two men in Knoware were the two men on the plane from Paris. They looked very different. But it was them. She was sure of it.

"What's wrong?" Marcus asked.

Should she tell him? If she did, what was he going to do about it? There were in a plane, up in the air, and he was on his way to see his dying father. Plus, she hadn't had the chance to sort out in her own head what it meant that the two men had changed their appearance. Or been in Knoware.

"Nothing's wrong," she said. "I just forgot to buy a water at the store."

"I imagine you can get a water from the flight attendant."

"Oh, sure," she said, settling back into her seat. "That's a good idea."

* * *

Gasdrig opened the door of Tiddle's Tidbits and Treasures and immediately saw the security guard. Oh, he wasn't dressed in a security uniform, but he carried himself like a former cop and Gasdrig would bet anything that he was packing under the loose shirt.

But since he was already halfway in and didn't want to draw attention to himself, he kept walking. Ivan trailed him.

Gasdrig nodded at the two young girls who were behind the cash register. They were new. As he and Ivan had watched the store, it had only been Erin McGarry and the older woman they called Jo Marie.

He walked over to a box of prints. Found one of the Pacific Coast. "I love this," he said. "But I'd like it in a larger size. Do you have that?"

The two girls looked at each other. "I believe all the available stock is out, sir," the blonde said.

"Sure, sure," he said. "But I think I was here the other day and overheard somebody say that these are all local artists. I wonder if the artist has other sizes. Would your manager know? Is she here to ask?"

The second girl stepped up. "Erin will be back in the store tomorrow evening. We'd be happy to pass that question on to her, sir. Can we have your name and number so that she can call you?"

Erin was not there and wouldn't be there until tomorrow night. Maybe she was with her sister. Maybe she'd left town for the night. Whatever the reason, it was a frustrating delay. "No problem. I'll just stop in another time. We're going to be here all week."

Over his dead body, he thought as they made their way out of the store. They needed to get to Washington, DC, by Thursday of this week at the latest and it was already Tuesday.

Ivan was scowling when they got in the car. "That was a waste of time."

"We found out that not only is there an alarm system, but there's also security in the store. If we end up having to hit her there, we will need to be prepared."

"She's back tomorrow night."

"I heard the girl," Gasdrig said, irritated beyond belief at Ivan. It was his fault that they'd been forced to lie low for a couple days and now they needed to twiddle their thumbs until tomorrow night.

They needed eyes on the woman. And he thought he might know just the person who could help them. He drove around to the alley that ran behind the store. The parking place behind Tiddle's was empty, but he didn't take it. He took a spot farther down, but still where he had a good view of the restaurant's back door.

"What are we doing?" Ivan asked.

"Buying some insurance," Gasdrig said.

"It's hot in the car," whined Ivan.

"It is likely hot in an American prison," Gasdrig said, not taking his eyes off the door. It was almost fifty minutes later before he was rewarded. The young man, wearing his white apron, came outside to smoke. Gasdrig opened his car door. "Stay here," he ordered.

# Chapter 16

The traffic was horrible from LAX to their hotel and the driver of the cab had a habit of accelerating too fast that made her nervous. Plus, during the entire ride, Marcus had gotten very quiet. She didn't think he'd said a word for the last forty minutes. Whatever ease and peace he had with the journey to see his father had dissipated when the plane touched down in Los Angeles.

She breathed a sigh of relief when she saw the sign for the hotel. The driver pulled into the circular driveway. It was a lovely place with beautiful flowers and lots of greenery. Doormen waited in anticipation. She did not stay in places like this when she traveled on her own. Marcus paid the driver and finally, they were out of the cab and in the fresh early-evening air.

"Beautiful," she said.

"Yeah," he responded, barely even looking around. His head was clearly somewhere else.

He held the door for her and they entered the spacious lobby that had shiny marble floors, rich-looking rugs and staff all dressed in identical blue blazers. There was a coffee shop in one corner and a bar in the other that had an attached patio where a number of people appeared to be partaking in cocktails.

"I'll check us in," Marcus said.

"I can pay for my own room," she offered.

"Don't be ridiculous," he said. "I've got it."

She decided not to argue. She took a seat in one of the available soft chairs while Marcus approached the desk. Once he was done there, he shifted over to the concierge stand. Five minutes later, he approached, holding two room keys. "We're on the same floor," he said, handing her one. "The concierge made us a dinner reservation at a place just down the block that they highly recommend. Is that okay?"

"It's fine." She was hungry, but grateful that she hadn't eaten before the cab ride.

They took the elevator to the fifth floor and he unlocked the first door. "This can be yours," he said. "I'll just take a quick look," he added, proving that he had not left being a cop at home.

Then he was back and stepping out of her room. "We need to leave in about twenty minutes. Does that give you enough time?"

"Absolutely."

"I'll knock on your door," he said, walking down the hall. She watched him enter a room four doors away.

Once inside her room, she stripped off her clothes and wrapped a towel around her head to protect her hair from getting wet. Then she stepped into the shower, using the lovely smelling soap provided by the hotel.

Five minutes later, she was drying off, feeling refreshed. Nothing beat a shower. She'd have been an absolutely lousy pioneer—a bath in a copper washtub once a week just wouldn't have cut it. She put a splash of perfume on and then opened her backpack, pulling out fresh underwear and the one dress that she'd brought. She hoped it met the dress code of the restaurant.

It was a sleeveless royal blue sheath that skimmed her hips and hit a couple inches above her knees. She slipped her bare feet into the same sandals that she'd worn on the plane. They would have to do. Then she brushed her teeth, added some eye makeup and lipstick, and was ready with five minutes to spare. She called the store. It would be closed but the girls might still be there, finishing up.

It was answered on the second ring. "Tiddle's Tidbits and Treasures, Raven speaking."

"Raven, it's Erin McGarry. How did everything go today?"

"Really good, I think. It was busy."

"Very good. Well, I just wanted to check to see if you needed anything."

"Nope, we're good."

"Okay. Thanks again for doing this." She hung up. Then texted her sister, letting her know that they'd arrived safely. Hopefully Morgan would be home by now, with her feet up, making Brian wait on her—and watch a romantic comedy on television. She didn't want to interrupt that.

Marcus knocked on the door right on time. She opened it. He'd also showered and changed clothes. He wore a button-down shirt and dress pants with the same sport coat that he'd worn on the plane. It was what she saw in his eyes, however, that made her shiver. Pure male appreciation.

"You look…really nice," he said.

"Thank you." *Something different.* Was that what this was or was it good old-fashioned lust? Because one look at him had her thinking that maybe she could forgo dinner and instead invite him in.

But he still had the shadowy look in his eyes, as if he was fighting a massive headache. Or maybe heartache. She wouldn't ask. If he wanted to talk about it, he would.

"Are we walking to dinner?" she asked.

"I thought we might."

She grabbed her sweater off the chair for later when they walked back. It took them less than five minutes to get to the steakhouse that had been recommended. There was a reservation under Marcus's name and they were quickly seated. It was a pretty place with lots of plants and light wood and a two-story skylight. There were white tablecloths and white napkins and candles on the tables.

"Our first dinner, you said you'd considered a steakhouse, but then decided on shrimp and grits. I guess we've gone full circle," she said.

"In less than a week."

How could that be? She felt that she knew him so well. That they'd known each other for a very long time. She was saved from answering, however, because the waiter came to get drink orders. When she ordered a pinot noir, Marcus said he was going to have the same. The waiter suggested a bottle and Marcus raised an eyebrow in her direction.

"We're not driving," she said with a smile.

"Bring a bottle," Marcus told the server. When the young man had walked away, he leaned forward. "Maybe we'll drink two."

She'd told herself she wouldn't ask, but she couldn't help it. "How are you doing?" she asked.

"I don't know," he admitted. "Between the time I got the news and we got on the plane, I really didn't have much time to think about what I was doing. But now that we're close, that I'm literally just twenty miles away, I realize that I'm going to see my father tomorrow. I don't have a clue what to say to him."

"I am confident that the right words will come to you."

He smiled and reached across the table for her hand. "You have more faith in me than I likely deserve. But I want you to know how much I appreciate you being here. It makes it…"

"Palatable?" she offered.

He shook his head. "It makes it doable."

The server delivered their wine and Marcus let go of her hand. Then it was a quick study of the menus and they ordered. She got a small filet and baked potato; he got the rib eye and a sweet potato. Both got Caesar salads.

"I've never been to California," she admitted once the server had walked away.

"I thought you'd been everywhere," he said.

"Not here. But it is lovely. Though that traffic. Yikes. Are we taking a cab to your dad's house?"

"He's sending a car for us. His personal driver."

She opened her mouth, then shut it, realizing that what she'd been about to say sounded bad. "Great," she said instead.

"You aren't thinking *great*. Tell me," he said.

"It sounds like something out of a movie. 'I'll have my driver pick you up,'" she said, in her best haughty tone.

"Welcome to my life," Marcus said.

"But you're so normal."

"It was only my life in very small increments. Most of the time I lived a very normal existence, very grounded. My mom drove a ten-year-old Buick."

"But when you were exposed to…well, let's just say, to excess, did it make you terribly sad to have to leave it?"

He shook his head. "I know this sounds weird, but even as a kid, I thought that whatever my dad had to do to make all that money probably wasn't worth it."

"Wow. Good head on your shoulders, young man."

He laughed. "I just hope his driver actually drives better than the guy in the cab."

"So you did notice," she said.

"I noticed you. I thought that I probably should have brought a second pair of shoes because you were going to vomit on the ones I was wearing."

"I was this close," she said, holding her thumb and index finger close. "Now tell me about California."

"Wikipedia might be easier," he said.

"Stop. You know what I meant. Tell me about your life here. Start at the beginning and don't leave anything out."

He left some things out. It was a meal, after all, not a two-day seminar. But he hit the highlights. Told her about college and why he'd chosen to study criminal justice. Talked about joining the Los Angeles Police Department and told her funny stories about the crazy things that a cop sees. He added in the details about the other kinds of things, the scary, sad, demoralizing things, but didn't dwell on them because that was consistent with how he assessed his chosen profession. Yeah, there were bad days and bad people and bad circumstances, but he also had a unique opportunity to do what was right, what was good.

And the meal was eaten and the wine was drunk, dessert was debated over, finally chosen and consumed. Cherry cheesecake for him, apple tart with cinnamon ice cream for her.

"I'm stuffed," she said. "But it was delicious and I loved hearing your story."

"I'm still waiting for you to reciprocate," he said, paying the bill with his credit card. "I only got the CliffsNotes version at Food Truck Saturday."

She pushed back her chair. "I suppose fair is fair. We'll see how far we get on the walk back to the hotel."

He held the restaurant door for her. Now that the sun had set, it was cooler. She put on her sweater. When she was done, he reached for her hand. She didn't resist. Perhaps she felt it, too, the need to be connected.

"It's perhaps best to begin by saying that I've always considered myself a bit of a rolling stone. Sometimes I'd be at rest, but it was a state that was not destined to last."

"A rolling stone," he repeated. "Rolling because?"

"Because initially it made me happy. I liked living in new places and I liked being able to try new jobs, learn new skills. I mean, I wasn't crazy. It wasn't one week here, another week there. But every year or so, I'd feel an urge to move on. I always gave my landlords and my employers plenty of notice so I left with a clear conscience and an optimism of what was to come next."

"You sure you weren't part of a carnival in another life?" he teased.

She smiled. "I think that I felt comfortable doing it because in the back of my head, I knew that Morgan was always there for me. Steady. Settled. I wasn't really just winging it out in the big bad world. I was spreading my wings knowing that there was a mama bird who would welcome me back to the nest at any time."

"Did you ever tell Morgan that?" he asked.

"I didn't need to. She understood. She always said that I was searching. And I would ask her what I was searching for. She said she didn't know, but that I would know once I found it."

"But you never did?"

She shook her head. "Before I came back to the States to help Morgan, I was in Paris," she said. "Working at a car dealership. Preston's Automobile Exchange."

He could tell her that he knew about Preston's Automobile Exchange. But then he'd have to admit the background check and whatever connection they had going was likely to be forever severed. "Did you like the job?"

"I did. Of course, dealerships work a little differently in France. Most people who have vehicles keep them for a very long time. It's not like here where people trade every couple of years. And there are other small differences, but in general, people would come, work with a salesperson to identify a vehicle, and the purchase would be transacted. I worked in the office along with one other person. She took care of inventory and I processed the paperwork on sales. There was no crossover in our duties. It worked fine."

"I think I'm hearing a *but* here."

She turned to look at him. "I imagine you're a good interrogator," she said.

Her glorious hair was blowing in the slight breeze and her eyes were shiny under the streetlights. She was beautiful. "I have my moments," he said.

"Yes, you do," she said, her tone very serious. "You know, I haven't talked to anybody about this, but I want to tell you. I really want to."

He felt as if there was an ax stuck between his shoulder blades. But there was no way he could be totally forthcoming right now. Just no way. "I want to know it all," he said.

"My boss went on holiday with his family and my coworker got ill. I didn't want her to fall behind so I jumped in. I didn't say anything to anybody, I just did it. It took me a couple days before I started to see something that wasn't right. Sales were getting reported for inventory that didn't exist. At first, you know, you assume it's a mistake. But then when I saw multiple instances, I was confident that it wasn't simply a mistake. Something was going on."

"What did you do?"

"I waited until my boss returned from holiday. By that time, my coworker was back at her desk and I don't think the boss even realized that she'd been gone. I let him get settled in for a day or two and then I showed him what I'd uncovered."

"What happened?"

"He told me that I was wrong and that he'd been unhappy with my work for weeks and that he'd made a decision to terminate my employment. He said I had fifteen minutes to leave the building."

"You were suspicious of the timing?"

"Of course. But my head was spinning. No one has *ever* told me that my work performance wasn't good. Not ever. Being fired was humiliating."

He could tell it had been a kick in the stomach. "I don't know much about French labor laws, but wasn't there a resource that you could have contacted?"

"Yes. And I thought about it. Then I spent a week watching movies on television. The next week I organized my photographs. Then I baked bread and took long walks in the park. I was just getting myself back together again when Brian called."

"Did you tell Brian or Morgan the truth about the Paris job?"

"Of course not. There was no need. I told myself I was over it. But I can't seem to put it behind me. I think there was something very wrong going on there."

"Because?"

"Over the months I worked there, I saw a couple people in the showroom who I was confident I'd seen months earlier. I remember asking my boss once if one particular man had returned his car, if he'd been unhappy with it, since I saw him inside the showroom. My boss told me I was mistaken, that he'd never been there before. But I was confident."

"What is it that you thought was going on?"

"I really don't know. I've tried to think it through. Recording sales for inventory that doesn't exist. That's overstating revenue. So that led me down the money laundering path. I mean, that's how it works, right? You get money from some illegal source, but in order to be able to move it through your business, you have to have a paper trail that explains the money."

She was smart. "That's the basics of how it's done," he said.

"But I don't know how the repeat visits by one individual fits in. And maybe there were repeat visits by more than one person, but I only noticed this particular guy."

They were back at their hotel. "Could you describe him if you needed to?"

She shrugged. "Why would I have to do that?"

"It's a cop question," he said, trying to dismiss it.

"Here's a civilian answer. I think I could. But really, I try not to think about Preston's too much. It was…hard to be told that I wasn't good enough. I didn't like it."

They walked into the lobby and got into the elevator with another couple. Then it was down the hall to her room. He took the key card she had pulled from her purse and opened her door, flipped on the light, did a quick visual check of the bath and the open closet. Then he motioned for her to come in. Once they were both inside the room, with the door closed, he turned to her.

"Your boss was a damn fool. You were definitely good enough. I suspect *too good* for him."

"Where were you when I needed somebody in my corner?" she asked, her tone slightly teasing. But her eyes told him the truth. Her experience in Paris had wounded her.

He'd be in her corner. He'd fight her fights. Every day. For the rest of his life. "You're pretty darn perfect if you ask me." Then he leaned in and kissed her. He could taste the sweetness of the cinnamon ice cream, could feel the smooth texture of her lips, could smell the scent of the perfume that she'd told him had come from Paris. It was a blast to his senses and need soared through him.

It was heat, each kiss building in intensity, until they were both gasping and pressed together so tightly there was no denying the need.

"Stay," she whispered. "Stay with me."

"Just try to throw me out," he growled softly, his mouth close to her ear. He walked her backward until her legs touched the bed. Then as one, he lowered the two of them down and slowly, ever so slowly, pulled up the hem of her pretty blue dress. "This is sexy," he said, his fingers lingering over the silky material.

She reached down and peeled the dress up and over her head. She lay there in nothing but a lacy bra and panties. Lime green, matching set.

"This, too," he said.

And then seconds later, when she was fully naked in his arms, he pulled back to stare at her. Breasts so firm and round, flat stomach, narrow hips. "Best yet," he managed, his throat feeling tight. She was so perfect.

"So get busy," she said, reaching up to pull him close.

And he did.

When he woke up in Erin's bed, it was light outside. She was still asleep, on her side, her bare back to him. It had been a hell of a night. They'd made love twice before exhaustion had finally claimed them both. It had been the best night of sleep he had in months, with her in his arms.

But now, as sunlight danced over her body, filtered by the mostly closed blinds, he needed to face the truth. He should not have made love to her. Not when he hadn't been truthful and absolutely forthcoming about the background check that he'd done or the FBI visit. But there had been no way that he'd have been willing or able to call a halt to what was happening between the two of them. Not with her giving him the green light the way she had. *Hey, Erin. I'm excited as hell, as you can probably tell, but can you hold on just a minute while I tell you about my new friend, SA Sargeant.*

Wasn't happening. But now, as he gently stroked a finger down her spine and envisioned many more mornings and nights making love to her in his bed, he knew that he was in a world of trouble.

"Good morning," she said, rolling over.

"Good morning," he answered. "How are you?"

She stretched and her breasts lifted, resulting in a quite predictable response from him. Thank goodness for a sheet. "Like I ran a 5K before I was ready," she said. "I detect a few muscles moving in protest this morning."

He wasn't surprised. By day, Erin McGarry was ladylike and polite and quite delightful. She was somewhat of a polecat in bed. At one point, he'd thought there was enough rolling around and position maneuvering that he'd been half-afraid they were going to end up on the floor. Had given as good as she got. It had been pretty damn exhilarating and a hell of good surprise. He'd expected it to be good. Hadn't expected it to blow the top of his head off.

She smiled. "I need a shower. You?"

"Uh…yeah."

"I've lived in places where water isn't always plentiful," she said with a seductive smile. "I try to make it a point to never waste it."

He was pretty sure he was picking up the drift, although most of the blood had drained from his head. "I can support that."

She took his hand. "What time is the car coming?"

"The driver can wait."

Ultimately, the driver did not have to wait on them. They were in the lobby of the hotel a full three minutes before the man arrived. Marcus had never been to his dad's current house. But when he saw it, he wasn't too surprised. Big house. Brick driveway. Real nice neighborhood with professional landscaping. Good roads in the neighborhood. It was like the others.

But that was where the sameness abruptly ended.

He wasn't quite sure what he expected but the pale, too-thin man in the leather recliner looked to be a cheap imitation of the virile, masculine father he remembered. "Uh, this is Erin," he said with a hand motion in her direction. He and Erin sat on the couch, on one side of the large living room, and his dad sat across from them. They'd been ushered into the room by a woman named Margie who identified herself as Theodore Price's home health aide.

His dad hadn't gotten up when they'd entered.

Neither of them had opened their arms for a hug. But then again, that had never been their style.

"Good to meet you, Erin," his dad said.

His voice was weak.

"Good to meet you, too, Mr. Price," she said.

"Good flight?" his dad asked.

"Uneventful. The best kind," Marcus said. This was starting to feel like every other short trip he'd ever made to see his father. Pretty soon they'd be talking about the weather.

His dad turned his head, looked out the living room window onto the manicured lawn, the pretty street. "Nice day to fly. Hardly any wind."

There it was. Marcus wanted to scream. And maybe Erin sensed his irritation because he saw her arm shift and suddenly, she was holding his hand. It was an infusion of courage.

"I'm sorry you're sick," Marcus said.

His dad nodded.

"Is there anything that we can do for you?" Marcus asked.

"I've had some of the best care in the world. Best that money can buy," his dad added with a sad smile. "It's been a good lesson in the limitations of a sound portfolio."

He didn't know what to say to that. "Is your wife here?" he asked.

His dad shook his head. "That's over. We were married less than a year. Zero for four."

It was so close to the thought in Marcus's head that it startled him. "That must have been difficult, on top of being sick."

"Marriage was never my strong suit."

Couldn't argue with that.

"Nor fatherhood," his dad said.

Marcus felt his throat close and he tightened his grip on Erin's hand.

"And I'm sorry about that," his dad said. "I've had a lot of time to sit and think lately and I've decided that I'm sorrier about that than I can easily say."

What now? Marcus thought frantically. Did he reassure his dying father that he'd done fine, that parenting was hard and that he should cut himself some slack?

Should he assure his father that he'd turned out fine, had a good job, good friends. Didn't a kid's accomplishments reflect something of a parent?

"You should probably focus on the things that can make you more comfortable," Marcus said. It was the very best he could do.

"My assets are in a trust," his dad said. "You're the sole beneficiary to that trust. It's a substantial amount of money, Marcus."

He didn't want his father's money. "I... I didn't come to have this kind of conversation. I came because you said you were sick."

"And that likely makes you a better man than I ever was," his dad said. "And a father, even a poor one, gets some pleasure from knowing that his child is a good man." Now he switched his gaze to Erin. "I'm glad you have someone who is important to you."

He could feel Erin tense and he rubbed his thumb across the top of her hand. "She is," he said. It was too early to make proclamations to his father or any other outsider, especially before he'd had the chance to talk to Erin about the future. But they were going to have one. It was nonnegotiable.

"I don't think you'll make the mistakes I made," his dad said. "Your mother is to thank for that. Good thing she could make up for my deficiencies."

Marcus said nothing. And they sat in silence for a long time. He could sense that his dad was tired. Perhaps sitting up in a chair was a big event. Maybe he spent most of his time in bed.

It was time for them to go. If he was going to say anything, it was time.

"Dad, like I said, I am sorry that you're sick. I am

also sorry that our relationship is less than ideal. But the thing I've learned over the years is that people don't set out to do poorly at something, whether that's working a job, or getting married or having a family. They generally want to do well, want to be successful. But a whole lot of things can mess that up. Sometimes in their control and sometimes not. But here's what I know. You provided financial support for me when I was a kid. You introduced me to California. You paid for my college. I got to stay in California, where I had wonderful years. You did things that allowed me to grow into the man that I am today. I am grateful for that. And I have made a decision that I will focus on what I am grateful for in our relationship rather than the things that I regret. I guess… I guess that I would wish the same for you."

Then Marcus got up, crossed the room, and gently, very gently, hugged his dying father.

# Chapter 17

A few hours later, when Marcus dropped her off at the store, Erin went inside to check how things were going. She waved at Jim, the security guard. Both girls were working and said that they were doing well.

"We didn't think you'd be back this early," Raven said.

"We got to the airport in time to catch an earlier flight," Erin explained. "What I'd like to do is run by and see my sister. If you girls can watch the store while I do that, I'll be back by four or so and can finish out the day."

They agreed. She drove to her sister's house. "You're supposed to be in bed," she said after walking into the family room and seeing Morgan on the couch. "Do I need to report you to the medical police?"

"Lying in bed or lying on the couch, same difference. I only get up to use the bathroom. Have pity on me."

"I do." She hugged her sister. "Where's Brian?"

"Working and then he's going to stop at the store for groceries." She sighed. "Did you know that your feet get bigger during pregnancy?" Morgan asked, studying her toes.

"You wear a size 7. What's the concern?"

"No concern. It's just that this baby really is a game changer."

"In so many ways, I expect."

"How was California?"

They'd talked in the car when she and Marcus had been en route to the airport, but really, how much could she have said with him in hearing range? "He was amazing with his dad. Kind. Compassionate. Forgiving."

Her sister smiled.

"What?"

"I think Erin might have an itsy-bitsy crush on Officer Price."

"We spent the night together," Erin said. She wasn't the type to kiss and tell, but this was Morgan, her sister and her best friend. She wanted her opinion. Needed her advice.

"I don't even have to ask how it was," Morgan said. She glanced over her shoulder. "Just had to do a Brian check. Men are so weird when you talk about other guys. But one look at Marcus and you just know that he'd be good in bed."

No argument there. She'd forgotten how great truly good sex was. Or perhaps, hadn't ever really known. Marcus was so physically fine, so strong, so confident that she hadn't held back. They'd pretty much destroyed the bed the first two times and the third time, in the shower, had been raw and needy and…exhilarating. That was the best word she could think of.

It was good she hadn't met him ten years ago. She wouldn't have been ready, wouldn't have been able to handle him. She certainly hadn't slept around, but she'd had lovers. After one morning in Marcus Price's bed, it was hard to remember their names.

"I really like him," Erin admitted.

"Like or something more?" Morgan asked.

Erin hesitated. "I don't know. I don't know what something more looks like. I've never been in love."

"I think you'll know," Morgan said. "Give yourself a little time. This might take some getting used to."

"I guess there's time," Erin said.

The door opened and Brian came in, juggling four sacks of groceries. "He's a good one," Erin said, winking at her sister.

"I know. That's why I snapped him up. So while there's time, don't dawdle."

Erin smiled as she went to help her brother-in-law put things away. If her sister had seen them at the hotel, dawdling would not have been the word that came to mind.

After Marcus dropped off Erin at Tiddle's, he went to his office. He had two interesting voice mail messages on his office phone. The first said that the Ford Explorer had been retrieved and was now being examined by the appropriate folks in the crime lab. That was good news. The second was a message from SA Sargeant asking for a return telephone call. He debated ignoring it, but knew that he could never do that. He dialed.

"This is Marcus Price," he said when the man answered.

"Our conversation ended rather abruptly the other day," the man said.

"I'm sorry. I had an emergent situation that needed my attention."

"I understand. It did give me a chance to discuss your situation up the chain of command."

*Your situation.* He had a situation? "Okay."

"But first, I wanted to let you know that I have something on the photos of the two men, the ones you call Talk and Hat."

"Tell me."

"Talk is Gasdrig Olimar and Hat is Ivan Smertoski."

The names meant nothing to him. "These two are known to the FBI?"

"And other agencies. They hail from the Ukraine, although Ivan Smertoski was educated in the States."

Marcus knew what his next logical question should be. Yet he hesitated to ask it. But he needed to know. "And what do these two have in common with Erin McGarry?"

"That is what we'd like to know. They're part of a small terror cell that has gotten some attention in recent years. Anti-American for sure. But also for a few attacks in Great Britain and France, too."

Erin had been in France. "Do these two have any known associations with Albert Peet or with Preston's Automobile?" Marcus asked.

"Not that we know of. But we're not happy that they're in the States."

"Not on a watch list?"

"Gasdrig Olimar is. But he traveled under an alias."

Marcus was pretty sure he could guess it. "Michael Stone or Scott Einstein."

"Michael Stone is correct. How did you know that?" SA Sargeant asked, his voice hard.

Marcus filled him in on what had happened to Serenity's sister at Pinetree Paradise and his subsequent conversations with the night manager.

"So let me make sure I understand this. Is one of them under suspicion in the attack on this woman?"

"They were persons of interest," Marcus said.

"And who is Scott Einstein?"

"He's the guy who rented the car that Michael Stone was driving."

He let that sink in for a minute. "Obviously, Michael Stone is an alias. He flew under that name. He rented the car under another alias, Scott Einstein."

"How did you know that?"

Marcus filled him in on why he was interested in the Ford Explorer. When he finished, he said, "I just heard that we have successfully retrieved the vehicle. It's at the crime lab."

"I want a copy of that report."

"Fine," Marcus said. He would save his arguments for things that were important.

"You were out of town," the agent said.

"That's true," he said.

"With Ms. McGarry."

"Again, true. Visiting family."

"I know."

Marcus didn't bother to ask how or what he actually knew. That didn't really matter. SA Sargeant was headed somewhere and Marcus was getting a bad feeling.

"We're going to bring Ms. McGarry in."

A slow burning started in his gut. "Are you charging her with something?"

"We're interested in talking to her. While we don't have any reason to believe that there was a past association between Ms. McGarry and Gasdrig Olimar and Ivan Smertoski, it does seem more than coincidental that they were on the same flight from Paris, all did a layover in New York, and then, once again, were on the same flight to Seattle. Then all three of them end up in Knoware and you yourself have admitted that they've interacted here."

Summarized like that, it didn't sound great for Erin. But he knew her. Trusted her. She was going to be scared when the FBI wanted to talk to her. "Let me tell her what's going on," he said.

SA Sargeant came back fast. "That's not a good decision on your part and quite frankly, it's not going to fly."

"Then let me be there when you question her."

"I'll allow that."

Marcus was happy the man wasn't standing in front of him. Otherwise, he might have put a fist through his jaw.

"If I needed to find her, can you suggest where I might first look?" the agent asked.

He could tell him he didn't know. But it was delaying the inevitable. And since later she'd be at his house, that would only look worse. "She was headed over to her sister's house." Marcus looked up the address and gave it to the man.

"Thank you. And Marcus," the agent said, his tone a little nicer, "don't call her or in any way communicate with her in advance to warn her about my visit. Doing so will only muddy up an investigation that you really shouldn't be a part of. It won't ultimately help her or help you."

"Where will you question her?" Marcus asked, letting the advice go by without comment.

"We'll do it at your office, assuming you're going to be there for a little bit."

Nothing was going to budge him. Just last night he'd vowed to be in her corner, to fight her fights; the only thing that had changed in the last day was that he was even more committed to that promise. "I'll be here."

Erin had helped put away the groceries and then Brian had cut the cake that a neighbor had dropped by. "I should get going," she said, once she'd practically licked the cream cheese frosting off the plate. She had hours of work ahead of her and it had already been an eventful day that started with waking up with Marcus in her bed, then the emotional visit to his father's house, and then the return trip to Knoware.

But she suspected that later, once they were back at his house, both she and Marcus would easily summon up the energy to make love again. He'd teased her on the flight back that she needed to bring a few more clothes into his house, that she couldn't live out of the trunk of her car forever. She'd reminded him that her initial plan had been to stay one night.

"Bad plan" was all he'd said.

She supposed it had been. She should have known that she'd never be able to resist him. They'd had no other conversation about the future besides the tacit agreement that she was definitely staying with him for the immediate duration. But that was enough for now. Her head was quite frankly whirling a bit even with that.

She heard Morgan's doorbell ring. "Want me to get that?" she asked.

"I got it," Brian said. "I can tear myself away from this," he said, motioning to the romantic comedy on the television.

Erin and Morgan just smiled.

In two minutes, Brian was back, standing in the doorway of the family room, a tall, dark-haired man in a suit with him. He looked very serious and Morgan immediately turned down the volume of the television.

"This is Special Agent Sargeant of the FBI," Brian said, a business card in his hand. "He needs to talk with Erin."

Erin stood up. The FBI? What the heck? "Uh…come in," she said.

"I've made arrangements for us to talk at the local police station," the man said.

It took a moment for the words to sink in. *Arrangements.* Marcus would be aware if the FBI was conducting interviews using his office. She reached for the backpack that she'd tossed on one of the chairs.

Morgan was getting off the couch. "Does my sister need an attorney?" she asked, her eyes flashing.

"Ma'am, we simply want to have a conversation with Ms. McGarry."

She wanted to demand why, but definitely didn't want to have that conversation here. Erin motioned for her sister to sit back down. "This is fine, Morgan," offering an assurance that she summoned up from somewhere. "I'll call you when I'm done."

"I'd like to drive my own vehicle," she said to the man as they walked out the door. "I need to go to work afterward. I have two sixteen-year-old girls waiting for me to relieve them."

"That's fine. I'll follow you."

She got in her rental car. Her hands were shaking, and she gripped her steering wheel. Even though Special Agent Sargeant had said that he simply wanted to talk to her, it was more than a little unsettling to have the FBI care enough about talking to her that they'd tracked her down at her sister's house. Her mind was whirling. The only thing she could think of that this could possibly be related to was Preston's. She'd suspected there was something illegal going on there. Did they think she could shed some light on the situation?

It was a short drive to the police station. Marcus's SUV was parked in the lot. He knew the FBI intended to talk to her. But he hadn't called to warn her. What did that mean?

She parked and waited for the FBI agent to get out of his vehicle. Without a word, he joined her on the sidewalk and they walked in together. At the front desk, he asked for Marcus.

She pressed her lips together. She watched as Marcus came out of his office. His eyes were focused on her. But he didn't greet her. Or hug her. Or touch her in any damn way. He simply motioned for them to follow him down the hall.

They went into a conference room. She took a seat on one side of the oblong table. Special Agent Sargeant sat at the head of the table. Marcus took a seat directly across from her. She did not look at him. Instead, she kept her eyes on the FBI agent.

"Ms. McGarry, it's my understanding that you know Interim Chief Price."

"Yes," she said.

"And you have no objection to him being present for this conversation?"

"No."

"I am interested in learning about the relationship that you have with Gasdrig Olimar and Ivan Smertoski."

She searched her recollection for names of customers at Preston's. But neither sounded familiar. "I don't know those names," she said.

The FBI agent stared at her. "Did you travel from Paris, France, to New York City last Thursday?"

"Yes."

"And then from New York City to Seattle that same day?"

"Yes."

"If I told you that I was aware that Gasdrig Olimar and Ivan Smertoski had that exact itinerary on that same day, what would you say?"

"I don't know what I'd say. It wouldn't mean anything to me."

Special Agent Sargeant took out his cell phone. "I want you to look at this photo. This was taken on Flight 425 from Paris to New York City."

Erin looked at his phone. It was a photo of her on the plane. She was in her seat, she was staring straight ahead, and she thought it had likely been taken relatively early in the flight when she'd been watching a movie. The two strangers who she'd finally placed just the previous day were sitting next to her. They were not as prominent in the photo as her, but definitely recognizable. "Who took this photo?" she asked.

"The flight attendant. At our request."

"Why?" she asked.

"We'll get to that later," he said.

Erin looked at Marcus for the first time, trying to read his face. What was going on here? But his expression was blank.

"Who are the men next to you?" the FBI agent asked.

"I have no idea. They were strangers. I'd never met them before the moment they sat in their seats."

"Have you seen them since?" he followed up.

She was suddenly pretty certain that Special Agent Sargeant knew exactly where she'd seen them since. "Yes. In Knoware."

She saw the muscles in Marcus's neck tighten, but he said nothing.

"For what purpose did you meet with these two men in Knoware?" Special Agent Sargeant asked.

"For no purpose. I first saw them inside my sister's gift store. They left without purchasing anything and within minutes, when I left for the day, I encountered them around my vehicle. They claimed to be looking for a car and thought my rental was nice-looking. The second time I saw them, it was just the older man. He was behind me in line at Food Truck Saturday. We had a brief conversation about my purse and that was it."

"You talked about your purse?" the man questioned, his tone disbelieving.

"Yes. He said that he was looking to buy his wife a purse and he liked mine. He asked if I'd gotten it in the store. That's not word-for-word, but certainly the general gist of the conversation. I do not understand your questions. I do not understand why this is important."

"Did it strike you as odd that you were running into people in Knoware who had been on your flight from Paris?" Special Agent Sargeant asked.

"I didn't recognize the men at first. It was just recently that I realized it was the same two men."

Special Agent Sargeant reached for the water pitcher that somebody had placed in the middle of the table. He poured himself a glass. Motioned to both Erin and Marcus as to whether they wanted some. Both shook their heads no. "How recently?" he asked.

"Yesterday, when I was on a flight to Los Angeles."

Special Agent Sargeant looked at Marcus. "So after you and I spoke the first time."

Marcus nodded.

What? Marcus had spoken to the FBI about her before their trip to see his father? How could that be? How could he have kept something like that from her?

It felt hard to breathe. She needed to get out of there. Fast. "What does this have to do with Preston's?" she asked.

"Why don't you tell us, Ms. McGarry?"

"I have no idea," she said, exasperated. Her chest hurt.

Marcus leaned forward. "Look, she said she didn't know the men on the flight. What else can she tell you?"

The FBI agent sighed. "This is Gasdrig Olimar," he said, pointing to the older man. "And his godson, Ivan Smertoski. Olimar is on a government watch list for known terrorists. We have recently become aware of a credible threat on US soil and find the arrival of Olimar and Smertoski to be especially concerning."

Terrorists. She'd been talking to them. They'd been in her sister's store. "How could they fly if they're on a government watch list?"

"They both used aliases that were carefully cultivated over a number of years. Their passports were not questioned."

"But you were watching them, right? Why else did you take their photo on the plane? Surely not everybody's row gets photographed?"

"It does not. But we weren't taking their picture. We were taking yours."

Nothing should have shocked her, but that did. "Because?"

"Because the FBI and other agencies have been monitoring you for a period of time."

"Me?" She cleared her throat, embarrassed that her voice had squeaked.

"Yes. Because of your relationship to Albert Peet and Preston's Automobile Exchange."

What did Albert Peet have to do with Preston's Automobile Exchange? Yes, he'd been a customer and yes, he'd been helpful in her securing an interview. But beyond that? "You must think that Albert had something to do with what was going on at Preston's?"

Special Agent Sargeant cocked his head. "What exactly is going on at Preston's?"

She told him the same story that she'd told Marcus, about covering the job for her coworker, finding the discrepancies and losing her job shortly after pointing out the problem to her boss. The FBI agent listened carefully, never interrupting. He took notes on his legal pad.

"You were in a romantic relationship with Albert Peet," Special Agent Sargeant said.

"We dated," she clarified.

"He helped you get the job at Preston's. Did you talk to him about getting let go from your position?"

"No. We had stopped dating by then."

He flipped back a few pages on his legal pad. "We have records that you called Mr. Peet's cell phone about a week before you left Paris."

They'd been monitoring her cell phone. Watching her. It was surreal. "If you were listening to my phone calls, then you must know why I called him."

"We weren't actively monitoring your phone. We did just recently review your cell phone records."

She supposed that was marginally better. She was willing to grasp any good news right now. "I called him because I had a turntable at my apartment. Albert had brought over a few records. I called to let him know that I'd dropped them off outside his front door."

"Anybody see you drop off the records?"

She shook her head. "My neighbor saw me carrying them out of my apartment."

"Okay, if we need that information, we'll get it from you." He flipped back to the notes he'd been taking of their conversation. "So you never saw either of the two men you encountered on the plane and then later in Knoware at Preston's or anywhere else in Paris?"

"No."

Marcus reached for the water. He poured himself a glass and then a second one. He pushed it in front of her. She didn't acknowledge the gesture.

"It just seems so odd, so unlikely, that they'd be making the same flight," Special Agent Sargeant said. "In fact, we've checked the airline records under the aliases they were using. They didn't buy a ticket from New York to Seattle until after they had already landed in New York."

What had suddenly made the men decide to come to Seattle? Had they followed her? But why would two terrorists possibly intent upon carrying out an attack be interested in her? She was a nobody. A woman traveling to help her sister. Surely they could have taken one look at her and realized that she wasn't all that interesting.

One look. That thought rolled around in her head. What would they have seen? She'd traveled in yoga pants and a sweater and comfortable shoes. She'd had her suitcase, which she'd put in the overhead bin, and her brown bag under the seat in front of her.

"Oh my God," she said. "I think I know something."

"What?" Special Agent Sargeant asked.

She reached for her backpack and she could see the FBI agent tense up. "I found a thumb drive. In my brown bag. I don't use that bag very often and it looked familiar to one I had." She pulled the manila envelope out of her backpack. "My first day at the gift store, I found a purse there that I loved. I transferred things I needed from my brown bag to my new purse and put a couple items in this envelope. I left it at the store. I retrieved it just yesterday because it had my passport and I was going to be flying. That's when I saw the thumb drive again." She dumped out the envelope. The device clattered onto the table. "There," she said, using the edge of the envelope to slide it across the table.

"Did you look at what was on this?" the FBI agent asked.

"No. I saw it, put it in the manila envelope and forgot about it."

Marcus stood up. "This makes sense. I told you that on Sunday night Erin was attacked in the hospital parking lot. She was pushed to the ground and her bag was taken from her. We found the bag several blocks away. There was no thumb drive in it, obviously because she'd already taken it out. The next day, the house where Erin had been staying was burglarized. Some money was taken, but it was obvious that the damage was most extensive in the room Erin was sleeping in."

"They were looking for it," Special Agent Sargeant said.

"Yes," Marcus said, pounding the table. "We need to see what's on that thumb drive."

"You've got a computer in your office," Special Agent Sargeant said.

"Let's go," Marcus said.

Erin wondered if the two men had forgotten that she was still there. "Are you done with me?" she asked, looking at Special Agent Sargeant. "I need to get to my sister's gift store."

"I'd like to get your fingerprints before you leave. You touched the thumb drive when you put it in the envelope. We need to rule you out."

"Her prints are on file," Marcus said, waving away the request.

She'd been fingerprinted when she'd been briefly jailed in South America. But how would Marcus know about that? She turned to look at him. "How did you know that?"

"I...uh...we can talk about this later," he said.

She didn't think so.

"You can go, Ms. McGarry," Special Agent Sargeant said. "I appreciate your forthrightness and I am damn grateful to learn about this thumb drive. This could be huge."

Huge was the hole that was starting to develop in her heart. She'd confided in Marcus and all he'd been doing was keeping secrets. "I know the way out," she said.

## Chapter 18

Marcus did not like the bleakness that he saw in Erin's eyes. He wanted to stop her, to hold her tight, to convince her that everything was going to be okay. But SA Sargeant was looking at him expectantly. They needed to see what was on the thumb drive.

They would talk later. He tried to telegraph that to her, but she wasn't looking his direction. He'd made a mistake by offering up that her fingerprints were on file. But she'd looked tired and stressed and all he'd been thinking about was that she didn't deserve to be sucked into this drama. She was so smart, however, that she'd latched onto his lapse.

And SA Sargeant hadn't helped when he'd let it be known that he and Marcus had had a previous conversation. But he supposed it was okay, even for the best. They needed to get things on the table.

He could explain his actions. They were reasonable. She simply had to see it that way. The alternative was... well, it was unacceptable.

SA Sargeant was holding the thumb drive with a handkerchief as they walked down the hall to his office. Marcus motioned for the man to take his desk chair and waited while the man put it in the USB port.

An error message popped up on the screen.

The FBI agent wasn't happy. He made a few clicks, trying something that seemed beyond Marcus's basic troubleshooting approaches.

"I've got an officer here who we depend on to help us with stuff like this," Marcus said. Serenity was the best of them on the computer.

SA Sargeant said nothing. Just kept focused on the screen and making additional attempts. "I think what we have here is an excellently encrypted device," he said finally. "I don't think your officer is going to have any better luck than me," he said. "We're going to need the best. Fortunately, we've got that."

Marcus assumed that "we" meant the FBI. "How is that going to happen?"

SA Sargeant pulled out his cell phone. "I'm not exactly sure."

Ten minutes later, they knew. A Bureau computer expert, currently stationed in San Francisco, California, was getting on a chartered plane. She would fly directly to Rainbow Field outside of Knoware where SA Sargeant would be waiting to pick her up. "Plan for us to be back here in ninety minutes."

Marcus looked at the clock on the wall. It was now just four. That meant it would be five thirty before they knew anything. A frustrating delay, but he knew what he was going to do with the time. "I'll be here," he said. "But I think it's important to remember that Olimar and Smertoski have not been seen in the Knoware area since Saturday night."

"But you have reason to believe they were here on Monday, when the woman was attacked at the hotel."

"Yes."

"They're still here. Maybe staying out of sight because of that situation. But I don't think they're leaving until they have this."

Which meant that Erin wasn't safe.

"Lock this up somewhere," SA Sargeant said. Then he pushed back his chair and walked out of Marcus's office.

Marcus locked the thumb drive in the middle drawer of his desk. Then he quickly waded through a stack of forms that needed to be signed and authorized a couple purchases before tossing his pen to the side. He needed to see Erin. Couldn't see Olimar and Smertoski making a move on her while the store was open and there was security in plain sight, but still, he wasn't feeling like he wanted to test his luck, either. He was just about to shut his office door when his desk phone rang.

"Marcus Price," he answered.

"This is the crime lab. We want to talk to you about this Ford Explorer."

Fifteen minutes later, when he walked into Tiddle's, there were several customers. He nodded at Tyson, who must have replaced Jim, whom Marcus had seen through the window when he'd dropped Erin off earlier. His friend and former coworker nodded back, but kept his distance.

Erin had to have seen him walk in, but she gave no

acknowledgment of the fact. She was 100 percent focused on her customers. He waited, impatiently studying a display of stone angels that he thought was new.

Finally, he was the only one in the store. "Hey," he said.

"Hello."

Her tone was frosty. "How are you?" he asked.

"Fine. How are you?" She was mad. He was off-kilter, too. The idea that she'd had the thumb drive this entire time made him feel sick. She'd been at such a risk. And the danger wasn't over. Not until the two men had been apprehended. He looked over his shoulder at Tyson. "Erin and I are going to step into the back. Let us know if somebody comes in," he said.

"I'm not interested in stepping into the back," she said.

"Erin," he said. "Please. I have information on the vehicle that hit Jordan Reese."

"Fine." She brushed past him on her way to the back room. "I'm listening," she said.

"A couple of things came together. One, at the scene, where Jordan was hit, we recovered a piece of plastic. We weren't sure what it was. But since she'd described the vehicle that hit her as a black SUV, we were fairly confident that it was relevant evidence. Then when we were investigating the attack on Faith Jones, Serenity's sister, we realized that there were two men who'd abruptly left their hotel room, earlier than expected, without checking out. They were driving a Ford Explorer that was rented on Thursday, the night you arrived in Knoware, and returned on Saturday, the day Jordan was injured."

"The two men were Olimar and Smertoski?"

"Yes, staying under aliases. But we hit a bit of a stumbling block because the intake form at the car rental company made no mention of damage. We had the vehicle picked up and examined at a crime lab. It has a broken piece of plastic underneath the front bumper. It was definitely Olimar and Smertoski who hit Jordan. We'll be able to charge them with a multitude of things when we arrest them."

"That's good news," she said. "Is that everything you wanted to tell me?"

He wanted to tell her that he loved her, but now definitely didn't seem like the right time. When she started back toward the front of the store, he quickly stepped in front of her. She set her jaw and her eyes were full of fire. It hit him wrong. Yeah, he'd had secrets. But she'd had some of her own. "When were you going to tell me that you recognized the two men in Knoware as being on your flight from Paris?" he asked.

"How did you know that my fingerprints were on file?" she asked, not answering his question.

He wasn't going to lie. "I did a background check on you."

She didn't appear too shocked, probably had had time to figure it out. "When?" she asked.

"After I saw you talking with the man at Food Truck Saturday. You seemed unwilling to talk about yourself and I had a bad feeling about the guy. Plus, we'd been made aware of a credible threat."

"So you thought I was a terrorist? At that moment?"

"No, I… I don't know what I thought. But I needed more information."

"And you didn't consider that you could simply ask

me? How about something like this. 'Hey, Erin. I saw you talking to that guy in line. Who is he?'"

He tried to unclench his jaw, but was generally unsuccessful. "I did not know at that point whether you and the two strangers were…together in some form or fashion."

"So you ordered a background check? Find anything interesting?"

"I found out more than you'd told me to that point."

"Well, then, congratulations. It was a good plan."

"It wasn't a damn plan, Erin. I'm a cop. Who had very recently been advised that there was a credible threat of a terrorist operation on US soil and to be watchful of strangers. You were a stranger."

She stepped close, perhaps more mindful of Tyson's presence than he'd been. "Yet," she whispered, "you took me with you to see your father. You made love to me. And yet you still didn't know."

"I knew, damn it. I knew. You told me about Preston's. I could tell that you'd been hurt by the experience."

"Again," she said, stepping back. "Another missed opportunity to tell me the truth."

"I was going to tell you," he snapped.

"I don't believe you. Get out, Marcus."

He didn't want to walk away. Not now when she was so angry. But maybe a cooling off period would benefit both of them. "We'll talk tonight, at my house."

"No," she said. "I'm not staying there."

"The two men, Olimar and Smertoski, are unaccounted for. There's still danger."

"You have the thumb drive," she said.

"We can't get it to open. SA Sargeant has sent for

a computer guru to help." He could tell that surprised her. "So you definitely need to stay at my house tonight," he added.

"No."

"Yes. I just told you that we're in the thick of this."

"I don't care."

"You better," he said, raising his voice. He could not, would not, let her be in harm's way.

She turned fast and almost ran back to the front of the store. He followed her more slowly, attempting to get a grip. When he entered, Tyson looked at him, his eyebrow raised.

He wasn't going to have this discussion with an audience. "This conversation is not over," he said. Then he walked out the door.

Erin desperately wanted to cry. But she would not. No. Instead, she threw herself into rearranging stock until she heard the door open. Her relief was short-lived, however, when she saw that it was Daisy Savick.

"Hi," Daisy said.

"How are you, Daisy?" She was just going to have to gut this out. She could not cry in front of the woman who everybody thought was perfect.

"I guess I should have checked in at home," Daisy said, smiling. "I thought Raven and Sophie were still here."

"They left a little while ago. We were able to catch an earlier flight home."

"I can't wait to get the full rundown. Sophie must have talked for fifteen minutes straight last night about the day. She absolutely loved it. I haven't talked to Raven, but I'm sure she felt the same."

"They are both lovely girls. You must be very proud."

"I am. How was Los Angeles? Marcus's dad?"

That question was all it took for the dam to break. Her eyes filled with tears. Everything had seemed so simple when they were in California. Now it was so complicated.

"Oh, Erin, I'm sorry. I didn't mean to make you cry." Daisy wrapped an arm around her shoulder. "I shouldn't have brought it up."

Erin glanced at Tyson, who had tactfully turned away from their conversation. "It's not your fault. It's…complicated. Marcus did a great job with his dad. I think he gave his dad comfort and acceptance and really everything that his dad probably had a right to wish for."

"But?" Daisy asked, rightly sensing that Erin wasn't telling her everything.

"I don't know where Marcus and I are right now. I just don't know. But I'm afraid it's not good," Erin admitted. "I can't really say much more than that." She could hardly tell her that Marcus had apparently consorted with the FBI regarding her and had investigated her background.

"I'm sorry," Daisy said again. "I don't want to intrude and I don't want to make you unhappy. All I know is that I believe my husband and he tells me that he's a hundred percent convinced that Marcus loves you and that you're the one he's been waiting for for such a long time."

Was it true? Did it even matter? "Thank you, Daisy. Thank you for caring enough that when you saw my tears that you didn't just beat a hasty retreat. You waded in with both feet. That takes courage and I think that

Marcus is a lucky man to have friends like you and Blade and Jamie. He's very lucky."

"Lucky to have you, too," Daisy said. "Now, how about some chocolate? I think I'm going to need a few boxes."

Erin was ringing up the sale when more customers came in. She gave Daisy a wave goodbye and was confident that she'd be able to maintain some sense of decorum, at least enough that she was confident that the new customers wouldn't realize that her heart was breaking. Tyson was another story. He watched her move around the store, his gaze thoughtful. She half expected that he might approach and plead Marcus's case—after all, they'd been friends and coworkers—but he did not.

She was thankful for that. It might have been a final straw. And she was pretty sure some of the stone angels could do some harm if she started throwing them around. Still, she told herself, they probably weren't as effective as the gun Tyson had tucked under his shirt.

It would be misdirected anger. She wasn't mad at Tyson. She wasn't even mad at Marcus. She was hurt. She felt foolish. She'd told him about Preston's. She hadn't even told her sister about it. How had she given so much of herself to somebody who was lying to her? How could she not have seen that?

Blade thought Marcus loved her. Well, maybe love wasn't enough. Without trust, what was love? He couldn't force her to stay at his house. She had her own vehicle and she was driving it to her sister's house. Then she thought about what Marcus had said. That there was still danger while the two men were unaccounted for. She knew it was true. There was no way for them to know that she'd given the thumb drive to the police.

Maybe she should post a note on the door.

It had a nice *now you take that* feel, but she knew she couldn't do it. They might be terrorists. She could not do anything that would give them any idea that the police were onto them.

But what that meant was that she couldn't go to her sister's house. She would not lead the men there. It was highly likely that they'd been the ones to break in. And unlikely they'd hesitate to attack again if they thought she was there and could tell them where to find the thumb drive.

Marcus had said they were bringing in an expert. Surely he or she would be able to access the thumb drive. And then they would know that none of this had anything to do with her.

"What is that?" Marcus asked, leaning over the shoulder of the computer specialist from the FBI to stare at the screen.

SA Sargeant didn't answer. Neither did Angela Richards, the deputy SA in charge, or DSAC, who'd made the trip with the computer specialist, who was slowly paging down. Again and again. To the very end. Thirty-two pages of schematics.

Finally, the senior agent straightened up. "I'm pretty sure it's the Washington, DC, Metro system," she said.

There were not a whole lot of great reasons for a known terrorist to have this kind of detail of a major transportation system.

"There are two other files on this thumb drive," the computer specialist said. "I can't get them to open. Quite frankly, I've never seen this level of protection. I can tell that they're big files, as big as this one. We'll almost certainly be able to break it, but it may take some time."

"We may not have time," SA Sargeant said. "We need to find Olimar and Smertoski. Now."

"I don't have any reason to believe they're still in Knoware," Marcus said. He wanted them to be. Wanted to be the one to give them the proper incentive to cough up how to access all the information and tell them what it all meant.

"I think they are," SA Sargeant said. "I don't think they're going to leave without exhausting every probability to retrieve this."

"Maybe they feel as if they have already done that," Marcus argued.

The FBI agent shook his head. "They haven't approached Erin McGarry directly. They haven't demanded the return of their property."

"Tell me what you're thinking." DSAC Richards jumped into the conversation, looking at SA Sargeant.

"We use Erin McGarry to draw them out."

"No," Marcus said. "Think of another way."

SA Sargeant shook his head. "She's the key. She's been the key from day one. We'll keep her safe."

Marcus had been a cop long enough that he'd seen those promises broken. "There's no way to keep someone a hundred percent safe."

"I want to talk to Erin McGarry," DSAC Richards said. "In the next fifteen minutes." She looked at Marcus. "And I need a landline to call my superiors."

He wanted to keep arguing, but he knew that he couldn't refuse to let them talk to Erin. "You can use the conference room next door. I'll contact Erin McGarry."

But before he could take a step, his phone rang.

Tyson. His heart rate shot up. Had something happened at the store? He stepped out into the hallway.

"What's up, Tyson?" he asked immediately.

"No immediate concern," Tyson said, clearly understanding that Marcus had assumed the worst. "The store is closed and all locked up. Erin is next door, at Gertie's. I… I wanted to talk to you when you were here earlier, but it didn't seem like a good time."

"It's complicated," Marcus said.

"Everything always is. I've got the two ex-wives to prove that. But I'm calling because I saw something last night. Jim was on security duty, but I relieved him for about a half hour so that he could get a haircut that he'd had scheduled and didn't want to have to reschedule."

"Okay." Jim had always been proud of his hair, proud that he had a full head of it when lots of guys his age were bald.

"I was just parking my car on the street when I saw two guys walk out of Tiddle's. They went to their car. I didn't think they were a good match for the two guys you showed us the photo of. But now that I've had some time to think about it and get past the stuff that's easy to change, I think their build was right."

Marcus understood. Hair and clothing were easily changed. Temporary tattoos applied. Fake beards and mustaches. Cops were taught to look past that, to the characteristics that couldn't be easily altered. Height. Weight. Bone structure.

"Anyway, they went to their car and drove away. I worked for Jim and when he came back, I took off. But when I drove past the alley, I saw their vehicle. Parked. They were sitting in it. So I watched them. It was maybe another fifteen minutes or so, when that new dishwasher Gertie hired, I think his name is Sonny, stepped out back for a smoke. The older guy got out of the car and approached Sonny, showed him something on his phone. Then there was some conversation. I was too far away to hear it, but I got the impression that Sonny was upset. The conversation ended, Sonny went back inside, and the two men drove off. I tried to follow them, but lost them on the far west side of town."

"Thanks, Tyson. This is helpful."

"Good. I'm glad. And you know I'm the last guy you should listen to when it comes to women, but I'd suggest that you don't give up too easily on Erin McGarry. I like her."

"Yeah. I like her, too," Marcus said.

He hung up with Tyson and used his phone to send a text to Erin. He had thought about calling, but decided it was likely that she wouldn't answer. Erin, call me ASAP. Very important. Regarding your earlier meeting here at KPD.

His phone rang thirty seconds later. It was her. "Thanks for calling," he said.

"What is it?" she asked. Her voice was cool.

"We've had a chance to look at some of the information you gave us," he said. He was going to choose his words carefully since they were both on cell phones. "But there are issues that our visitors need to discuss with you. Can you come here?"

She sighed. "I'll be there in a few minutes." She hung up.

Marcus's phone buzzed with another incoming call. Blade. He thought about letting it go to voice mail, but Blade didn't usually call unless it was important. "What's up?" he answered.

"How did it go with your dad?"

"It went about as well as could be expected. I'm glad I went."

"Good. I'm glad, too. Uh…listen, Daisy stopped in at Tiddle's just a bit ago. She said Erin was upset. She evidently didn't tell Daisy much, just that it was a complicated situation."

"I screwed up. Erin found out that I met with the FBI about her and that I ordered a background check on her. Unfortunately, she learned this after we'd…gotten to know each other pretty well in Los Angeles."

"Damn."

"Yeah. I'm not sure I can fix this."

"You can," Blade said, his tone urgent. "You can fix this. Apologize. Grovel. I know you love this woman, Marcus. I can see it."

"Of course I love her," Marcus said. "But it may not be enough. Listen, I have to go. Thanks for calling, Blade. I know you mean well. It's just…"

"Complicated," Blade supplied.

"Yeah." He hung up and went back inside to update the FBI agents. They were both in his office. "I have some news," he said. He brought them up to speed on what Tyson had told him.

"It makes sense," DSAC Richards said when he finished. "Olimar and Smertoski would need some way to monitor her. We need to feed information to Sonny. We were just discussing how we could get Ms. McGarry into some situation where Olimar and Smertoski felt comfortable approaching her. We would, of course, have agents waiting and ready to arrest them."

It was too dangerous. She didn't have to do it. They

couldn't make her. She was a civilian. "Put somebody in her place. A decoy."

"We considered that. They have interacted with her on several occasions. It won't work."

*I won't let her.* The words were on the tip of his tongue. But he stopped himself. First of all, it was highly unprofessional. Second of all, it was insulting to Erin. She was a smart woman who'd been living on her own for more than ten years, in multiple countries. She had good judgment. His opinion was not needed.

Or likely wanted, from the sound of her voice as they'd conversed. If he lost her over his sheer stupidity, his failure to be frank with her when it mattered most, he had only himself to blame. It would haunt him forever.

He was watching out the window and saw her pull up. He met her at the door of his office. "Don't let them pressure you into doing anything you don't want to do," he said. It was all he had time to say. SA Sargeant was already headed their direction.

She gave him a quick nod, but then everybody, with the exception of the computer specialist, was moving fast toward the conference room. DSAC Richards introduced herself. "Let me bring you up to speed, Erin," she said. Then she told her about their suspicions about the information on the thumb drive and their inability to open two of the files. Given that it was the Washington, DC, Metro system and one of the largest Fourth of July celebrations in the country was just days away, there was a consensus that time was short.

"We need your help," the senior FBI agent said.

# Chapter 19

"I'm listening," Erin said, never taking her eyes off the older woman.

"Olimar and Smertoski have been unsuccessful in their attempts to retrieve their property. They need you to tell them where you put it. It only makes sense that they're going to come for you."

To Erin's credit, she didn't flinch. Marcus wished the DSAC would soften it up a bit, but then again, there was nothing to be gained from sugarcoating it.

"We think you're most vulnerable in your vehicle or at night. We are proposing that we have you stay somewhere where we can insert agents in advance and they will be there to apprehend these men."

"Where would I stay?" she asked.

"We're working on that," SA Sargeant said.

"I might be able to help there," Erin said. "Less than

a half hour ago, I spoke with Gertie Biscuit who owns Gertie's Café. She has a few properties that she rents out and one was available. I'd made arrangements to rent it, beginning immediately. I planned to stay there tonight."

Both of the FBI agents looked in Marcus's direction. Was that pity he saw on their faces? He worked hard to keep his own face neutral. But he was dying inside. She had taken immediate steps to ensure that she didn't have to stay at his house tonight. "Which one of her properties?" he asked, grateful that his voice held steady.

"On Prospect Road."

"I know that place," he said, looking at the agents. "It could work. There are some woods that back up to the property. Agents could hide there and in the house."

"Any other properties nearby?" DSAC Richards asked.

He knew what she was worried about. Was anyone living close enough that they might get caught in cross fire?

"No."

"Did anybody hear you talking to the landlord, this Gertie?" DSAC Richards asked.

"We were at the counter. I think several people could have."

"That's good, that's good," DSAC Richards said. "The dishwasher, perhaps? I think his name is Sonny."

Erin shrugged. "I don't know. He might have been gathering dishes. I couldn't say for sure."

The senior FBI agent looked at Marcus. "Do you know Gertie?"

"Yes."

"Trust her?"

"Implicitly. Gertie Biscuit is an institution in this town. Everybody trusts her."

DSAC Richards and SA Sargeant shared a look. Then DSAC Richards turned to Erin. "Are you comfortable with this?"

"I don't even understand what you expect me to do," Erin said.

"Tyson called me," Marcus said. "He saw Olimar interacting with Sonny outside the back door of Gertie's. We all believe that it's possible that Olimar is somehow using Sonny to spy for him. Most likely, your comings and goings. You park behind the store and it would be easy for Sonny to know when you were at the store or when you were leaving."

"What does Sonny say?" Erin asked.

"We just learned this information so we haven't spoken to the man," DSAC Richards said. "I'm inclined not to. I think we have enough that we can be fairly confident that he's the watchdog. But what we don't know is whether he definitely heard that you're renting Gertie's house." She paused. "We need to ensure that happens."

"How do we do that?" Erin asked.

"I want you to return to your store. We're going to engineer another exchange between you and Gertie about you renting her house. This will occur in the alley, some distance apart, so that you can raise your voices. Interim Chief Price can work with Gertie so that she understands her role in this, which is to make sure that Sonny is outside on a break. All you need to do is stay inside the store until you get a text telling you it's time to go out to your car."

"Once I leave the store, I would normally swing by

the bank and put the deposit in the night depository," Erin said.

"If that's your routine, then do that. It will give Sonny a chance to make his report. Now, of course, if we're wrong about all this and Sonny isn't on their payroll, stay alert. The bank may be a place where they'll be waiting, intending to follow you from there and intercept you before you reach your destination. However, they'll either be expecting you to go to your sister's house or to Interim Chief Price's house. When you head somewhere different, I suspect they'll hang back, waiting to see where you're going."

"If you think it's possible that they're going to be outside the store or at the bank, why don't you simply arrest them then?" Erin asked.

"We weren't able to get any prints off the thumb drive," Marcus said. "And the computer specialists said it might be difficult to trace it back to a specific computer."

"So you need them to demand it from me, to verbalize that it belongs to them," Erin said.

"Exactly," DSAC Richards said, clearly pleased that Erin was catching on quickly.

"If they follow me, what do I do if they stop me before I get to Gertie's?"

"They're going to want to know where the thumb drive is. Pretend that it's in your vehicle. Tell them it must have dropped between the seats or something. We'll have agents trailing you. You won't be alone for long."

Marcus hated this. He absolutely hated this.

"Assuming I make it to Gertie's property, what do I do?" Erin asked.

"Go inside. In whatever room faces the road, turn on the light. Move around, as if you're unconcerned. We'll have agents hidden in the back rooms. Also outside. Everybody will stay hidden. We want to make it as easy and nonthreatening as possible for Olimar and Smertoski to get to you. They're not going to be scared of you. There's two of them, they'll be armed, and they'll think you're easy prey. As soon as they verbalize what they want, we'll apprehend them."

"It sounds easy," Erin said.

"It's never easy," DSAC Richards said. "But it should work well enough."

"Are you going to mic her?" Marcus asked.

The two agents looked at each other. "We could," DSAC Richards said. "It's a risk, though. What if Olimar and Smertoski see it before they've issued their demand?"

Erin studied all their faces. Finally settled on Marcus. "Do you think I should wear a mic?"

"I do," he said, grateful that she cared enough to want his opinion. It wasn't much, but it gave him just a little hope. "You won't be able to hear us because you won't have an earpiece. But we'll be able to hear you."

"I want one," Erin said.

Marcus turned to the FBI agents. "I'm going with her. Back to the store and then to Gertie's."

"You can't," DSAC Richards said. "They won't approach if they see you."

"They aren't going to see me. I'm going to be in the trunk of her car."

Both agents stared at him. "It's too warm to be in the trunk of a car," SA Sargeant said.

"She parks so that her trunk is up against a wooden

fence that borders the alley. I'll pop the trunk just enough to let some air in. Nobody will notice. It's the best way to make sure that somebody is with her."

"You need to square things with this Gertie woman," SA Sargeant said.

"My officer Serenity Jones can do it. Just give me five minutes to read her in."

Ten minutes later, Erin was on her way back to the store. She knew the wire that was taped between her breasts was thin and light, but it felt like a heavy log chain. It was nerve-wracking. She had to pretend that nothing was going on. But she knew there was a flurry of activity behind the scenes. Serenity would be talking to Gertie, bringing her up to speed. FBI agents would be descending upon Gertie's rental property, hiding themselves away.

And what would the two men, Olimar and Smertoski, be doing? That was the real question. Where were they? When would they strike?

And was she a good enough actress that she could get them to utter the necessary words so that an arrest could be made?

She had better be. The DC Metro system. Yikes. It was beyond horrible to contemplate the damage that could be done if she failed.

It was good, she supposed, to have a lot to think about because it helped to keep her from thinking about Marcus, who was now in the trunk of her car. He had betrayed her, sure. But he had done it because he was an officer of the law and he hadn't known whether she was a threat. Now he was willing to do whatever it took to keep her safe.

She parked in the alley, went inside the store, and

waited, her cell phone in her hand. The minutes ticked by. Finally, almost a half-hour later, the text came.

She took a deep breath, set the alarm, walked outside, and turned to lock the door. From the corner of her eye, she saw that a young man, who must be Sonny, was outside, leaning against the building. He lit up a cigarette. She heard a door slam. Gertie had come out the back door. She was twenty feet away. "Hi, Gertie," Erin said.

"Honey, did I tell you where I put the key? It's under the front mat. And you've got the address, right? It's 4040 Prospect Road. First white house after you cross White Road. Easy to remember. White and white." Gertie laughed.

"Got it," Erin said. Man, Gertie was good at this. She seemed so relaxed. Erin felt like she was strung tight. "Thanks again for letting me stay there tonight."

"Of course. I'm sure you and Marcus will make up soon. Good night." Gertie went back inside. Erin got in her car and pulled out of her space. She drove down the alley and risked a look into her rearview mirror. Sonny had his cell phone up to his ear.

Gasdrig's phone rang. He recognized the dishwasher's number.

"What?" he answered.

"She's staying at one of Gertie's rental properties tonight. Address is 4040 Prospect Road. White house." He paused. "Nothing bad is going to happen to her, is it?"

"Of course not," Gasdrig said. The destination change bothered him. "Why is she renting a new place?"

"I heard Gertie say something about her and Marcus needing to make up. Maybe they had a fight. I don't know. Listen, I did what you asked. You're not going to show that video to anyone, right?"

"Relax. I'm a man of my word." Gasdrig hung up. After they dealt with the woman, they should probably circle back and eliminate the dishwasher. No loose ends.

"It's time," he said to Ivan, who was eating a sandwich. The kid could eat twenty-four hours a day. He checked the airline website on his cell phone. "We've got enough time to get our property, deal with the dishwasher and get to the airport in time for the eleven o'clock flight to DC. We'll be there by morning."

Ivan tossed his sandwich wrappings aside. "Let's go," he said, his mouth full. "She deserves to die. She's caused us a lot of trouble." He picked up the gun that had been resting on the table and slipped it into his waistband.

"You take the car and stay behind me," Gasdrig said. "I'm going to drive the old lady's truck." The vehicle had been about the only really pleasant surprise at their new home. It was at least fifty years old, built sturdy before vehicles became an accumulation of plastic parts.

"Why?" Ivan questioned.

"You'll see why," Gasdrig said. "Let's go."


Erin drove to the bank and put her cloth pouch in the night depository. "At the bank," she said, mostly for Marcus's benefit. "I don't see them."

Of course, nobody could answer her. Although she did get a knock from the trunk. Marcus was letting her know that he'd heard her loud and clear.

Maybe this was all a bad dream. Not likely, she thought. Even the worst bad dreams weren't this scary.

She entered the address of Gertie's house in her GPS.

It was a ten-minute drive. She kept her speed at forty, just like the sign on the road stated. Every bump she hit she wondered how it felt in the trunk. Her GPS said she was a mile away. The next crossroad was Frost and then there would be White. "Couple minutes," she said. She got a knock in response.

She saw the old truck too late. It shot out from the crossroad and hit her broadside, the rear of the vehicle taking most of the hit. The impact sent her car spinning and the airbag popped, hitting her with a powerful force, pinning her back. She could do nothing.

When the vehicle finally stopped moving, she was facing the opposite direction than she'd been traveling. It was only then that she realized that a side airbag had also inflated, cushioning her from the worst of it. Both bags had deflated, leaving a powdery substance. She felt disorientated and ill, and she swallowed hard, praying she would not vomit.

"Marcus," she said.

There was no response. No reassuring knock.

And before she could utter his name a second time, her door was whipped open, her seat belt was cut, and she was yanked out of the car by the man she now knew as Gasdrig Olimar.

"Ms. McGarry," he said.

Gone was the pleasant veneer she'd seen at Food Truck Saturday. Now his face was hard and the veins in his neck were raised. His eyes were filled with... hate. "Mr. Olimar," she managed before she swayed.

He grabbed for her, to keep her upright. And in the process, saw the wire. He ripped it from her chest and then ground it into the gravel with the heel of his boot.

Had her mic worked for that brief second? Did the

FBI realize what had happened? Oh, God. Marcus. He'd taken the brunt of the hit, without an airbag to cushion the blow. He was likely badly hurt, maybe even dead.

And she hadn't told him that she loved him, that she forgave him, that she wanted a life with him.

"We don't have much time," Olimar said.

At first, she thought he was talking to her. Then realized that the younger man, who had to be Ivan Smertoski, had joined him. "What the hell?" Smertoski said.

"It seemed convenient to me that she and the cop had broken up. I was concerned we were going to have company at our destination." Olimar shook her. "I want my property back. Where is it?"

"What property?" she asked. The FBI would come. She just had to keep them talking.

He looked at her if he wanted to wring her neck. He grabbed her arm. "Change of plans," he said, looking at Smertoski. "We're taking her with us."

Panic flared and she could not think. "The thumb drive," she said. "I think it fell between my seats."

But they weren't listening. They didn't believe her. Energy surged and simultaneously, she jerked her arm away and brought her leg up to kick Olimar. She was going to fight with everything she had. They would kill her eventually. She knew it. She thought about Serenity's sister. There were some things worse than death.

"You little bitch," Smertoski said, stepping forward. He hit her and it felt as if her face exploded. Now they were dragging her toward the car. Olimar had the back door open and Smertoski pushed her toward—

"Police. Step away from the woman and put your hands in the air."

Marcus.

Both Olimar and Smertoski whirled around, letting go of her. She turned. Marcus was standing by the trunk, his gun pointed at them. She saw Smertoski's hand slip under his shirt and suddenly he was holding a gun.

"Get down, Erin," Marcus roared.

And she did exactly that, her knees crumpling.

And bullets flew.

# Chapter 20

Erin sat on the ground, her back against the tire of a vehicle, reminding her very much of the aftermath of when she'd been attacked in the hospital parking lot. That night it had been relatively quiet. Today, there were cops and FBI agents, ambulances and fire trucks, even a helicopter.

Evidently the FBI had some folks on speed dial when they'd realized it was going to go badly.

She had an ice pack and every time she lowered it, Marcus, who sat next to her, gently put it back up to her face. "If he wasn't already dead, I would kill him for this," he said, gently probing her wounded cheek.

Marcus had killed Smertoski and shot Olimar in the shoulder and had managed to avoid getting shot himself.

"I thought you might be dead," she said, watching

FBI agents circle her rental car, taking pictures from every angle.

"It was a hell of a hit. Remind me to never complain about all your clothes. They were pretty good padding. I think I might have been out for a minute," he admitted. "When I woke up and realized what was going on, it was…not good," he said. "I can't lose you, Erin. I love you."

"I love you, too," she said. "I knew it and I was afraid that I was going to die before I could tell you." She put her hand on his leg. "If you hadn't stopped them when you did…"

"I'd have come after you," he said simply. "I'd have never stopped."

And she knew it was true. He would protect her with his life. "What's next?" she asked. She'd already given a statement to the FBI and knew Marcus had done the same.

"You go back to my house. Take a shower. Get some rest. There are a few things I'll need to wrap up before I'm done for the night. And then tomorrow, maybe you could go shopping."

"Shopping? Are my clothes getting confiscated?" she asked, eyeballing the agents around her car.

"For a wedding dress," he said. He shifted, so that he was on bended knee. "Marry me, Erin. Marry me and I promise I will love you forever. I am not my father. He was right when he said that I will not make the mistakes he has made."

She smiled. "I'm not worried about that. But are you sure you're not worried that I'm a rolling stone?"

He shook his head. "You know what happens when a rolling stone comes to rest? She settles in," he said, answering his own question. "Certain that the years have brought a polish and a luster to her life and now content to nestle up to another rock, someone who will be there to weather the storms, to watch the sunsets, to raise the baby pebbles that will hopefully grace their future."

"That sounds nice," she said, lowering the ice pack so that she could lean forward and kiss him. "I think Morgan was right. I was searching. For you. All this time, I was searching for you."

This time he took the ice pack away so that he could kiss her long and hard.

"When do you want to get married?" she asked.

"Soon. As soon as it can be done."

"Can we get married in the harbor and have food trucks at the reception?"

He laughed. "I'm sure that can be arranged."

She leaned her head against his shoulder and closed her eyes. "I'll bring the chocolate."

\* \* \* \* \*

*Don't miss the conclusion of*
*Beverly Long's*
*Heroes of the Pacific Northwest miniseries,*
*available soon*
*wherever Harlequin Romantic Suspense*
*books are sold!*

He paused with the blade hovering over the crack between
boards. "Are you sure you want to keep prying up planks?
Whoever did this could have loosened any number of
boards in this floor."

The truth of his comment clearly daunted her. Her
shoulders dropped, and her expression sagged with sorrow.
"Yes. Continue. At least with this one, where I know
something was amiss earlier." She raised a hand, adding,
"But carefully."

He ducked his head in understanding, "Of course."

An apologetic grin flickered over her forlorn features,
softening the tension, and he took an extra second or two
just to stare at her. Sunlight streamed in from the window
above the kitchen sink and highlighted the auburn streaks
in her hair and the faint freckles on her upturned nose. The

bright beam reflected in her pale blue eyes, reminding him of sparkling water in the stream by his cabin. A throb of emotion grabbed at his chest.

"Matt?"

"Do you know how beautiful you are?"

She blinked. Blushed.

"What?" The word sounded strangled.

"You are." He stroked her cheek with the back of his left hand. "Beautiful."

Her throat worked as she swallowed, and she glanced down, shyly. "Um, thank you. I—"

"Anyway…" He withdrew his hand and turned his attention back to the floorboard. He eased the pocketknife blade in the small crack and gently levered the plank up.

As he moved the board out of the way, Cait shined the flashlight in the hole beneath.

She gasped at the same moment he muttered, "Holy hell."

In the dark space they exposed was a small plastic bag. Cait moved the light closer, illuminating the contents of the clear bag—a large bundle of cash, bound by a white paper band with "$7458" written on it.

When she reached for the bag of money, he caught her wrist. "No. Don't touch it."

When she frowned a query at him, he added, "Fingerprints. That's evidence."

*Don't miss*
Mountain Retreat Murder *by Beth Cornelison,*
*available April 2022 wherever*
*Harlequin Romantic Suspense*
*books and ebooks are sold.*

Harlequin.com